THE MAGIC OF TIÉGA
Marcel Souris

CALEBASSE PRESS

First Published by Calebasse Press 2022
Copyright © Marcel Souris

Marcel Souris has asserted his right under the Copyright, Designs and Patents Act 1988, to be identified as the author of this work.

ISBN 978-1-3999-3172-4

Cover Artwork © Kata Martell

Cover Design by Calebasse Press
Typesetting by Calebasse Press

Printed and bound in Great Britain by
Clays Ltd, Elcograf S.p.A

For Sabrina
thank you for always believing

In memory of
Paul Souris & Daniel Souris

'Memory, I see your game: you take root and form in the imagination, and the latter blossoms only through you.'
Patrick Chamoiseau, *Childhood*

THE MAGIC OF TIÉGA

Bill

I hope you enjoy the book

[signature] x

Prologue

The Maroon Hunt

Behind him there was a trampling of feet, the panting of both men and dogs. Branches snapped, and machete blades hacked away at the undergrowth.

'Ey, Celestine, laba,' *hey Celestine over there.*

The voice came from below, deeper in the forest, its reverberation creating confusing echoes among the trees. The voice was full of excitement.

Titon was slick with sweat, his body patched with dirt and bract.

He squinted as dripping sweat stung his eyes, his vision blurred. His shoulder struck the trunk of a tree; he stumbled, feet spilling from beneath him and toppled to the floor.

For a moment he lay on his back staring up through the forest's canopy. High above, flickering between leaves and branches, a kestrel swooped as it rode the thermals.

Then he was on his feet again, running, wiping at his eyes with the heel of his palm, glancing over his shoulder expecting to see the dog within biting distance of his behind. But there was nothing, only the dirt sprayed from the bottoms of his feet.

His lungs felt as if they would burst and his head thumped with a constant heartbeat. Each inhalation brought in too little air.

The once steady ascent increased so dramatically he was forced to grab onto roots and branches to assist his climb. His feet sought out rocks and footholds where before they had skipped and darted over forest floor. His fingernails were bloodied and clotted with mud.

When he next looked behind him, the first members of the *détachement des noirs* were visible, their white shirts unbuttoned to the waist and greyed with sweat, the cotton moulded to their sable chests.

They scanned the undergrowth for any movement that might betray the whereabouts of the maroon. Titon peered down from behind a clutch of bushes, on a ridge backed by the sheer face of the mountain.

Among the men of the detachment was the captain of the local *gendarmerie*, his cap abandoned, although he still wore his blue jacket. Its buttons scintillated with flashes of sunlight. It was dirty and unfastened, revealing a cotton chemise in the same state of undress as that of his men, the rump of his paunch pressing against its fabric. His cheeks and pate glowed red with exhaustion. His chest heaved like bellows.

Nevertheless, he stood composed in a commanding posture before his troupe. With the raising of a hand he ceased his men's agitated chatter.

The next figure to appear made little sense to Titon, who at first thought it a hallucination brought on by exhaustion.

She was almost as tall as the gendarme, dressed in a cotton dress its pattern bleached grey by the sun and torn to a height just above the calf.

He had never seen a white woman so attired.

Her feet were bare; the right atop a clump of black rock, toes curling around its crest in simian fashion. She held a shading hand to her brow and inspected the landscape for signs of the fleeing quarry. With the same hand she fended off stray locks of copper-coloured hair, blown into her face by the wind. It was a face of wearied beauty, youth's sparkle replaced by the lines engraved by hate and despair. Beneath her golden complexion lay a rosier hue, as if she had not long become accustomed to such jaunts in the sun.

The men about her stood mesmerised, like disciples in awe of a deity.

Titon crouched, his backside pressed against the mountain wall. Its ledge continuing for fifty or so feet before it curved northward and disappeared among the trees.

He began to edge along the rock face. His hands and feet moving with animal like synchronicity.

Below lay a drop much steeper than the one he had ascended; one that prevented scaling by all but the most accomplished of climbers.

The air no longer carried the voices of men or yapping dogs.

The chatter of birds filled his ears. He heard the wind, the swaying exhalation of the forest, a strange silence, a rifle crack.

He saw the jagged line of the adjacent mountains cut along the horizon, a pelt of green covering all but the most precipitous outcrops; the plantations that bit uncouthly into the fringes of the forest; the stone fort perched on the edge of the littoral. Beyond that the sea.

As the echo faded the scattered birds lit on new boughs and branches.

Blood poured from a small wound in his side, seeping between his fingers and from beneath his palm despite the pressure he applied.

He felt no pain.

There was an absence of thought; neither comprehension nor incomprehension as he regarded the gore that escaped his damming hand.

He sat with his back against the mountain, resting on his haunches, and strangely no longer fatigued by the chase. With this freedom came such lightness that he was forced to look down at where he sat, amazed when he found himself still grounded.

As the second crack sounded he felt himself falling forward and then down into the precipice; caught in a chaotic tumbling, moiling, spiralling as his body flung itself over the hips of rocks and into the flanks of trees.

His descent ended at the foot of a calvaria tree, a sudden and shattering termination. His body lay still, ochred by dust, breathless from the grounds merciless pummelling, yet his mind continued to tumble.

And the kestrel called to him from high above the tree tops, 'come home, come home, come home.'

A REUNION
OF STRANGERS

Chapter One

Pirat

How it happened, well— As I gazed absent-mindedly upon the succession of feet, I caught sight of the most beautiful pair of ankles I'd ever seen. They were the warm brown of coconut shell – without the hair, of course – and as slender and shapely as a cerf's. That's a deer to you. Cowry anklets glowed against the skin. The feet, although bare, were still too young to look like they spent their whole day crushing rocks. And the calves, O the calves... of these I caught only a glimpse. As my grip relaxed the guava I was placing in Ti Marie's basket fell from my hands, struck my foot-top and rolled out into the street.

It rolled in its own off kilter kind of way. Not quite a zigzag, not quite straight and seemed to weave between the feet of all and sundry. Almost as if it were aware of what a shame it would be, were it to be stepped on.

From behind me there came a skittering of paws and then a flash of golden brown. I'd thought Pirat was asleep, with good reason, but how wrong I turned out to be.

The dog moved between passers-by like a lizard, his body seeming to glide into the ever-moving spaces, but he was always a pair of legs away from the fugitive fruit. Then came the cries and the kicking feet. My heart beat in my head and my stomach dropped to below my knees.

Ma-Jo and Ti Marie stopped their chattering. Not a teensy-weensy *ayo* nor a solitary *c'est vrai* escaped their lips. Without even turning my head I could see their jaws drop, almost expected to hear them clatter to the floor. But I remained transfixed by the turn of events, in awe of the dog's sudden charge.

'Al rode lichien, la,' *get the dog*, came a cry from behind me, rousing me from my torpor.

It was then I saw the horse and chaise approaching. Hooves that looked certain to clobber Pirat – although not the fleeing fruit, I might add – were but a few yards away. And if the horseshoes only managed to concuss the dog, the wheels were certain to finish him. So off I went, attempting to weave in and out of the market goers with the dog's finesse. I might as well have just barged my way through, for all the success I had. But there was hardly time for a shove or a cross word to be slung at me, before I made a dive for Pirat. The collision knocked him out of the carriage's path and we rolled in the dirt like a pair of quarrelling rummies. A most unceremonious rescue, indeed, but what else was I to do? A few scrapes and a little wounded pride were far preferable to serving of *crêpe au lichien*.

All in all, a performance to set tongues about the market a wagging.

As I lay in the dirt, dog in my arms like a sweetheart, I caught sight of the carriage's passenger. She was old but not decrepit, sturdy looking for a *blanc* of her age. I am not saying she was built like a washerwoman, no, no, not this nabob. With a width of shoulder more common on a sporting man and a posture not easily flounced by the jerk of the road, she appeared to have once been an active sort. She rode the bumps with an ease to rival that of her driver. No mean feat considering Clarel, who drove the chaise, had a backside mapped with every dip and mound of our town's streets.

Despite the heat she sheltered beneath no parasol and wore only a black lace mantilla on her head. The white of her frock was so white it could have been made just that day. Uncommon attire for such a dusty thoroughfare whether one was travelling by carriage of not.

The look she gave me was not what I expected, though; not one of anger, annoyance or disdain. Instead, in those widened eyes, green like the clear deep sea when you can still see its sandy floor, there was surprise. And not because of the commotion she had just witnessed, or so it seemed to me. For I, and I alone, was the subject of that unremitting gaze, a study that caused her to turn in her seat. Not the usual behaviour of a woman of her standing, believe you me. The merest turn of the head should have been more than enough to devote to my sort and that turn would likely have been in the opposite direction.

The chaise trundled on and I got to my feet, dusting the dirt from my clothes. It was with trepidation that I wandered back to Ma-Jo, expecting a right good ear bashing from her. What I found was something very different. There she was packing away our stall and it not even midday. We had a good deal of produce left, too. Not to mention regulars who would be along in the afternoon for their two mangoes and a manioc. I had never seen Ma-Jo so spooked.

'Aller vini, done ene coude main ramasser,' *come on help me pack up*, she said, without once taking her eyes off what she was doing.

'Kieter sa, Ma, ki problem?' *What is it, Ma, what's wrong?*
I asked.

She stopped, looked at me and then in the direction of the
receding carriage.

'Ti pou li sa, mo garçon,' *that was her, my boy*, was all Ma-Jo
said, 'aller,' *let's go*.

And off she went, wares balanced on her head, without even a
glance over her shoulder.

*

Looking back, the day was not without its omens.

It wasn't usual for Pirat to follow us to market. Upon waking
he'd eat breakfast then amble over to his spot beneath the tamarind
tree. A patch of dirt to the right of an ant's nest, and a little to the
left of a huddle of rocks that seemed to have burrowed their way
up from beneath the earth. A haven that saw no sunlight until
early afternoon.

That morning the old dog woke later than usual, dreaming
dreams of more sleep, I suppose. After wandering over to the
tamarind tree he didn't settle in the shade, though, instead he
stood barking at his favourite snoozing spot.

It teemed with ants.

To you this might not seem at all strange, lying next to an
ant's nest as it did, but before that day no more than a few had
ever strayed into his territory – as if by some treaty borders had
been agreed.

But it's what you least expect that surprises you and just
because a thing is rarely seen it doesn't mean it's no longer there.
(A most pertinent maxim given the day's later events.) Let's be
honest, though, an ant's nature is to invade and perhaps in lieu of
opportunities missed the little guerrillas decided it was time Pirat
surrendered his claim.

Anyway, Pirat's barking had little effect on the ants, so much thunder lost in the noise of the battle. Ants crawled over the dog's feet and up his legs, and he charged about the yard trying to shake off the usurpers.

This kind of tomfoolery Ma-Jo could have done without.

After tripping over the Pirat three-four-five times and seeing her neatly arrange produce set in disarray she'd had enough. The dog was kicked out of the yard, followed by a flurry of curses and the gust from the swinging gate. So, as you can imagine, Ma-Jo was none too pleased when on our way to market Pirat appeared beside us.

At first, she refused to acknowledge him, her eyes fixed on any point but the out of favour hound. The basket usually so secure atop her head swayed like a drifting pirogue. She stopped and adjusted, then adjusted some more, but it just would not sit right. A sign, some might say, of something more than irritation.

'We haven't seen the end of it yet, mo garçon,' said Ma-Jo with a shake of her head 'mark my words, there's more to come.'

Yes, maybe she was ticked off at our mangy dog or miffed about a few mushy mangoes, but the way she said *there's more to come* – with a look in her eye that said she'd glimpsed some future occurrence – set butterflies, dragonflies and a moustik or two loose in my stomach.

Though it might only have been the manioc I'd eaten for breakfast.

Chapter Two

Le Gamin Noir

There were few things as breathtaking as the view of Grand Port from the sea.

On her departure from La Belle Horizon it seemed all but the cockerels and the stable boy were asleep. Bird and peon were yet to be roused, only a glimmer of the day visible on the horizon. Even that hint of light was absent from the blue-grey world of the estate.

As she rode out towards the district of La Rivière Sèche, there was already a promise of the heat to come on the morning air. When she had passed the settlement and headed down to the embouchure of La Grande Rivière the morning had broken, and promise had turned to fact.

A coasting pirogue waited at anchor for her.

She was used to the sidelong glances. Heads would bow rather than meet her stare. Without a word her horse was taken to be fed and watered, and she made her way to the awaiting boat.

After so many reclusive years it was as if she had been revived like the beauty from Perrault's tale, if only, as with that damsel, her body had been overlooked by time. She remembered the saddle, but her muscles ached from the ride. It was only after dismounting that she felt the toll it had taken. Had she forgotten old age was now her companion or just remembered it had not always been so?

On taking to the sea the life fled back into her, the exhilaration which she felt on the ride again roused within; rejuvenated as much by the anticipation of the trip, as the experience itself. The swift tranquillity with which the craft seemed to skim atop the water's surface; the heave and sway when the skipper took the boat out closer to the reef; the arc of the sail against blue sky; the splash and spray of wave against hull. She felt as giddy as a child, like a girl escaping the disapproving stare of her guardian.

And maybe it was so. To pretend one has not been abandoned by youth, to remember the clear vision and the body so welcoming to pleasure and strain, and not despair at their loss; neither to mourn their passing or pretend they had never been. Was this not escape? How soothing memory can be, she thought, how fickle the subjects of her attention?

She could have almost forgotten the very reason for her journey.

And that view, the mountains and the sea. If she looked past the habitations and smattering of unruly shacks, it was possible to catch a glimpse of the coast of Cerne as the Portuguese had seen it. Those ranges whose green flanks were so pleasing to the eye and seemed to promise entrance to a fantastical world; a land lost to man or never before glimpsed. Ashore its beasts would be the rare sort, whose peculiarity encouraged observers to use a little too much imagination when depicting them. Flora with fronds, fans and waxen leaves, and forests with black impenetrable hearts. Forests she was not unfamiliar with, into which she had indeed stepped, and in good stead she might add, to pursue a two-legged beast. Through such jaunts she had become more master than many of the island's monsieurs who ascribed themselves this title.

What a woman she had been. Not untameable, no, just unwilling to allow the world her Alexandre had built to crumble around her. A mantle she had borne and wielded with theretofore undiscovered courage.

With the turn of the boat towards Grand Port bay, the starboard roll pitched her towards the sea. She laughed, she actually laughed, and leaned into the roll dipping her fingertips into the water. Then she submerged her whole hand, the pull of the sea tugging her arm way behind her, the spray soaking her sleeve. What world had she restricted herself to when pleasures like this lay but a few hours journey from her veranda? Could be seen, no less, when one stood upon the terrace. Had she become no more than a replica of the old man? Engrossed so completely in the plantation's administration that life beyond the confines of La Belle Horizon ceased to exist.

But after all, had this not been her plan? To safeguard their world, her world, and a way of life that had been on the brink of being surrendered to uncivilised hands.

Wasted thoughts, nothing could be changed. And anyway, was it not so, that frivolities too often tasted became bland and ordinary; that pleasure could become rote if experienced every day. Maybe it was to savour moments just as this, that she had sacrificed so many of life's other joys, ensuring Alexandre's legacy was not left to dwindle. And she had not toiled in vain. Instead of declining the plantation had prospered more than it ever had during her husband's lifetime. Of course, there were many contributing factors, but truth be told, her dedication had been chief among these.

And she had not been so alone.

From debarking in Mahébourg she planned to travel up through town to the workshop of Dubois, the old coffin maker. Not an errand a *Grand Blanc* such as herself would usually undertake. In fact, the carpenter had received his instructions from an emissary;

one whom she knew could be trusted with more delicate matters. The delivery of messages was not part of the notary's usual bailiwick, but she had been confident he would make an exception for her. And of course, he was suitably remunerated. For the old official was not so secure in his dotage that he could refuse an easy commission.

The inspection of the casket, the purpose of that day's journey, was a different matter. This she preferred to do in person. For was it not but a small inconvenience, to ensure a person one was fond of received a fitting habitation for that last abode. A kindness she had been unable to perform for Alexandre.

There had been the shock when receiving the news of Alexandre's death, the feeling that with such loss one's own life would also cease. With this most recent passing it had not been so. There were weeks of decline during which the necessary arrangements had been made; the inevitable was accepted and no matter the anguish it was possible to see beyond the event.

Even so soon after the fact her pain seemed to have resolved itself into a dull ache; the space in her life where there had been another, was not so large that she felt its constant pull. In fact, she appeared to have developed an appreciation of life which had been absent from her day to day existence for more than a decade. Was it not germane that in old age she should have rediscovered the will to live, at a time when life's precariousness was all too plain?

Maybe so.

The streets of Mahébourg were crowded; she had not anticipated the market. There were sellers and hawkers of every kind; covered stalls and push carts, goods spread out on woven mats that sprawled out into the roadway; men and women with baskets who jabbered and bellowed out ear-splitting calls. With this came the inevitable drove who wandered among the sellers like untended cattle, without consideration for others who might need passage through the streets.

The *nègre* who drove the chaise she hired proceeded with similar carelessness. He headed straight into the stream of people, trusting in providence, rather than good sense, to ensure the safety of pedestrians. That the vehicle passed through the crowd without serious incident seemed an indictment of his choice, a synchronicity between man and his locale. That was until the appearance of the *gamin*.

First came the dog. She was sure that was what she had seen, darting through the gaps in the crowd. The shape, the colour, the movement; fractions of second captured by the eye; a creature with purpose weaving in and out of a directionless horde. It emerged before the carriage, was almost beneath the horse's hooves; the dog's fate about to be realised through death or mutilation. Then it was gone, vanishing like the fragments of a receding dream.

Next came the boy.

They rolled to the side of the road; dog and boy. She could not believe what she saw, but the proof was undeniable? As the boy sat up, this *gamin noir*, this black urchin, before dusting himself down or cuffing his mongrel, he looked straight at her. It was as if she had been hypnotised, she was unable to turn away, powerless to avoid his gaze. His eyes seemed to delve into the very heart of her; disturbing memories, if not forgotten, then hidden in places not easily uncovered.

It was like the rising of an unwelcome Lazarus, and again the tranquillity of all she had fought to achieve, to preserve, seemed under threat.

Was it him?

Furthermore, after she had passed the *gamin*, she recognised an elder black who had been eyeing the boy and calling out to him in her crude tongue. A woman tending a stall at the entrance to the bazaar. This woman had been one of theirs, yes, yes, she had, a *nègre de Lousteau*. It was a face she'd seen in the fields or otherwise idling about the plantation. Who this woman was she had realised, only later, so greatly had the black been changed by the years.

As for the *gamin*, the more she replayed their brief encounter, the more she became convinced of his provenance. His reddish-brown hue sat somewhere between the coal tar of his father and the unnatural paleness of his mother. The skin of the *mulâtre*, the boy's mother, had been so light; almost as white as her own. This was countered by the girl's hair, course as a *nègre's*, and a face bearing the same exaggerated features. There had, however, been something unexpected in this melange. A comeliness she could only attribute to the *sang français*, this white blood having some civilising effect on the face's overall composition; the swollen curve of nostril and lip curtailed by their being petite, that unwieldy hair somewhat redeemed by its rich brown colour.

A recollection rendered with such clarity that she feared the revival of other dead memories; those she thought consigned to coffers whose keys had been long discarded.

Of the father— that degenerate did not bear thinking about.

In the boy she saw the mother, it was there in his childish beauty. A transient thing, soon lost to manhood in those adolescent years, but which the *gamin* retained despite his no longer being a child. The long curling lashes and eyes more brown than black. The whites of his eyes so white they gave him a constant look of surprise. She had made a study of him, circumstance made it inevitable.

Had there been a hint of recognition, is that what had prompted the glare? Impossible, she was a stranger to the *gamin* and he had been dead to her; had never lived, in fact. It was as if she expected some residue of memory, something passed on by flesh or soul, a memento of their connection.

On her return from visiting old Dubois both woman and *gamin* were gone. The woman's stall no longer there, its space occupied by some other idlers.

LOVED ONES

Chapter Three

Elise's Story

The story wasn't given to me freely. Though it would have been revealed sooner or later, I suppose. When I was older, maybe, and my head wasn't so easily cloyed with words. It was a lot to take in at seven years old and I am sure I've lost a bit here and embellished a bit there – making the story a little more my own. For how do you know if a child is ready to hear a tale that will forever change them? A story hidden in the child's heart though it had never been told.

The answer could be summed up with a shrug, perhaps.

Pas coner – *I don't know.*

It's just as much a mystery as to why I chose that moment to ask Ma-Jo, 'Ma, what happened to mami and papi?'

Twas eight years before that day at the market.

Ma-Jo – my guardian and the only parent I'd ever known – didn't so much as break stride at the asking, but kept moving, carried on as if I'd said not a word. From one task to the next she moved in seamless transition; plucking, picking, brushing, sowing – pealing a manioc or two.

I gave her dress a tug, followed by another pull.

'Eay,' she said.

'Ma.'

'Ur.'

'Tell me about mami and papi.'

'Ayo, you'll have to wait, garçon.'

'When?'

'When chores are done, and dinner is cooked. Later.'

'By the fire?'

'Ur.'

'Ma-Jo, by the fire?'

'Garçon?'

'Ma!'

'Ayo, perhaps. We'll see.'

So, instead of letting lose my usual torrent of words I attempted to stay quiet for the day – no mean feat, believe you me. Instead I mumbled to myself, whispered secrets to the trunk of the tamarind tree, had an interesting conversation with a chicken behind our shed – all this unnoticed by Ma-Jo.

You see, by keeping tight-lipped I thought she'd be more likely to remember the last thing I said. Little did I know that grown-up mind's need a bit of prodding, so that things don't get lost in the mess in there.

When evening came, supper was served: fried fish, bouillon brède and rice. Now, I know what you're thinking – couldn't I have been more imaginative and thought up a dish with a little more pizazz. But mo cousin, what *kreol* doesn't love their *brède* and *poisson frire*, ey? Anyway, once we'd scraped our scraps into Pirat's bowl and picked our teeth with the bones, we settled beneath the tamarind tree. Ma-Jo resting on a large, flat sided stone, her mouth rolling like that ill-fated guava as she chewed on a tamarind fruit. Me, I sat at her feet, watching the first stars wink their hellos, my head resting on her knees.

'Ayo garçon, mo fatigué,' *oh, I'm tired*, she said between chews, 'phff.'

I felt the movement of her body as I rested there, what I'm sure was an exaggerated stretch; heard her yawn, felt the slap of her hands upon her knees as if readying to stand. She sighed again.

'Phff.'

Maybe she took my silence as a signal that I was tired, too. I admit I was a little drowsy though not ready to drop off just then.

'Ay, dormi mo piti?' *Time for bed?* Ma-Jo asked.

'Ma!' Was all I managed to say.

When I turned to look up at her, panic in my eyes, she gave me a wink and smile then ruffed my hair, let out a chuckle or two. But then she assumed a look of intensity. Her brows furrowed, her mouth set straight and she bade me, 'shhh, be quiet and listen.'

She cleared her throat.

'Your mama's name was Elise. Her mama, your grand-mère, was fourteen years old when she bore her – still a child. Your grand-père, well, your grand-mère never mentioned his name. But when your mama was born we had our answer – or so we thought,' Ma-Jo shook her head, spitting the seeds into her hand and tossing them into the fire. 'Garçon, it's not unusual for a babe to born pale, but this one was a little too white. And the child's hair, though thick and curly, a little too brown. Her eyes the same grey as the master's. Your grand-mère, she was as black as me.'

The world about us seemed to change with the story's telling. Dusk hovered above the horizon, the afternoon's long shadows melting into a brief twilight. From the mountains to the north a squall of bats swooped beneath the cloak of descending darkness, their squeaks agitated and excited.

In the evening's half-light Ma-Jo's skin was the colour of the night to come, her beauty radiant as the day just passed.

She explained that *grand-mère* worked in the Grande Maison but was banished from the master's house soon after mama was born. So too was the fate of every black in that home; from cook to maidservant all sent out to the fields. And this during harvest time, with cane waiting to be cut and the rollers of idle mills soon to be oozing with cane juice.

'Garçon,' Ma-Jo said, 'Peeling potatoes and scrubbing floors is no easy life. But work in the fields was nothing like tending our little plot, no, no. It was a curse too wicked even for your worst enemy, an evil that made the promise of death seem like relief. Take my hand, Liberté.'

Ma-Jo lent forward, slipping her left hand under my arm so it poked out before me. I gripped it with my own tender mitts. Unlike her almost flawless face, the hand was sown with scars and as thick as a man's. The palms and fingers as tough as a foot-bottom. A solidity which had never seemed unusual as it was all I had known.

'I was about your age when I began bundling cane. This, garçon,' she said, wiggling her fingers, her words breath in my ear, 'is more than twenty years working the fields from darkness to darkness, waking before the cock crowed and finishing long after the bats had taken wing. Can you imagine what it did to the hands of your grand-mère, unused to the travails of the field?'

To be honest I didn't even want to guess.

It so happened that *grand-mère* was sent back to work just days after giving birth to my mother. 'That she survived that first day was a miracle,' Ma-Jo said with an acknowledging nod. An old Malgache poultice was used to soothe *grand-mère's* hands, salve rubbed on the muscles of her arms and back. The morning after she was out in the fields again facing the same misery.

I wiped the tears from my cheeks, unsure if I wanted to hear more of so wretched a tale. Though I made no move to halt Ma-Jo's recitation.

Not only were blacks dismissed from their domestic duties, she told me, but they were forbidden to step foot in the Grande Maison. Their employ assumed by Malabars, all male and dressed to the nines in turbans and finery. Even visiting messengers, if black, were refused entry – met at the door, their dispatches delivered by an intervening tongue.

This new order, it appears, was instated at the mistress's decree.

'You see,' Ma-Jo said, 'it was not only those in the camp des noirs who realised. The lady of the house had her own suspicions about the identity of the child's father.'

The fire crackled and snapped, sending out constellations of cinders into the night air. We shuffled closer to the fire and I sat on my own rock by Ma-Jo's side.

A ceaseless pulse of crickets pressed in upon us.

From a bonbonne she poured herself a measure of tilambik, giving a satisfied smack of the lips after her first sip. She rested the cup and jug of spirits between her feet and fished a pipe from the pocket of her apron. A pinch of tobacco was pressed into the bowl then lit with a taper first dipped in the fire. Smoke puffed from her nostrils like steam from beneath the lid of a bubbling pot.

I edged towards the fire, mesmerised by the hocus-pocus of its flames.

'Not too close,' she said.

I remember the push of the blaze; how its heat made my skin feel like it was roasting; the floating embers that bit at my legs like red ants. But I endured its heat, a supplicant to those slithering daggers.

'For seven years,' Ma-Jo said, 'your grand-mère worked in those fields before smallpox took her in the epidemic of 1820. Mo ti croire, sa letemps margoze la zamai pou fini,' *we thought those bitter times would never end.* Ma-Jo lifted her cup and drained the liquor in one gulp.

For a moment she said nothing.

The silence was filled by the barking of a dog, the skittering of paws along the dirt road in front of our house; the pat of human footsteps. Pirat following along the fence line, offering his own chorus in return. A voice hailed from the blackness. Ma-Jo, her face lighted by the fire, raised a hand and replied, 'bonsoir Bernard,' to the disembodied call. The footsteps carried on, soon lost to the night.

'Around that time,' Ma-Jo continued, 'your mother began to work in the mistress's garden, she was apprenticed to an old Malabar gardener, Narram. A job more like play to child born in those days. She tended to the flowers and plants like they were her children. And was at her happiest when her fingers were in the soil or cupping the muddy roots of a seedling.'

Ma-Jo smiled, absently rubbing one foot atop the other and staring out towards the mountains now lost in the dark. When she spoke, it was as if her words were intended for some presence in that unseen place.

'Seven years passed, and Elise blossomed into a fine young woman. Her skin had browned a little with all that time in the sun. But when she wore that brown hair of hers in braids or had a wide brimmed sapo on her head, she could have been mistaken for white. Well, at a glance, anyway. Garçon, can you imagine how mouths went dry when a near-sighted visitor addressed her as maîtress? Not a blunder any self-respecting *blanc* would care to make, nor an oafish one for that matter. Your mama might have been given the best hand-me-downs and blessed with easier work, but she still lived in the camp with us. Who she was and what she represented would never be acknowledged. Her colour was just an accident of birth.'

A yawn escaped Ma-Jo's mouth, a deep lowing that seemed not only to belie the weight of the day, but that of the story she recounted.

It was then she told me about mama's pregnancy and how it had been four months before they realised that she was with child. Just like *grand-mère* her lips remained sealed as to the father's identity, immune to a glut of artful prying. I, however, struggled to fend of sleep with the same success. My head had begun to flop like a rag doll's and my eyelids were low and heavy.

'Ey, garçon,' Ma-Jo said, 'you sleeping? Al dormi, don,' *go to bed*, 'we'll finish tomorrow.'

'Si ou plait, Ma,' *please*, I said, 'encor en tigit,' *just a little more*.

She lifted me from where I sat, as if I were a mere babe, sitting me down carefully on her lap. There was a clink as her heel struck the cup at her feet and it in turn knocked against rock.

'Shhh,' she said to my murmurs, my head beginning to drift into sleep's murky shadow. In an effort to stay awake I shuffled and fidgeted in the woman's arms. Ma-Jo tightened her grip around me, her embrace now bordering on restraint.

'Arete bouzer, don,' *stop wriggling*, she said. I stopped moving, tried to sit up straight in the hope she wouldn't carry me off to bed. The air was still warm, though with a faint chill about it and a hint of brine on the breeze. It was less than half a mile to the sea and I often fell asleep listening to its whisper.

'That's better,' she said, stroking my head the way I have seen many mothers do.

The mystery, as Ma-Jo told it, was that not a soul in the camp recalled seeing mama alone with a man – none other than old

Narram that is. 'And bolom la,' *that old man*, she said, 'was almost seventy years old. He could hardly raise himself off his knees, there wasn't a chance of him raising anything else,'

Her laughter echoed in the night. I shook upon her knees.

Ma-Jo's face grew serious.

'But old Narram loved your mama like she was his own and would never let any harm come to her. I saw with my own eyes, the pride in his face as he watched Elise nurse that garden. And he wasn't the only one who felt that way.'

The other, it just so happened, was the master of the estate, a man feared and respected throughout the district of Flacq. Yes, it was true mama lived with the other slaves, but through extra rations and gifts of the best brand-new hand-me-downs, the old man made his feelings for her clear. Would you believe that despite dismissing any paternal liability, he felt responsible for the modesty of this girl? Funny, ey? Such a strange thing is the heart of man. Or perhaps his cataracts extended only as far as one eye and the other held a more benevolent lens. And it's just as likely you'll see wild boar perched upon the branches with pink pigeon.

Anyway, like any good despot the master had eyes and ears among his multitude, namely one Geté: an old Malgache who had long had the heart beaten out of him and loved the master like a crippled dog loves his keeper. There wasn't a plot brewed or an insurrection planned that the old tell-tale didn't apprehend. No matter how conscientious the plotter Geté had the habit of cropping up when anything interesting was afoot. Now, with mama looking the way she did, she stuck out among the camp residents, making it easy for the old spy to keep his beady eye on her. From behind trees and rocks; from round corners and the shadows he watched, but no illicit rendezvous did he witness. That was until—

By this point in the story my tiredness had begun to give way to confusion. All of these names, that weren't names at all. Mama, *grand-mère*; master, gardener, spy; bastard children: one of them me, one of them mama; fathers whose identities remained unspoken as if their very mention would bring down a curse. It was enough to make an alert mind swirl, let alone my sleepy head. But I was captivated by Ma-Jo's words and that I struggled to make head or tail of the yarn didn't matter. Because through the magic of childish intuition I realised the story was as much about me as those it described. So, I employed every trick for staying awake that I knew: I bit my thumb knuckle, pinched my forearm, used my fingers to lever my eyelids open – determined to hear out the tale.

The moon was high overhead, so I knew it was late. Despite my best efforts I couldn't help but snuggle into the softness of Ma-Jo's body, comforted by her familiar smells. Pipe smoke and arrack; garlic, onion and tomato from her cooking; the mixture of earth and spice from our garden, along with the freshness that seems to accompany everything green; the underlying musk of her skin. There was a moaning upon the breeze, the faintest hint of voices and words in an indecipherable tongue; both strange and familiar. There was something desperate about the sounds, like the grunt of an animal amidst the fury of a chase. Yet I was unafraid.

'It was but a month before the master's death,' Ma-Jo said, 'that your mama's tryst was finally observed. While the camp slept she had crept from her hut. There were rumours of magic – that by some spell she was given the power of invisibility; bestowed by this or that gris-gris or incantation. That she moved unseen in the moonlight; a gossamer through which the moon's rays shone, leaving no shadow; no suggestion of her living self. But in the shadow, bereft of the moons glare, she once again became whole, her beauty aglow, a beacon easily located in the darkness. Whether this was true, mo piti, or it was her own cleverness that kept her liaisons secret, who can say? But in the end, it was her moonlit figure in the shadows that betrayed her secret.

'After all his sneaking it was by chance that old Geté caught sight of your mama. There the Judas sat doing his business among the bushes, looking for a landmark or two so he wouldn't stumble into his own dung the next day (he might have been a sneak, but he was no fool), when who should he spy? Nestled at the edge of the forest's shadow, was Elise, and not alone. With her a companion who was no more than a shape against the trees.'

I opened my eyes and looked up at Ma-Jo, her face painted orange by firelight, and then screwed them shut, in an attempt to catch a glimpse of the two figures. But my imagination failed me, storing away its fantasies in readiness for the creation of dreams, I suppose.

'Geté held his breath,' Ma-Jo continued, 'clenched those muscles necessary to keep in his putrid air and prayed a sly fart wouldn't surprise him. He wet his lips in anticipation of the arrack the master would supply. Or so the story goes. Caught by the light of a stray moonbeam your mama's paramour was revealed, but only for a moment, this glimpse enough for Geté to get his eye-full. His bowels almost deserted him. The man he saw among the trees cut an unmistakeable figure; his muscles, taught and sinewy, glossy in the moonlight; his profile wild and handsome, yet on this occasion softened by a smile. He was no stranger to the old fiend. His deeds were camp legend. Its residents would have given him the very food from their table, had any of them had a table to begin with. In the arms of this figure was your mama, her face pressed against his chest.' Ma-Jo paused, and I listened to her heart beat with an excitement that matched my own.

29

'And when your mama's love knelt before her, like a supplicant before a shrine, even old Geté was moved by the scene – though, it turned out, not enough to stop him blabbing to his master. The figure in the shadows placed his hands around Elise's belly, as large as ripe watermelon. He kissed it and laid his forehead against it, uttering some unheard and unfathomable prayer. She pressed her hand gently upon the back of his head, like you would a child, stroking it as if to console him. Then like a phantom he was gone, submerged by the forest. Not even a shadow of him visible in the darkness. So too did old Geté flee, forgetting in his haste, even to search out a leaf or two before he pulled up his drawers.

'Only your mama remained, breathing deeply, as if to catch one last breath of her departed love, seemingly unaware that she was alone.'

'Was he my father, Ma? What was his name?' I asked, mumbling into the softness of Ma-Jo's Chest. I inhaled the salty taste of her skin and felt her body shudder as she nodded. 'Where was he going? Why didn't he stay?'

'He didn't stay, because he couldn't,' she said, 'he lived, in the forest, in the mountains, in the gullies, in caves; in the places inhabited by birds and animals and spirits. The places men shy away from and where nightmares congregate. And his name, mo piti, his name was Titon.'

'I don't understand,' I said, 'was he a ghost or monster?'

'No, mo piti, he was no ghost. He was a maroon, a runaway. One who could not live the way that we were forced to. His heart wouldn't allow it, refused to surrender itself to the life of an ox.'

'A maroon,' I said, from a place that was not quite dream and not quite consciousness. I knew the word though not its meaning.

It was a word from a time before I was born, or from a time when words were mere sounds to me and nothing more.

'Oui,' Ma-Jo said, 'a grande marron, with a bounty on his head of 500 piastres offered by the master himself.'

Chapter Four

Alexandre

The Lament of Mme Lousteau

It was a rock that did it. This is what they tell me. A thing that fit so easily in the palm of a hand. A piece of that black rock which litters this God forsaken place.

What was the old fool doing out there anyway? Is it not a young man's sport? And if not a young man's then an active man's.

Yes, yes, I concede it was his business, for it was his stock they chased. But there are trained blacks and dogs for this. And what of the *maréchaussée*, what do we pay them for? Do we just throw away our subsidies expecting nothing in return?

Vanity sent him out chasing stray *nègres*; vanity and that mule of a girl. He is too soft with her, I have seen his looks. Of course he has good reason. And I do not deny she is comely. There are occasions when her type inherits some gentility from their donor. She is so very pale and strangely this does not stand at odds with her flat face and that briar of hair. She is marked upon his heart, there is no denying it.

This island eats away at the civilised, the heat invades you. And living in such close commune with these savages awakens something in our men, something that would be better off left sleeping.

If it were not for Balteau I might not see a white face for weeks. Of course it's different now, with every *petit propriétaire* thinking it their duty to come and pay their respects; expecting conversation and refreshment for the duration of their visits. Pah, leave me to mourn in peace. Go and drink your own wine and take tea with yourselves; bid your own servants – if in fact you have any – bring you cake. I do not feel up to socialising.

Why did he not leave it to Balteau and his little circus, instead of venturing up into the mountains where a *Grand Blanc* has no business going? Why this time if not for that girl?

He did not join the hunt after Guyot's murder. And he was a white man. Maybe not a man of distinction, but exemplary in the pursuit of his craft. And as far as may be judged by my feminine eye, he was a credit to this *habitation*. There are always those less tractable creatures, the ones with thick hides and even thicker skulls, but a good overseer has an eye for them and he had that. Well, apart from that last time. But for the most part the *nègres* obeyed him dutifully.

The slave my husband died chasing was the same one who killed Guyot, you know. It was the girl's condition that drove him up into the mountains and to his end. What a fool, and what comes of fool but a fool's death?

He leaves me here, stranded amongst mountains and sugarcane and blacks. And now what? This oasis is no oasis at all. They are everywhere. I feel the scrutiny of their averted eyes; hear their snorting breaths while I sleep and the songs which disguise mutiny. In my dreams I hear cries like those of the doomed planters of Saint Domingue.

They run away and make camp amongst the trees. They surround us, all but their eyes and teeth hidden by shadow. Do you see them, do you not see them?

In the fields and in their hutches they laugh and smile; sing and dance their licentious jigs. There is much beneath their feigned docility and none of it good. Mark my words their freedom would mean the end of us, *he told me so*.

He was not wholly absent of sense. No, he was not blind, not to everything.

If they are freed they will make us pay. There will be no curtsy, no '*oui mo maître*,' our throats will be cut as we sleep and our babes cast into the sea. I ask you, does a man beat his dog and then release the mutt that it might bite him?

God made them what they are, cursing Ham with his own divine tongue. It is the nature of things, the nature of creation. Their right is to be used not civilised.

I feel them seething. I feel their heat, their wantonness, their sanguinary lust. They are watching. They are talking. They are making ready. They are everywhere.

The casting of a single stone, that one unlucky shot, has left me stranded; stranded and alone with them; alone with her.

I loved him.

OLD WOUNDS

Chapter Five

The Notary

'Madame, M. Gallard is here to see you.'

Mme Lousteau looked up.

Sandi stood in the doorway. His turban seemed to hover above his pyjamas, cuffs and trouser legs ending in nothing, like a suit of hanging clothes.

To her eyes, which had not so much cried rivers but been submerged and gazed up at the water's surface, the world appeared to have lost its edges. One thing being not quite separate from another.

Mme Lousteau wiped her eyes as she saw Sandi clearly for the first time.

'What is it, Sandi?'

'M. Alfonse Gallard is here to see you.'

Gallard, the name's familiarity surrendered no clues. How was she supposed to remember? Sorrow had swallowed up so much of her memory and the things she could remember hurt too much to recall.

She pressed her fingertips to her temples. It made no difference.

Yet another salver of condolences, no doubt. Another visitor whose concern would fail to mask their self-interest.

When the man entered of his own accord, and he must have for Mme Lousteau could not remember summoning him, she thought, *oh that Gallard.* With this came further recollections, fragments that arose without prompt from some forgotten repository: M. Gallard kissing her hand. A vision of him in the study with Alexandre. The door being closed. A long-heated discussion the door could not conceal. His farewell smile, genial but one that spread no further than the mouth.

The strands of grey that flecked Gallard's hair mimicked the cloth of his suit, its black weave threaded with strands of silver. The suit, despite its obvious quality, betrayed signs of M. Gallard's proclivities; the buttons of the jacket beginning to strain and seams stretched in ways unintended by the tailor.

It occurred to her that she had thought him handsome. His skin as clear as a woman's, its lines as superficial as sleep marks lacking the inscribed permanence that inflicts many an aging face; that oiled hair combed into waves. So different from her Alexandre; who although not weathered had bore the look of one not afraid of the outdoors, the look of a country man.

Where had all this come from? Memories that would have proved unreachable if searched for floated to the surface of her mind like the rising of swollen dead.

Gallard hesitated just inside the doorway, as if unsure whether to continue.

He bowed.

'Madame.'

'Do you intend to bellow at me from across the room, monsieur, or will you perhaps enter and conduct your business like a civilised man?'

She was surprised by the sharpness of her words, how direct she had become. Metamorphosis is only natural when confronted with the tragic, but this acidity was an altogether new development. She put it down to the appearance of another unwelcome guest, although, in the wake of Alexandre's death the arrival of a man such as Gallard was to be expected.

One could only be amazed, she mused, at the speed which news travelled through these rural enclaves. Even pigeons would struggle to carry news as rapidly as it was spread by chattering tongues.

'Forgive me, madame,' he said striding to meet her.

'Your apologies are unnecessary, M. Gallard, what can I do for you?' Mme Lousteau asked as she rose from her chair.

'First I must say how sorry I am. Alexandre was fine man who loved you dearly. Your husband and I may not have always seen eye to eye, but our differences were never enough to sour our relationship,' again he hesitated. 'These are difficult times for you, madame, I realise this, and what I must tell you brings me no joy. However, it is better you know now, that swift action might be taken.'

'I'm tired, M. Gallard, please do me the courtesy of getting to the point.'

M. Gallard reddened, cleared his throat.

'Very well, Madame. In my position as notary I oversaw the drafting of your husband's will, I am also its executor. Three months ago, Alexandre summoned me and requested an addendum be added. This he entrusted to me for safekeeping. With the instatement of this codicil, which I must say was a creation of his own hand and had already been drafted on my arrival, you would no longer be the major beneficiary of his estate. All other negligible bequeaths, notwithstanding. You would share his estate and the greater part of his holdings with another; namely his daughter.'

The trembling started in her left foot, travelling up one leg and then infecting the other. She stepped back, stumbled, found the arm of a chair, managing to take hold of both rests before the remainder of her began to shake.

M. Gallard rushed to her but she waved him away, risking a fall rather than accept his assistance.

Mme Lousteau shook her head, continued to shake it as she began to speak.

'How dare you.'

'Please, Madame, if you will just allow me—'

'His daughter? You are well aware we have no children.'

'I realise, Madame, that—'

'Get out, now. Leave my home, immediately.'

She fell back into the chair, gulping back a sob, hands still grasping the armrests. The air around her seemed to thicken so that every breath became a struggle. There was a pressure within her head, pushing at the temples and behind the eyes, as if her skull had reached its capacity and everything inside was trying to escape.

It was Sandi's hand upon her shoulder that saved her. The words he breathed into her ear that helped Mme Lousteau recover her senses. 'Hear him out,' he said, in no more than a whisper, so subtle it could have mistaken for a thought.

Sandi nodded to M. Gallard, who, despite Mme Lousteau's commandment, had remained firmly rooted to the spot. He blinked as if it was his turn to bring the world back into focus, anticipating, maybe, yet another interruption from Mme Lousteau.

When he again began to speak, it was haltingly, as if each word was twice contemplated.

'I should not have been so bold in my pronouncement, considering your recent bereavement. But it is exactly because of your current circumstances that my impatience got the better of me.'

Mme Lousteau waved away Gallard's regret, not wanting to speak, that he might hear her voice crack.

'The one of whom I speak is no stranger to you, she lives here, in the camp at La Belle Horizon. You cannot be ignorant of her identity.'

*

A child was born, as begins that oldest of tales, but this birth brought no joy – not for her, anyway.

For a *nègre* to bear such a fair-skinned child would indeed have been a miracle.

Mme Lousteau had heard of such goings on, in fact, they were said to be quite commonplace. Although, as with many things one has heard of but never seen, it was a surprise.

Not on their *habitation*, no, it could not be.

Her immediate thought had been of Guyot, for whom else could the father be, but there was something in the glances of the house slaves, a question she could not, or did not want to ask herself.

At first, she had put this down to her own imagination, the kind of fantasy that might arise when cooped up for too long with only blacks for company.

After a little investigation, however, Nanette – a disagreeable looking thing but one of the few blacks she had ever taken to – told her it was the child of the kitchen girl, Florine.

'Sa mem tout ki mo coné, maîtress,' Nanette had said, refusing to meet her mistress's eyes, staring instead at her own bare feet.

'En français, ma fille, en français,' Mme Lousteau replied.

'C'est tout ce que je sais, maîtress,' *That is all I know, mistress.*

40

She had shaken Nanette and lifted the girl's face, fingers pressing into the flesh of her cheeks that she might look into the girl's eyes. And what she saw in them, the fear, set her own heart to racing.

But she got nothing more from the girl.

Alexandre had been in his study reviewing the plantation's ledgers. The door was ajar. Mme Lousteau knocked, and entered on hearing him mumble something which could have been either *allez* or *vini*.

He sighed and looked up from his book, peering at her from over the top of his spectacles. He said nothing, only stared, eyes full of figures and wearing an expression as blank as an empty page of his ledger.

The room was light and high ceilinged and seemed to suck the words from her throat before she had time to consider them.

'There is a child living among the blacks,' she said. Alexandre resumed the study of his ledger, 'a white child – no something else.'

'An albino, maybe,' he said, amending an entry with a flourish of his pen.

'It has brown hair. Should an albino, even one born of a *nègre*, have brown hair?' she said, her voice rising, 'would it not be white?'

He sighed.

Her gaze followed the streaks of brown that crested and troughed the silver waves atop his head. His hair had grown long, touching his shirt collar. One side swept behind an ear, the other partly trapped behind the arm of his spectacles, stray strands draped before his brow. Quite the old swashbuckler, even in age there was some of her young man in him.

'The child's welfare is of obvious concern to you,' he said. 'Perhaps you should visit *le camp des noirs* and put your mind at rest. And of course, pass on my blessing.'

She should have taken her leave, allowed Alexandre to complete his business and abandoned her pursuit of the foolish notion. There she was lost in her mind's own intrigue while he was steeped in the very workings of the plantation.

But it had been important, hadn't it?

'Alexandre, please, I am—'

'This information comes from whom?' he asked, his voice all exhalation.

'I know it exists.'

'So, it exists,' he said, again looking up from his ledger, 'what is your point? Would you have it brought to the house to live with us?'

'Alexandre be serious. The mother is a *nègre*. And the child, well— Someone is responsible for this. Are such things now acceptable on this *habitation*?'

'*Cherie*,' he said, his voice softening, 'do you know how many children are born in the camp? How many of those make it through infancy?' He paused but continued without awaiting her response. 'This child represents a successful birth at a time when such things are rare. Whatever you might imagine it to be, it is certainly an increase to our holdings.'

He continued to watch her, waiting she guessed, for her to leave or to say something. He picked up his pen and rolled it between his fingers, inspected its nib.

'The seas are full of British patrols,' Alexandre added, filling the space where her words should have been, 'ships are captured, their cargoes confiscated. There are very little in the way of good slaves these days. You cannot work a good *nègre* too hard, but the mozambiques we receive are weak and infirm. We're lucky if they last one season. If they were horses most would be shot as soon as they stepped ashore. So, in a way the child is a blessing, the negation of a future expense. Now please, *Cherie*.'

42

This said he returned to his bookkeeping, as if with this dismissal all her concerns had been allayed. Oh, if only this had been the case – that such suspicions were banished so easily.

She stood before Alexandre's desk waiting like a child before a schoolmaster, hunched over his ledger he carefully followed each entry with the tip of his pen.

'It is Florine's child,' she said.

This sounded so strange to her, the familiarity with which she used the name, like the mention of an old friend. She smiled, and was not sure why, but when he looked up this is what he caught on her face.

'Florine?' He asked, frowning now.

Yet at the sight of her smile, she was sure it was the smile that did it, something happened. Those eyes, which over the years had acquired a master's appraising stare, softened, as if begging she go no further.

She had stood for a moment and then turned, leaving the room. She felt his eyes follow her as she disappeared into the parlour, leaving him only the echo of her footsteps.

It was impossible for her to remain in that room. Not if she wanted to preserve whatever love she still felt for him. And she did love him.

She remembered a younger Alexandre. The one she clung to as they ascended the gangplank, all those years ago in Marseilles, and wondered how and when they had been separated. She remembered the life that had once grown inside her but had been taken from her – leaving a place forever empty.

The Alexandre she knew did not work at a distance from his concerns. The plantation was his livelihood, not a pastime or some remote investment. He was well acquainted with his slaves. That is to say he was a good judge of their suitability for this or that task.

Perhaps his evaluation had gone further than the perfunctory, on this occasion. Had he cooked up a little soufflé with the kitchen girl, or was she making too much use of her imagination? He was certainly not ignorant of Florine as his reply had suggested.

Old Modeste, the cook, had been happy when Florine was assigned to help her in the kitchen. The girl was a good worker. She was obedient and made little nuisance of herself, gladly performing whatever task the old woman gave her.

(Apparently it was not only the old Cook's orders the girl obeyed without hesitation.)

But really, for all her speculation what did she have? Evidence pieced together from imagined looks and whispers – whispers, that maybe, she had given too much credence. From possibility she had derived certainty; she had seen a tapestry where only mere threads existed. Was it not more likely that her fears had gotten the better of her? This was her Alexandre, after all.

Whatever her suspicions it was not wise to fixate on one possibility and dismiss all others out of hand. There was no sense to it. And it was not as if it were the most plausible of scenarios.

For all she knew his indifference was the result of overwork, his disinterest not affectation but a symptom of a preoccupied mind. Well this made more sense, didn't it? This she had seen with her own eyes. Was it not the industry of one man, her Alexandre, that made their *habitation* flourish – that ensured its profitability even during those leanest of years? If he were not sitting hunched over his books he would be out touring the plantation; inspecting mills and culverts, or just regarding the work of slaves and foremen, (let us not forget the kitchen girls), looking for ways in which the plantation's great mechanism might be improved.

And was it not more likely, as she had first concluded that Guyot had fathered the *mulâtre?* Guyot was a man whose proclivities erred towards the brutish. In fact, were not such qualities essential to one whose trade was dependent upon the use of a severe hand? What overseer ever profited from leniency?

The more she considered it the more the possibility of Alexandre's involvement seemed preposterous and she, herself, became the culprit.

Could she really have gotten it so wrong? Were all her notions nothing but flights of fancy?

They must have been.

All those who corrupted with their glances and whispers, and maybe even their very presence – it could not be allowed to continue. They must go. There was to be no more opportunity for them to spread their seeds of intrigue. (His seed spread so intriguingly.) Who would have guessed hearsay and insinuation could prove so destructive; so seductive? Averted eyes, hollow answers, the quickening of steps on their mistress's approach; mutterings not quite in earshot but which could definitely be heard – insignificant incidents the imagination might make much of but which disappeared like smoke at the grasping.

Little more could be expected of servants, of blacks, but of her? To fall foul of such whisperings; to be influenced by such ideas, what was happening to her?

They would have Indians. Yes. She had seen Indians serving in the home of M. Malpass, his servants dressed in turbans and satin costume. There had been a bearing about them, neither haughty nor above their station, more pride in duty. As if they were aware of what an honour it was to serve such people.

What a wonderful change such a retinue would make. And what more fitting symbol of one's status was there than servants of suitable stateliness?

Of course, there would be no girls, definitely no girls. Their loose lips bred gossip (and brown skinned bundles) – enough of that. It was such idle thoughts which had led her astray, (it was him who was led astray), idle thoughts born of an idle mind. What was to be done with her? How was she to curtail such wistfulness?

The question hung in the air like a dream not quite remembered; its clarity dissolving with every concentrated thought and coalescing when sort to be forgotten.

There was only one thing she could do: help him.

Such an industrious soul as her Alexandre would never ask for help; not from her, nor from anybody. He was a proud man, not prone to displays of what he would call weakness. But that did not mean she should not offer her support. She was literate, not ignorant of the art of bookkeeping and for years had observed the running of the plantation. (Apparently not close enough.) There must be some way she could assist him. They were a partnership in God's eyes, weren't they? For richer, for poorer; in sickness and in health. And it would mean less time for her mind to wander. (And for his— to wander.) It would be remedy for both of their conditions. Yes, she was a woman, but what of it? Isle de France was a place where, if circumstance demanded, one might be excused from the old ways. (And he had certainly excused himself.) And circumstances did demand it. She could save them both.

A grandiose sentiment to be sure, but this did not prevent it from being true. She would need to be careful how she broached the subject with Alexandre, however. A certain amount of diplomacy would be needed. She should stress her own need for occupation rather than his for assistance. (He certainly had no trouble keeping himself occupied.) Yes, she would apologise for her outburst and tell him it was all to do with her mind. No, no, that would not do, what she meant was all those idle hours she had. And the isolation – no, not the isolation, she would rather socialise with the furniture than with one of those plantation wives – for she knew this was what Alexandre would suggest. Those women were all so dull, so dreary, locked in a world of pretence and frivolity, heads full of frocks and parasols and inconsequential things. (For him nothing so dreary, it had been the exotic that piqued his interest.) Not to forget the children. (How would she ever forget?) Whose presence was always to be felt whether or not they were present. There were those tell-tale signs of occupation, a door hastily closed, the scurrying feet of a child or nursemaid or both; an irritation in the manner of a hostess who usually affected so distracted an air. She knew this, had seen this, felt it through the walls.

Mme Lousteau had felt an adventurer when she set out on her journey with Alexandre and now what was she, a bystander in a story that had carried on without her. (Yes, he had carried on his adventuring.) How could she help but be distracted when she had nothing to arrest her mind – nothing of purpose, anyway. She had never been one for embroidery or dabbling with watercolours and had no intention of being drawn any further into literature's intrigues; she had proved more than capable of constructing her own fictions. One could dedicate only so much time to riding, travel only so far and remain within the bounds of safety. There was of course contemplation but look where too much of that had gotten her – all entwined in her own loose strands. But if she could just do something, anything just to help him, it would help her to keep her own mind straight. She would be no bother, she promised. She had a sharp mind, he knew she had a sharp mind and only need be told something once before grasping it.

'Please Alexandre, and if I do make a nuisance of myself I promise you I'll leave it all well alone and never ask again.'

*

'M. Gallard, I am no stranger to the rumours which surround that girl, but to suggest she is Alexandre's child— I would think twice before making such a claim.'

The notary glanced at Sandi.

'Forgive me, Madame, but this is not the time for keeping up appearances. I am here to help, to prevent further catastrophe, not engage in speculation. It was your husband's decision to take responsibility for the girl and to provide for her future; a belated and somewhat misguided gesture, but one that also leaves no question of misinterpretation.'

'So, you are telling me I must give half of La Belle Horizon to this— this bastard?'

Gallard reached into his jacket and produced an envelope, which he held up before her.

'I have here the aforementioned codicil – a legally binding document. Despite raising concerns about the wisdom of your husband's decision, he was adamant that the amendment be added, and I was left with no choice but to accept it. I did, however, decide to delay adding the document to my register. A measure I took both as a notary and a friend. There seemed little doubt emotions had gotten the better of him, and in my experience, it is at such times we need a friend who has our best interests at heart. Someone who sees things with a clarity impossible for those more emotionally involved.'

M. Gallard had begun to pace back and forth, emphasizing each point of his address with a flourish of the envelope.

'Please, M. Gallard, you are making me feel giddy.'

'Ah, yes, forgive me. I planned to reconvene with Alexandre, a week or so later, to give him time to consider his decision. But circumstances worked against us and we were unable discuss the matter again, before tragedy struck. What this means, however, is that officially this document does not exist,' the notary said, waving the envelope once more, 'and is known to none but those present here today.'

'Un verre d'eau, Sandi,' *a glass of water*, Sandi, said Mme Lousteau, the waver disappearing from her voice. She released her grip of the chair arms and took her refreshment. After two sips she passed the glass back to her servant, who placed it on its salver and took his place beside her. It was as if she felt the return of herself. No longer hunched she sat erect, chin in the air; eyes still glassy but her cheeks devoid of tears.

'A commendable speech, monsieur, but please forgive me, what is it you really want? You paint a picture of impending catastrophe yet with your final flourish there is not a storm but blue sky. How much is required for your silence?'

'No-no, Madame,' M. Gallard said, dropping to one knee and placing the envelope in Mme Lousteau's hands, going so far as to close her fingers around it. She allowed him this indulgence, before removing her hands from his. The notary got to his feet, brushing at his trousers as he stood. 'You do me a disservice by suggesting such a thing. My ties to your family go beyond duty; there is little I would not do to help. Please, just take the document and read it. After that, well, my advice would be to destroy it. For as long as it exists so does the possibility that it might find its way into the wrong hands. You understand that in handing over the codicil I am entrusting you with my reputation.'

Mme Lousteau nodded, wondering what else was hidden among all those words.

'Thank you, M. Gallard, and my apologies. You have proved yourself a true friend of the Lousteaus. And trust me; no evidence of this insanity will remain.'

M. Gallard, cleared his throat.

'There is one other thing, Madame.'

She resisted dropping her shoulders but could not help but let out a sigh.

'Is there no end to your tale, Gallard? How much longer do you intend to torment me?'

'It is better I tell you now, Madame, rather than wait for you to discovery it yourself. In the codicil there is mention of a letter, one your husband wrote to the girl. What it contains, I do not know. When I pressed him on the matter all he would say was: "I have said all that can be said and it is now in the hands of providence," an answer which provides little clarity.'

'And I should be concerned?'

'There is every possibility your husband made his intentions clear to the girl. And if his language was specific in nature, the letter, itself, could be judged a valid addendum.'

'So, the codicil's existence is moot, as the letter may prove just as good.'

'It is in no way a fait-accompli, but possible, yes.'

'I take it you have devised a plan to acquire this letter.'

'The matter of the letter, as the codicil, is in your hands. The girl is still your property and remains a resident of this estate. Does Madame not have someone in her employ that she might commission to retrieve the letter?' The notary's eyes flittered towards Sandi. 'A person who might move about the estate without arousing suspicion.'

Chapter Six

The Trophy

'It stood at the entrance to the camp, mounted on a spear – a message to us. We were told: "Don't move it. Don't touch it." Nothing was further from our minds.

'Gris-gris, hidden in pockets and beneath clothing, were sought out and held tightly. Prayers whispered to the gods of older times.'

Ma-Jo straightened, her hand resting at the crook of her back. She looked up towards the sun.

The heat was a heavy weight, an invisible burden we could not put down. Increasing the effort needed for each task tenfold. Stiff shadows blackened the earth, their edges as precise as lines drawn on a slate.

She wiped her brow with the corner of her apron.

Her head was wrapped in a blue scarf, the same blue as her dress, the blue of the sea beyond the shallows of Blue Bay. The cloth, once darker – almost indigo, had faded, beaten relentlessly by sun and stone. Its seams and creases were lighter, white against the darker plains of fabric. Dirt clung to the hem of the dress, dust puffing upwards when it brushed against the floor.

'Hot today, ey, mo piti?'

I nodded, and ran to fetch Ma-Jo a *calebasse* of water from the well bucket.

The previous night I had succumbed to sleep, ending the story's first instalment. But as if by a will of its own, the story began again the next day, drawn to us like waves are drawn to the shore.

'You're a good boy, Liberté.'

She took a sip and handed it back to me.

With her basket balanced on her hip she trod off towards our house, resting in the shade of its eaves. I struggled with my own basket; *calebasse* lodged under my arm, and sat down beside her.

'Fouf,' she said, fanning herself with her hand, sitting wide legged and straight backed like a man, 'even rest is hard work in this heat, ey?'

Ma-Jo lit her pipe, drawing in deeply.

She continued her tale.

'Flies crawled over it, making it shimmer like sun-stars on the surface of the sea. And then suddenly they'd fly away leaving it naked, exposing the terrible thing. We cringed at its sight. Hid from those unseeing eyes that stared at us without blinking. Yet we were drawn to it, unable to prevent the glimpses that caught in our eye-corners and twisted our necks to meet its gaze.

'A foul odour – sickening yet familiar, like spoilt meat and rotting mango; sweet but with a tang that threatened to bring up even yesterday's food – filled the air of the camp, coating our skin and nostrils. Women cried, men shook their heads and stared at their feet as they kicked the dirt. Teeth were gnashed and whispers of dissent passed between those men whose limbs bristled with the constant dream of escape. All living colour had left the thing. It was grey and wretched and sidled by nightmares of the wandering dead. There was no escape from it. It would not leave us.

'On the overseer's orders Dominère, the slave commander, returned to camp twice daily to check it was still there, would repeat his many warnings of punishment, his voice muffled by the cloth covering his nose and mouth.

'On the second day the skin began to squirm and wriggle, as if piece by piece the thing was coming back to life. The stink worsened following us to our huts and lying beside us on our pallets as we slept. It whispered things. Told us to get up and run; to flee to the forests and mountain caves. Told us stories, and the names and natures of places we had never seen. We all heard the voice, mo piti, yes, we all heard it.

'On the third day the spear was empty. The thing had disappeared.

'It couldn't have gone far. Or so we thought. For the stink still surrounded us and crawled up from the earth beneath our feet and edged into the spaces between our skin and clothes – trailing over our bodies like an army of ants.'

She stopped. The words seemed to hang in the air and then disappear like the smoke from her pipe. As the silence opened it was filled by sounds from the world outside of Ma-Jo's story: a banging hammer that seemed to echo from every direction; the snoring of our dog Pirat, who slept on the porch behind us; chattering women whose appetite for gossip was unaffected by the heat; and, of course, the trill of birds.

Even the air of that outer world seemed fresher, full of the scent of the growing things and the bounty which lay in our baskets. It was a world I had forgotten existed.

I sat embracing the *calebasse*, the coolness of it pressing against my chest, waiting for Ma-Jo to carry on. With her fingertips she touched my forearm and lifted the *calebasse* from my embrace. She took a long swig, tossing her head back so far that when she handed the thing back I was surprised

53

it still contained water. I drank too and despite the heat I shivered.

'Let me tell you, mo piti, the habitation was not run by empty threat.' Ma-Jo shook her head. 'Dominère told us we would feel his whip if we touched the thing and none of us doubted it. Five men were chosen and with them their women. There were puffed chests and squared shoulders but all wore a look of uncertainty in their eyes. We stared, shook our heads and mumbled only to be silenced by the crack of the whip. In turn each woman was taken to the post, their hands bound to the ring at its top. They were both there, the overseer and Dominère. The overseer seething with an anger which bordered on delight, fondling his rifle like it was a newborn child; while the slave commander cursed us, each word followed by rotten breath and a shower of spittle, and finished with "where is it, ey? tell me and I stop at one." No one spoke up and I doubt a soul knew of its fate. For who could keep quiet and allow such affliction? It's likely a maroon crept down from the mountains and took it, one of his men. And it wouldn't surprise me if the overseer and Dominère thought the same.

'Those mountain men had the footsteps of ghosts. Could steal the dirt from beneath your feet and you wouldn't know it until you found yourself knee-deep in a hole.

'Dominère threw his whip at the chest of the first man. It hit him and fell to the floor. "Take it," Dominère growled, but the man said nothing staring past the slave commander as if he didn't hear him. There was no warning. The man dropped to the floor with the first blow of the rifle butt. Claque!'

Ma-Jo clapped her hands making me jump and drop the *calebasse*. It wasn't full but my eyes watered when it hit my toes. I screwed up my face in pain. Ma-Jo turned to look at me, nodding, the pain of her story – by some accident – reflected in my face.

She looked away, returning to that other place, the water already just a stain in the dirt.

'No one saw the overseer move, only heard the crack of wood against bone. Dominère, he laughed, laughed as the man lay there – not moving. Even clapped the white man on the back to congratulate him, but the overseer gave Dominère a stare so cold he nearly choked on his own laughter, he swallowed it so fast. This enraged the slave commander. He kicked the fallen man, stamped on his back. "Get up, get up you lazy nègre," he shouted, "move when I tell you!" With the help of another the man struggled to his feet, bloody faced, his cheek torn asunder.

'The next man took up the whip without hesitation, pleading in Malgache for God's forgiveness. He was made to flog the fallen man's woman before meting out the same punishment upon his own. And if a blow was not brutal enough, Dominère would add another, making sure that the stroke left its mark. So it went on, the men's faces wet with tears as they beat their women.'

With this my own tears erupted, my heart unable to bear the thought of such cruelties.

True it might seem unkind to persist with a tale that tore at such a young one's heart, but as I have said by this time the story had taken on its own life, leaving me and Ma-Jo unwilling to let the tale go.

'Mama, what about mama?' I asked, fearing the worst for Mama Elise.

'Ayo, mo piti,' Ma-Jo said, taking my hand, 'what your mama saw the day that thing appeared, it was too much. At first, she would not believe it, could not believe it was him. Such a sight,' Ma-Jo shook her head, 'and your mama so heavy with child. But as it is with such things, her head saw through her heart's deception. For almost three days she would not eat, taking only the smallest of sips when water was offered to her. Who would perish first, we wondered; girl-child or the child she carried?'

Despite the blazing sun above Ma-Jo pulled me closer. The smell of summer heat radiated from her body.

'That thing – black with flies, flesh torn away so you could see both teeth and jaw – had terrified us. Who would not be frightened by such a curse? But your mama fell before it like a penitent at the cross; cried for your papa to come back, not to leave her.

'She cursed the overseer, spat at him and beat at the chest of the commander. This only seemed to increase their enjoyment.' Ma-Jo turned her head to me, giving me a blink and a nod. She bent over, her mouth level with my ear, lowering her voice to little more than a whisper, 'there was talk you know, mo piti. And yes, there is always talk. Idle gossip, maybe, but as I did not see I can only tell you what was said. It was said she visited it that first night; kissed it, whispered into that single ear, made plans for their escape. Spellbound, some said; mad, others. But likely these are just stories, works of mischief. They were always to be heard from this one or that one and when you questioned that one it was always another. There were those within the camp who loved to feed our ears with titbits of hearsay and so-and-so. Yet who but God knows what is true?

'I saw your mama the first day, watched our people drag her from before those devils, when the amusement of overseer and camp commander threatened to become something more sinister. Although there was little they could do to her, for we know who she was, ey mo piti,' she said, giving me a wink.

'I will not say we were great friends, me and your mama, but neither were we enemies. Our greetings were kindly. We would nod and smile and share a few words, but nothing more. I held no grudge against the girl, although I admit I was a little jealous of her. But who didn't envy that ti milâtress? Her work was easy and the old Malabar brought her food from the kitchen of the white house. And there was your father.'

With this utterance she stiffened. I felt a tightening in the muscles of her arm where it pressed against my own. And she dragged so deeply on her pipe I expected jets of smoke to come shooting from beneath her toenails. I wondered where the tale would wander off to next, what strange and unseen path it might take. I sensed a change, a turn.

I looked up at her, at Ma-Jo, not an old woman, yet old to me. When she talked I always wanted to hear more and more and more, never wanting her to stop. But this story, my own history, you could say, was threatening to become too big for my little head. Although as it turns out my little head was bigger inside than I thought.

'I remembered him, you see, mo garçon, the young rebel,' Ma-Jo said, looking down at her hands as she spoke. As if the words to her story lay in her palms. As if those lines and calluses mapped out the lives she recounted. Her voice, no longer full of a storyteller's energy, had lost its song and rhythm. 'Before his back was striped with the history of his dissent. When two ears balanced his handsome face and the blister of the fleur de lys was absent from his skin.

'He charmed me, you know garçon—'

I shook my head, although her question didn't seem directed at me, but to some other invisible ear.

'—bewitched me with words I'll always remember.

'He said that when I smiled it was like watching the first rays of sunlight fall upon the flowers of a bois de boeuf. Such a beautiful flower. Such a beautiful thing to say. Imagine that, mo piti.'

The corners of her mouth lifted but the smile travelled no further.

I donned my own uncertain smile.

'I had not long left childhood behind but the ways of men were new to me,' she said, 'his smile: wide and toothy, and yes, a little cunning, and those darker than night eyes, made me nervous. Made me want to run away – but at the same time they made me want to stay.

'But I turned,' Ma-Jo said, 'or I would never have stopped staring. I pressed my lips together trying to hide my happiness. But I couldn't. It didn't want to be put away.

'He laughed, it wasn't a mean laugh, I could hear that and it made me want to look at him again so I could enjoy it, too. Silly girl, ey garçon?'

She sniffed. This time I took her hand, my own no more than the span of her palm. I twisted my neck so I could see her face, but there were no tears.

I looked away, watched the ants as they marched between my feet, some tickling my toes and instep, heading in the direction of the tamarind tree. While others weaved around mountain-like rocks no taller than my ankle, inspecting tomato leaves that had fallen from our baskets.

The freshly picked fruit lay beside us on the porch, plump and red, the air scented with the spice of their leaves and stalks; a happy smell of harvest that clung to our fingers and clothes.

'It shouldn't have, but it always surprised me when something so beautiful came from one of our mouths – us whose lives contained so little beauty.' She said. 'Forgetting there were those who remembered a different life – a life often easier to forget than relive in your head. What good could such memories do, anyway, but make our lives harder? Or so I had thought.

'Your papa never forgot, though. He might have hidden it from the whites, but we could see the old place still lived inside him; its dirt still under his nails, between his toes. That he was unwilling to let go of the one he was before. Dangerous, ey?'

I nodded my head, and tried to picture this man again, mo papi. Not the wild-man; the half man, half spirit who lived in the forests – the hero depicted in Ma-Jo's earlier stories. But the man of before: young and unmarked with the coast of Madagascar in his eyes.

It is funny, I tell you, because the person I saw was me. A little older, a little darker, yes, but it was definitely me. But it's not as if I thought it was me, I knew it was him – like a memory had awoken inside me.

I looked up at Ma-Jo, my mouth open as if snot clogged my nose, wanting to say something but not sure of the words. Not even sure of what it was I wanted to say. And Ma-Jo looked down at me, like I had tapped her shoulder or spoken her name. And I could tell by her smile that she understood. Her smile was different this time. I'm not saying it was full of happiness; but understanding, yes.

'They worked us hard back then,' she said, 'and our rations would hardly have fed a child. Our children died and the ones who survived we mourned because of the life they would lead. Every last drop was wrung out of us and when we fell to the ground our bodies were little more than dust.'

At that very moment a gust of wind cut across the yard, lifting the fallen tomato leaves and their ant passengers off the ground, sending them on spins and gambols through the air. Grains of dirt stung our eyes and tickled our throats and nostrils; one coughed, one sneezed, who did what I cannot say. I shut my eyes and held my breath. With the same immediacy the breeze was gone, the leaves lost in the sweep of the yard.

'For them, you see, a storehouse of blacks lay across the ocean ready to replenish our numbers. Their dogs, their cattle, their asses suffered less than us – made in God's image just like them. I wanted no more of that life, that life of no life – none of us wanted it. What fool would? So your father's words, and that smile, set me to hoping, hoping that if he escaped the habitation he'd take me with him.

'You think I could have lived that wild life, ey,' she said, 'me, not much more than a child? Perhaps, I don't know. But all of this was already old by your mama's time, although, not completely forgotten. Ah, it's all foolishness, mo piti,' she said, shaking her head, 'it's funny, though, the games life plays. For now here I am mother to his child, in all but blood.'

'You don't have to tell me more if it makes you unhappy,' I said.

She shifted round to face me, our hands once again clasped together, and lay her lips upon my forehead.

'You're mo bon garçon, ey Liberté,' she said.

Those black, almost Asiatic-shaped eyes blazed with a light that shines only in the darkest of irises; their surface a watery film which stubbornly refused to become tears.

She added:

'Memories can surprise us with feelings we'd long forgotten,' I nodded as if I understood but my face must have betrayed my ignorance. 'Ah, I see,' Ma-Jo said. 'Listen. If you fall and cut your knee it hurts, yes?'

I grimaced.

'You cry but the pain fades away, and soon you're playing again. But later when you bathe and water washes away the dirt the graze stings again, also true, ey? Well, this is how it is when I think of these things. A little pain is awoken with the memory.'

My head bobbed forwards with more enthusiasm.

'Come,' she said, gently patting my knee, 'we're nearly done.'

Over the previous week we had gathered tomatoes, maize, margoze and manioc; picked the ripest zak and breadfruit; harvested three different kinds of brède: mouroom, malbar and songe; and wrested over three dozen eggs from our feisty hens. We would set off for the bazaar the following morn, before the cock let loose its first crow and the moon still winked down upon us. Ma-Jo with a great basket on her head and the rest of our stock arranged in paniers in my pushcart.

'I didn't see your mama about the camp after that thing appeared,' Ma-Jo said, as we stacked the day's pickings in our storehouse, under the cooling shade of two badamier trees. Pirat had roused and wandered along behind us as we carried our baskets, only to lie down in the shadow of the trees.

'Although as she was with child this was no surprise. The whispering voices persisted, saying that some witchcraft had sealed her fate. That with a kiss she gave up her life and signalled for your papa's return, so she might accompany him on that last voyage.'

'Was it true what they said, Ma-Jo?'

She gave a shrug of her shoulders.

'Maybe so, who can tell, mo piti? Hearsay is often no more than sweetmeat for the ears. But that said, at the centre of even the most outlandish tale there is a seed of truth.'

'But did you believe it?' I asked Ma-Jo, her winding words leaving me frustrated as well as enthralled.

A truth, when issued from her lips, would become a story. And a story was told with such conviction it became an unquestionable truth. Her wonderful descriptions were often entwined with strange and foolish notions whose understanding lay beyond my years. I lacked the knowledge to fully comprehend the grown-up world her tales depicted. A world whose characters became involved in situations that even a child would steer clear of.

Why would mama want to die? Why would she want to leave me?

This was something I would surely never understand. What but sorcery could have driven mama to wish for such a thing? Me, I never wanted to die, of that I was certain. Heaven and angels, I was happy to wait until old age before thinking of such things. The life I had was fine by me, I was in no hurry to visit the afterlife. All I wanted to do was climb trees and eat mangoes; to run and sing and swim. And I wasn't sure how much of that would be going on after I died.

Maman had coped with her own mother's death, and she was just a child then, so why was papi's death too much for her?

I was yet to experience the death of one so close to me, but even at that young age I was not wholly ignorant of such pain.

*

The year before my best friend Hypolite had drowned over near Le Chaland. He'd been fishing with his brother when a wave swept him away, dragging him straight out to sea. César, Hypolite's brother, hadn't even known he was gone. It was as if God just reached down and plucked him from where he sat.

The two brothers had climbed along the rocky outcrop until they reached the last of the boulders. Here they sat back-to-back in the midst of spume and waves; waves that slapped the rocks with the viciousness of Dominère's famed whip.

The sea out there is hungry, its swells are like slathering tongues. The last place you'd expect to catch fish, ey, but Hypolite swore it was good fishing. His big brother's words, I suspect.

Me, I never fished there, so I can't say if this is true of not. One look at those waves and I'd step back from the water's edge and into my own footprints, following them from where I'd come. Even the shallows contained the wickedest of currents, pulling seductively at ankles like the fingers of a siren, daring you to wade out just a little further.

There'd been an almighty crash when this particular wave struck the rock. César turned, laughing, his back wet with spray, thinking he'd see his brother sitting there sulking like a wet dog. But all he saw was an empty rock and Hypolite's rod riding the waves, already 20 feet or so from where he'd been sitting. It was clear what had happened, but this didn't stop César searching the entire outcrop: rocks, filao trees and all. When darkness fell, and there was still no sign of Hypolite, César ran home, hoping to find his brother there waiting for him.

Truth be told, when I first heard I'd wanted to laugh. Because it couldn't be true, could it? Hypolite, like me, was just a child. Impossible. Only the day before he'd invited me to go with him – fishing with his brother. That was just the day before; I'd seen him. He couldn't be dead. He was fine, then. This is what my heart had told me.

But when I realised it was true, I cried. It felt like a hand had been stuck down my throat and all my insides pulled out.

I lay on my coconut hair mattress, overcome by a cold and empty feeling, remembering the times we'd shared – finding it impossible to believe we'd make no more memories together.

As I squeezed my eyes shut I could still see his face, and I swear I heard his laughter. But with him gone I wasn't sure if the things in my head had really happened. How could I ever know if they were true?

It was a strange place I found myself in, and for the first time in my young life it occurred to me that I was not forever.

But this had made me want to live, not die.

Before Hypolite died, death had been only a word to me. I'd heard it in Ma-Jo's stories, but these were often tales of the already dead. Lives connected to me by little more than speech.

Yes, her stories were important, alive in my imagination and my heart – who can say these imaginings were not real? – but there was a difference.

Can you feel loss for those whose breath you never shared?

Can you mourn the passing of a ghost?

When death entered a story, I noticed the change in Ma-Jo's expression. How a frown, a grimace or a smile lost its power and the emotion was replaced by something else. A kind of acceptance, maybe; an understanding that death couldn't be undone, that loss is a thing which never leaves us.

But even this was a different thing. The touching of a wound that, although not fully healed, had long ago lost its sting.

When death wandered into my path it stopped being a stranger, it became as real as the emptiness it left behind.

Where had Hypolite's smiling face gone?

Where was the hand of my friend?

What of all that could not be touched: the love, laughter and happiness; all the hopes and sorrows and dreams that would never be – were they also buried with him at sea? Was death so wasteful?

I fell into a gully with banks too steep to climb, floundered in a swell of unanswerable questions. I could do little more than sleep but this provided no escape. It brought no solace, only nightmares.

In my dreams I saw shapes beneath the water; black silhouettes that spiralled down into the deep; a whirling current of bodies whose clutching fingers seemed inches from the surface, no matter how deep they sank. But when I delved into the water to save them there was nothing there, nothing more than my disturbed reflection.

For days I lay in my bed fevered by loss, unable to escape the weariness that overcame me. But even at the height of my suffering I never wanted to die, just the opposite; I'd wanted to bring Hypolite back to life. It was my helplessness – for what could I change? – that was the root of my despair.

It is only now, looking back a thousand-thousand footsteps, that I see it was Ma-Jo who rescued me from this place and helped repair the seams of my heart.

Maman had no Ma-Jo to save her. All that she had loved was lost and all who loved her had retired to the other side of the dark ocean.

*

'Ey garçon, to sourde?'

'No,' I said to Ma-Jo, 'I'm not deaf. I've been listening, I've been listening since the beginning— Ma?'

'Ein?'

'You think she meant for me to live? Because I could've died too, couldn't I?

She tapped the bowl of her pipe against the door frame, inspected the bowl's chamber and scraped the inside with a fingernail. She put the pipe back in the pocket of her dress.

I closed the door and we sat to the right of the shed, in the shade of a badamier tree. The ground at our feet felt so hard, so clustered with stones you'd think nothing would grow there. Yet, only a dozen feet behind us lay the furrows of our vegetable garden, filling the hot afternoon air with the scent of leaves and ripening fruit.

We fanned ourselves with our hands.

Sweat ran down our cheeks like rainwater.

'You're here. This tells you something, no?' Ma-Jo said.

I shrugged.

I ground my heels in the dirt and tossed a stone out into the yard, watching it bounce and roll to stop in front of the veranda. Pirat raised his head, alert, and then lay it down again, closing his eyes.

'Maybe she couldn't stop me leaving,' I said.

'It's not easy for a mother to let go. You were part of her.'

'But he was a bigger part of her life?'

'I don't know, mo piti, all I know is the story. People's thoughts, I can't see. I just piece bits together, things I've seen and heard, like patchwork. Add in a few tit-bits of my own for good luck. You know?'

My eyes searched out the stone I had tossed but it was lost among many others.

'What do you know, Ma-Jo? Tell me, please,' I said, still convinced the answer to my question could be found in her story. If not in the actual words, then in the breaths and pauses between them; or the rhythm and inflection of her speech; or the glances, frowns and half-smiles – the gestures of hand and body that are almost as important to storytelling as the words themselves.

To me her powers were supernatural, steeped in good magic. If she could draw so many things back from the past – people, places and sensations – as if the past were a secret room she had just stepped out of, then why not more? Why not the thoughts of another? I didn't think she was lying about her gifts, only that she was being modest; for who wants to be thought of as a witch – good or otherwise?

Our backs rested against the tree trunk, feet pulled in towards our backsides or maybe stuck straight-out in front of us. We sat on flat-faced rocks between the tree roots. Rocks which were cool to the touch, being out of direct sunlight.

I looked across at Ma-Jo. She chewed on something and stared hard at an object I could not see.

'It was Noone, the midwife's assistant, who led me to your

mama's hut,' Ma-Jo began, 'Noone was little older than Elise, but she dragged me by the arm like I was a child. I stumbled along not knowing where I was headed, or from where I had came; this despite having lived my whole life in the camp. So strange, I felt like a character dropped into an unfamiliar story, lost in a world not my own. My stomach turned, my head ached, and a sweet, musty smell hung about me. It was like a pleasant odour that had been locked away, and on its release brought with it the staleness of imprisonment. "Come," Noone said, "hurry, she needs you." When I asked her who needed me she said nothing, only walked faster. I could have stopped her, pulled away, but I let myself be lead. I was still weak from—'

Ma-Jo stopped short, as if suddenly remembering some forgotten detail, shook her head and then nudged me with her elbow.

'Ey, you know what day that was?' She asked, her voice shorn of all its gravity.

I shrugged and pulled a face; a little annoyed she had stopped the story. Ma-Jo grinned.

'Your mama was about to have a baby.'

'My birthday?' I said, letting the words out slowly as if checking each syllable.

'January 31st 1835, that right?'

The thought of becoming a year older made me smile. I nodded.

'There was something else, too, you know what?'

'Mama died?' I said, with the same reticence.

'Yes, that's true,' Ma-Jo said, her tone low and consoling, 'but not what I was thinking of. You know the word emancipation?'

I shook my head. Where would I hear such a thing? It was a word whose sound gave no hint of its meaning and was made of so many parts that it sat awkwardly within her speech.

'It's like liberté. Freedom,' she said.

'Like my name.'

'Just like your name. That day was supposed to be the eve of our freedom.'

I was pleased that such a big word lived inside my name, and that in its heart was something of great importance to us: *les kreols, lepep noir*. But that word, liberté, caused Ma-Jo's brow to wrinkle, the happiness I associated with freedom absent from her face.

'We were full of joy,' she said, 'but also angry and confused. They told us we were free, we were truly free, and we belonged to no one but ourselves.'

I thought of the wind and the sea, the song of a martin, the walk to Mahébourg with no hand to hold.

'But they also told us we couldn't leave. If we left we'd be maroons, like your papa had been. But we were free. But we couldn't leave.'

'You're turning my head around with riddles again, ma.'

One corner of her mouth lifted in a half-mustered smile.

'Mo piti, this is not one of mine. I couldn't understand it, either. None of us could.'

Ma-Jo explained that it had been decided – by whom, whites of course; British whites, French whites, Creole whites but not us – that we would work four more years before being allowed to leave our masters. We would serve this term not as slaves, but free people, apprentices. Apprentices to what, she did not know. Freedom, maybe, but how could serfdom teach you to be free? It was a conundrum which made sense only to those who conceived it. If a habitation was sold, the apprentices would be part and parcel of the deal, part of its inventory like cattle or a plough. I was just as stumped as she was.

'We were free,' Ma-Jo said, 'but could only leave if we bought our freedom. If we were industrious, they said, we could hire ourselves out on our day of rest; save and buy our freedom. Why should you have to buy something that is already yours? This we never understood.

'It only taught us what we already knew: that whites could not be trusted and they had the freedom to change the meaning of their words whenever it suited them.'

It was late afternoon and shadows reached across the yard like fingers stealing away sunlight. Voices of men returning from work sang out around us. There was laughter and greetings of ki manière. Wood smoke was carried on a light breeze, along with the aromas that follow the lighting of a cook-fire. Mouth watering concoctions to tempt men home before their eyes become too misted by tilambik.

Ma-Jo lit our own cook-fire and we ate salt fish and rice with a rougaille of fresh tomatoes.

'That name of yours, Liberté, I would have changed it if I had the power – but when a name has been spoken to the wind there is no calling it back.'

'Why?'

'Why what?'

'Why did you want to change my name?'

A grasshopper chose this moment to land on Ma-Jo's knee. He was the bright green of a bois matelot leaf and a bit longer than my longest finger. He seemed to study us, and despite those hinged legs that looked ready to leap, remained perfectly still.

In my eyes he looked plucked from a tree. His body, with wings gracefully folded atop one another, was a long thin leaf complete with veins and creases. His legs were like the delicate shoots of newly sprouting shrub. And his head like the tiny bud that becomes a lychee.

When he jumped it was a thing to be missed in a blink. He sprang from knee to shoulder as if to get a better look at Ma-Jo, or whisper to her some secret intelligible only to the ear of sorceress.

Then he shifted round to inspect me. I don't know if he was satisfied or unhappy with what he saw, but he sprang off, heading towards the rear of our plot.

We watched our visitor bounce away.

'Hmm, well now,' Ma-Jo said. Leaning forward, elbows rested on her knees, 'they told us this and that and something else, but what we heard was the rattle of the same old chains. This wasn't all, however. We felt a change, like the passing of the darkest hours of night when the promise of day brightens the horizon. There was an end in sight.

'We were wary, yes, there'd been rumours before: after the révolution française, and when the British first arrived, but these had come to nothing. This time we had heard with our own ears, and the story from neighbouring *habitations* was the same, "you are free and in four years you can leave." And we came to believe it.

'An air of celebration crept into the camp. As it darkened and the fires were lighted, anger gave way to joy. The tambour thumped out its rhythm like a beating heart, there was the tink-tink-tink of knife against bottle-glass, and the rattle of bouquet banan. People sang and clapped and danced like it was the fête banané.

'Noone dragged me away from these sounds, towards what I did not know. A swig of tilambik and the heat of the campfire would have been as a salve to my broken heart.'

*

I saw nothing clearly, not at first, only bits of things exposed by the candlelight. The hut was dark, full of flickering shadows that held ghosts and ill omens.

It was so hot and the air so thick I thought the candle would soon be snuffed out.

My head was thumping.

Among the earthy smells of blood and sweat was something else: sweet, fermenting, it brought bile to my throat and made me want to back out of the hut. This other odour travelled up my nose, straight to my brain, sticking to everything in between.

The earth caught hold of my feet and refused to let them go. I wanted to leave... run away... be out of that place... but when the room began to sway it was the earth's grip that kept me upright.

Then I saw her: Noone. It was odd, but her tears stopped the swaying in my head – helped me control my fear. There was not only sadness in that look of hers, but distance too, as if she saw past the darkness into some other place.

She was kneeling just within reach of the light; part of her revealed by candle flame, while the rest of her merged into the surrounding shadow. A pale child lay bundled in her arms. I could see its crown of curly black hair. Yet it was still – so, so still. The woman's hands and forearms glistened black and slick like the sea at night, staining the child's swaddling.

I did not look for Elise, though I knew she must be there.

Noone continued to stare at me, rocking the infant in her arms.

'La piti mort?' I mouthed, aware that even a whisper would be too loud for the silence; forgetting I stood in almost total darkness – my lips impossible to read. But by some magic my face must have been lighted for she nodded and then shook her head.

She looked down.

I followed her gaze and saw the child move as if animated by the woman's eyes.

A hand touched my arm.

My body stiffened. I glanced over my shoulder, no more than half a look, but that was enough. Piss ran down my leg, pooling at my feet.

Noone was also behind me.

When she whispered in my ear 'come,' the sound more breath than words, it was the lips of the figure kneeling before me that moved. I was given a gentle push. I did not look back.

My feet finally obeyed me and I took a step forward, and then another. I felt the mush of newly wet earth as I began to walk.

I knelt opposite Noone.

Between us lay Elise. She did not move.

The candlelight, as if out of respect, seemed to shy away from her, to cast its light on different things: Noone's knee, her elbow, her chin, her nose – but not her eyes, for they shone with some light other than the orange flame; the child, its ear and crown of nubby hair, skin not much darker than Elise's; an arc of dirt floor pitted with tiny moon craters; a cockroach that scuttled along accompanied by its big brother shadow.

But she was there, Elise, made up of shades of not-quite-darkness. And as my eyes became accustomed to the gloom I saw more of her.

I shouldn't have looked. I should've looked away. It wasn't a woman who lay between me and Noone.

She was only a girl, a child. Yes, I already knew this but—

Everything is taken from us.

That beauty, it could have been the dark, maybe I wasn't seeing right, but it wasn't there. Maybe it left with her life. Maybe that is where beauty lies and it's foolish to expect it to linger.

—but not that, I still see it and such visions are supposed to fade, aren't they? Like the faces of loved ones who've passed away.

All I saw was emptiness and fragility, like a husk left behind by fire, which falls apart when touched.

It was there in the child, though, in the baby. So maybe it had just passed on to him.

Noone spoke and I wanted to cry.

'It's alright,' she said, lifting up the child, 'look, look at what she has given.'

And I looked, but cried anyway. How could things be alright?

I snorted, wiping my eyes then my nose on the forearm of my sleeve.

There was the child.

I was holding it. I felt the tiny tugs and punches, its jerks and uncontrolled kicks. My arms were folded around it, its head resting in the crook of my left elbow. How had it come to be in my arms? Had I taken it? Was it given to me? I was unsure, no, I didn't know.

Young Noone smiled, showing me two rows of uneven teeth, yellow and unsettling in the room's strange light. I ran my tongue over my own teeth, aware, as if for the first time, of their perfection.

Her grin widened. What madness would inspire such a smile in a place like this? I felt the answer wriggle against my belly.

'Take him and go, now.'

I asked questions, questions I did not speak because, somehow, I knew the answers before my lips could move: is she dead? Why me? At what time shall I return with the child? Does he have a name? What will happen to her? Can I love him?

The corners of Noone's mouth slackened, her pink gums disappeared but the light remained in her eyes.

A hand was at my elbow and Noone helped me to my feet.

The one who knelt before me now stared into the darkness where Elise lay.

When I stepped from the hut it was like emerging from beneath the sea after chasing a trompette or a school of pavion;

when so engrossed in the chase you almost forget the need to breathe.

I took a deep breath and shivered as the sweat that covered my body began to cool.

*

A light breeze caressed my skin.

A moustik fizzed somewhere near my ear, my face, my other ear. I swatted at it. There was silence. The buzzing started again.

I searched the darkness for women's faces but was unsure of what I saw.

There was a light not far from where I lay. It was hazy like the sun seen through cloud. It hung there shimmering.

I tried to blink the world into focus.

Beneath me coco-hair pricked my skin.

My head ached. I shuddered, screwing my eyes shut.

The breeze stopped and again the heat ambushed me. Outside I heard the pat of a dog's feet.

When I tried to sit the insides of my head took a moment to follow, slurring like drunken words then shooting back into place. The world continued to move as my brains sloshed about my skull.

Things slowly regained their places, my vision began to make sense, but the ache in my head remained.

I saw the ripple of a curtain as it was caught by the resurgent breeze, the glow at its centre sending out orange light. Where the light faded it turned to grey and blackened with night, at its edges.

I knew the room and the room beyond the curtain.

I felt like I'd fallen out of that other place and landed on my head. I was confused thinking of all the things I had seen. None of which I could say were real or imagined, as if I'd emerged from a place where the two things met.

Could it have been the place where stories are born? Was it

there Ma-Jo visited to retrieve her tales? I felt as if I could reach into the darkness and be there.

But with each blink, with each strayed glance into the darkness I feared seeing Elise's, mama's, face. It was as if what I had seen with my own eyes – had I seen it with my own eyes? if not, through whose eyes had I seen? – had left an even greater hole. No, not a hole, but a greater sense of unknowing. In all my imaginings I had never really seen her, and when I finally did, she was not there. My absent mother absent from her own body.

I had not yet realised that we rarely find the answers we seek, they come to us in their own time, what we often find are more questions.

Sometime later, years maybe, when I next dreamt of mama, it was not a death mask I saw, but a young and beautiful woman. In her face, a face you could not help but love, there was something of my own: the arc of her nostrils, the curve of her upper lip, the folds that rode the corners of her mouth when she smiled. And something so familiar about her it seemed impossible that we had never met, that she had never planted a kiss on my cheek or squeezed me tight to her breast.

There are indeed places and mysteries whose origins are beyond this world, which can only be glimpsed in a dream, or day-dream, or in a look that looks nowhere at all. And here the dead can walk and talk with the living – for there is no difference between them.

The light beyond the curtain flickered. Was Ma-Jo in that other room?

I called out.

'Ma. Ma-Jo.'

The sounds that emerged were more like gasps than words, like a spoon scraping the last morsel of food from a marmit. My mouth was dry and my throat ragged.

On a stool next to me was a cup of water. I swallowed it down in two gulps.

It seems strange that I remember these things so clearly – the coolness of the water, the buzz of the moustik, the vividness of my dream – as if they happened just yesterday; when my youth lays so far behind me.

Or maybe it's not so strange. I was taught to hoard memories; these being precious things, things to be kept close to your heart, markers on the map of our lives. Things that can be remembered with fondness or reborn and remade into new things, like songs or stories. Things which remind us of life's joy and struggles.

I called out again. The croak in my voice still there, but the sounds more rounded, more like my old voice. There was no reply, nothing beyond the darkness and the flicker of the candlelight.

As I sat there I wondered about the story, and whether it was so much a part of me that it had entered my real life.

Chapter Seven

Sandiman

Sandi seemed to have come to them as an old man and never aged, despite his being no more than thirty years old, on arrival. What it was, she surmised, was his demeanour. That very air she had imagined essential in a good servant. One immediately felt at ease in his presence and never intruded upon. If any task were assigned to him, were it to fetch a book or pick a flower from the garden, it would be performed with the utmost care. And on assigning this duty, one could immediately forget its existence; happy in the knowledge Sandi would be carrying it out.

They were told he hailed from Pondicherry or maybe somewhere along the Malabar Coast. His people of a servant caste whom for generations had served his country's princes and nobility. He had ended up in the service of Captain Declare, as all such possession do, through bargain, deceit or plunder; or as forfeit when a gambling debt could not be paid. This was the story that accompanied him, one not necessarily to be taken at face value. Any purchaser with even a modicum of experience knew tales as these for what they were; half-truths at best, but more often fictions composed for the amusement of both teller and listener.

Although such details should have mattered little, she had to admit with Sandi her curiosity had been piqued. But on the occasions she had questioned him he would add no more to this story, answering with feigned incomprehension. His head would wobble from side to side as if independent of his neck and he would mumble 'sorry Madame, I do not understand.' In the end, she had refrained from asking.

However, such obvious prevarication could be forgiven, for in a way he was protecting her from her own curiosity, preventing attachment where it would have been inappropriate. She was fond of Sandi, yes, but not in the wistfully sentimental way that a mistress might become attached to her attendant. He was not a sibling, friend or confidante – she did not harbour such misplaced endearments – to her Sandi was the embodiment of dependability and warranted, if not her respect, then a high degree of appreciation.

Of course they had acquired him from no seaman. It had been the merchant Latande who brought Sandi to their service. M. Latande was also the propagator of the accompanying mythology. For his part he admitted the Captain's purchase of the Indian was likely no more fantastic than any similar transaction. And that the discovery of a bondsman of Sandi's pedigree was not uncommon in India's ports. Although straight away he proceeded to contradict these observations.

'By the same degree our Indian friend here could well have been press ganged by old Declare,' Latande had said, 'I wouldn't put it past the old salt to have had this fellow on board and out to sea before he knew whether it was a headache or a hangover he was suffering from.'

Alexandre had found this amusing and not unlikely.

As Latande described it, those territories which did not fall under the direct control of the British East India Company were the fiefdoms of hundreds of petit princes; Rajas, whose disputes and petty differences the company artfully exploited. There were those princes who held allegiance to the company, and those who did not. Some found their status elevated, even if their power was somewhat diminished, and became the recipients of the administration's favour; others were not so fortunate. And it was from one of these less fortunate principalities, Latande surmised, that Sandi had sprung.

The more the merchant indulged in speculation, the more it became evident he had little idea of Sandi's origins. And very likely Latande, himself, was the author of the tale.

Whether Sandi's abbreviated biography bore any resemblance to fact was neither here nor there, as without doubt this was a man with service in his blood. It became apparent when Latande first introduced Sandi to Alexandre. The bondsman entered, it seemed, without a word from the merchant. Dressed in a turban and pyjamas of pearl white, Sandi's creaseless attire flowed about his body as he moved, as if carried along by some other-worldly wind. There was a silence about him and not only in the tread of his bare feet, but in the tranquillity of his being. A calmness with which one imagined he approached every situation. He glided like a boat upon water, endowed with the mast's bearing and the serenity of a placid sea.

This was perhaps the reason Sandi was not as imposing as he should have been.

For he was a tall man, and not slight of frame, with a tall man's long face whose features were allied with the rest of his appearance. His eyes slim and wide apart, with irises of mottled brown; between them a long, straight nose any European would have worn with honour. Its proud bridge bowed out from the brow, returning its curve as it approached the tip. Here blossomed a ball exactly twice the width of its bridge, sidled by two arching nostrils that curved back with the gentlest of flare. Beneath, a moustache the blue-black of night, oiled and twisted and turned up at the ends like the prow of a ship. All of this upon the bedrock of a wide, thin lipped mouth and a square chin.

What was perhaps most intriguing was that his appearance seemed in no way incongruous with his position as a servant. It only proved that when one acted with the proper decorum and remained within one's station even the humblest could attain nobility.

Social stratification was an important part of India's culture, according to Latande's account, their ancient social mores maintained for a thousand generations. Whether such strict adherence bred stability or stagnation, was something else altogether. For despite all their great history the oriental races remained trapped in a bygone age, living forever in the shadow of their past achievements. Not that this was in any way exclusive to the people of the Sandi's continent, Latande had contended, for in the end was it not the fate of every nation, every man, to end in such decline. After all, there was no forever and destiny showed no favouritism, no special dispensation, whether king or vagabond.

Sandi had looked Alexandre straight in the eyes as he bowed, but not with the empty gaze of the cowed or the glare of the quietly dissatisfied, rather with that intelligent glint one often catches in the look of an eager student. As yet absent of arrogance but informed enough as to have left childishness behind. He said not a word and stood in attendance not at attention. Two things often confused but which are vastly different. The latter describing the vassal vacantly awaiting orders; the former waiting at the ready in the hope of anticipating his master's wishes.

There had been no need for evaluation, Alexandre had seen all he needed.

'So—' Latande had begun before Alexandre interrupted him.

'This is a good man. I have an eye for such things and it has failed me but once,' Alexandre clapped Sandi's shoulder and squeezed it like they were old companions, 'this one will be coming with me.'

Now middle aged, Sandi had been with them almost 20 years. Although no less taciturn than in those earlier days, his presence was a comfort to her, a constant in such volatile times. For in all those years his dependability had not waned, proving himself to be as exemplary as his history suggested. Gallard's hint had been unnecessary; there was no question as to whom she would entrust so delicate a matter. Sandi would retrieve the letter. Sandi would banish that shameful addition to her already troubled life.

But what of the other damage? Had the door not already been opened and the ghosts wandered in?

It was true, she never fully abandoned her suspicions. But they had lain dormant, a part of a life that was ever receding. Obscured by doubt and uncertainty, distorted by the past's murky lens. Who could be sure what was true? With the passage of time incidents in which complete confidence was once held, might prove no longer so conclusive. And it was not as if things had ever been that clear.

With Gallard's revelations a new clarity was added to proceedings. It was impossible to deny what she had once suspected. The last chance of refuting the notary's story dissolving when the codicil was produced.

'Destroy it,' he had said, 'destroy them both.'

And it was impossible to miss what had been inferred, whether it was Gallard's intention or not. Would it indeed be better if she removed those two souls from her life? One she had loved and one she would forever despise.

And the papers? Those, yes, without question.

Too many questions. Too many answers waiting to be discovered.

And with the opening of the door also came a key. Another thing grief caused to be put aside, but which circumstance now insisted be remembered. Unlike the door, the entrée to things she had shut away inside herself, the key was something tangible, and who could predict what other secrets it might unlock? What else might have been hidden just beyond the world she inhabited?

With her past in ruins, what would she take to the future? There was a danger it would be only those things best left behind, which like burrs snagged onto you without your knowing and often remained despite the effort made to rid yourself of them.

The key lay forgotten on the shelf of her armoire, hidden beneath clothes she no longer wore. After Gallard's disclosures the key had called to her, the voice of providence beckoning her towards more heartache, but she had become powerless against her curiosity. The distance death placed between Alexandre and herself proving to be no fixed point, but a gap that was rapidly widening.

It was in drawing room that she received Gallard and there she returned key in hand.

When the key had been given to her after Alexandre's death it had taken little investigation to find its purpose. But with key in lock she had decided against turning. Had this been a premonition of what she might be freeing. Like Pandora, would she find her powers extended only as far as loosing what lay within – their retrieval impossible.

This time, however, the lock turned; bolt sliding with ease from its socket. Like it wished itself to be opened. The moment for hesitation had passed and she opened the drawer to Alexandre's desk before good sense could prevail.

In the drawer were those things one would expect to be stored in a writing desk; a pot of ink, a rule and pencil, quills. Along with these sundries lay a leather bound journal, fastened with a leather thong. It was not a book in which she had seen Alexandre write. She had always found him hunched over one of his many ledgers, immersed in the study of figures that represented the plantation's success.

Likewise she had never seen the drawer open, the rectangle of its front appearing as nothing more than a pattern of elegant geometry. On opening it was as if she'd unearthed a tomb and to disturb the things within would be a desecration of sorts. Though, after so little rest Alexandre's ghost had already been awoken, and it was unlikely what she sought would send him back to sleep.

She removed the journal and closed the drawer, sitting herself at the bureau. The room was dressed with the afternoon's long shadows. It always seemed hottest in those hours before the sun was lost behind the mountains that backed the estate, the heat unwilling to surrender its sovereignty over the day. A slant of sunlight lay across the book giving it the imagined significance of a sunbeam breaking through the clouds. A significance it no doubt deserved.

In the book's opening pages, for the first third actually, she found little of interest. Nothing more than notes on the health of the estate, areas of improvement and experiment Alexandre explored in hope of improving efficiency or crop yield; the progress made after the update of the mills. Things which could not be captured between the lines of a ledger but that might find some correlation with the figures.

These entries were occasionally interrupted by instances of beauty that captured his eye. Descriptions of small birds whose intricate colouring, Alexandre said, rivalled Titians, whom she understood to have been an artist of some mark; a flower that in form and hue stood in stark contrast to usual ostentatious nature of the island's flora. These descriptions themselves rendered in a language she thought to have long deserted her husband. Not since those days of courtship and their early years of marriage had she heard such lines.

And the pain caused by his lapses into romanticism was only tempered when she discovered an entry, no more than a few lines, about herself.

It is a rare beauty indeed, that once scorched by fire refuses to crack, instead becoming more radiant; as if the heat, once absorbed, allows the heart to shine brighter. My winter rose, now a summer violet, not only enduring but blooming, despite the pain I inflicted.

Watery blotches of ink and swirling words unformed by tears, magnifying and blurring, told her she was crying. Her rigid veneer dissolving like a powdered remedy. Was it fair that he had been taken from her not once but twice, never to be delivered back to her?

If only she could shut the book and forget the girl's existence. And escape to what life? The estate was all that was left; the looming mountains, the blue of the distant sea; her garden, a place whose solitude saved her from sliding into her own nothingness, a place whose association with the girl, Elise, remained elusive due only to the girl's absence. It was all at stake.

So further pages were turned and what she came upon after Alexandre's observations on the Estate's management ended, was something altogether more personal; something she could not shut the book upon.

Chapter Eight

The Rape of Florine

From Alexandre's Journal

I remember.

I remember she cooked fish that day, the air heavy with its aroma. It seemed to saturate all it touched, the wood, the drapery, my skin. The smell drew me in, led me to search out its source; led me to her.

She stood in the kitchen.

The afternoon sun filled the small window, painting the edges of things with light. But she remained a silhouette against the window pane.

I had already drunk a measure or two of wine. For just a week earlier I had the good fortune to procure two cases of Château Rauzan-Gassies, a rarity in these climes; a panacea for one who has by necessity become accustomed to coarser spirits.

She sang to herself, shoulders hunched, the clack of the knife blade against board rhythmic, as if in accompaniment.

The soft lines of her shoulders were exposed by the neckline of her dress. It was a crude cotton thing, drawn in just below the breastbone.

I moved from the doorway, away from the sun's cast to get a clearer view of her.

The string of her apron sat in a neat bow at the small of her back, giving shape to the old frock, revealing the curve of her hips and the arc of her buttocks. Her feet and ankles were bare below the hem of her skirt; their tops as rich and dark as the floor's stained boards with an edging of yellow ochre just visible above the sole.

It was not apparent at first, so engrossed was I in this study, that both the singing and the tap of the knife had stopped. There was no movement from her, the folds of her dress hung in rigid planches; the only sound that of my own breath.

From this new position I could see the side of her face: temple, cheek and jawbone leafed in sunlight, and the corner of one eye that was closed. Or I imagined it must be so.

When she gasped I took it for play, for she was certainly aware of a presence in the room before she turned.

'Maître!' *Master*, she said, wiping first her palms and then the backs of her hands down the front of her apron, 'ou étonne moi,' *you surprised me*. 'Ou bisin moi, missier?' *You need me, sir?*

And was that not it, the invitation? Was there to be any misreading? After all what invitation was necessary – do I wait for my horse's permission before mounting? My resolve strengthened and I surrendered to a yearning I had long managed to restrain.

It was not love. Of course it was not love. But from the first glance I was ensnared, unable to rid her from my mind. Her face seemed to follow me in waking dreams; her form, hardly able to contain its womanliness, stoked within me that which has to be released.

I ventured further into the kitchen, the strength of me draining from my pores; as if the succubus siphoned off my lifeblood. I told the girl to make me a restorative.

She placed a cloth over her preparations and made for the larder.

There was a grace about her. Not the perfect equipoise of a white woman, studied and refined before practice, but something altogether more exciting. Something the switch had not yet banished, something native to that dark land of hers. I continued to regard her, stealing her beauty with my eyes; from instep to crown, inspecting every curve and undulation.

The air felt heavy and viscous, to be ingested rather than inhaled. My shirt stuck to my chest, my armpits, my stomach. Sweat ran down my forehead into my eyes, and as I rubbed them, she passed by me and disappeared into the storeroom. I cursed under my breath, turned as if to follow her, still wiping my eyes. But instead I stood, waited.

The storeroom was much darker than the kitchen. Its rows of provisions - condiments and preserves, and all manner of concoctions - no more than vague shapes wreathed in grey. Yet she used no candle. There was a shifting of jars, a drawing along the shelves; the touching of glass no more audible than a kiss. The ease with which she found the things she needed amazed me.

On emerging, arms bundled with the ingredients for her nostrum, she smiled, her teeth catching on her bottom lip.

'Ou paret malad, missier,' *you do not look well, sir,* she said, 'al repose ou siouplait,' *please go rest.* 'Mo pou amene medicine pou ou,' *I will bring medicine for you.*

I could find no words, neither nod nor shake my head. I could only watch as if bewitched; stare as she first retrieved the mortise and pestle from a shelf in the kitchen, then a bowl and finally ventured out into the courtyard to fill her bucket from the hand pump. A light breeze passed through the open door bringing me momentary relief from my anxiety. But as she re-entered closing the door behind her, the latch clicked with a finality that seemed to augur the arrival of some graver event.

The room began to swim and I felt in real need of the restorative. I walked towards her, stumbled almost, struggled to loosen my cravat. But as the girl turned, alarmed at my distress and rushed forward to meet me, something was revived within. One weakness was substituted for another.

She caught hold of my elbow.

'Vini missier, vini siouplait,' *come sir, come please*, she said ushering me to the table in the centre of the room. I rescued that old thing from the galley of a ship; three heavy trestles, buttressed feet and an oak top whose planks could have come from the ship's hull.

I allowed her to lead me, but before reaching the table I halted, clasping the girl's wrist. Although I saw fear replace concern in her eyes, she did not abandon her earlier solicitude.

'Kieter, kieter,' *what, what,* she said, but my grip only tightened, fingertips pressing into the flesh of her forearm. She did not cry out, only gritted her teeth, eyes fixed upon mine as if awaiting my reply.

I was surprised. Surprised at my strength and the ease with which I pushed her against the table. I cannot remember hitting her. But as she sat before me, legs exposed from toe to knee with just a hint of thigh – such an invitation – I saw the welt on her cheek and reddening beneath the skin. So black yet still you could see the deeper red. There was blood in the corner of her mouth which dripped from chin to apron. She pushed back against the trestle, both knees raised revealing a hint of the darkness between them, but she did not fight. She did not fight.

The noise of the world was gone from me; her breath my breath, her breath my breath. Even the voice in my head was silent. Yet there was a ringing in my ears as after cannon fire.

Something within me escaped.

Upon finding her voice, the girl's pleas, muffled by sobbing, fell upon deaf ears. Those cries that escaped were soon stifled by a palm pressed against the mouth, my hand big enough to grip the whole jaw.

I left her in the kitchen.

When days later, I returned, I found not my young cameo limned by window light, but old Modeste bending over a basin. Taken ill, she said of the girl, a malady of the stomach, her diagnosis. Thereafter, when I passed the kitchen the old woman was always there. Even the girl's eventual return failed to lessen old Modeste's attendance.

The old woman dismissed my suggestion that she rest more and let the girl take on some of her workload. For her age and long service deserved some good grace.

But no, the girl was not ready yet, her reasoning, and the responsibilities of the kitchen too much for one so young.

I have found my appetite somewhat reduced by the constant presence of the old chaperone. Now, there is barely a rumble when I think of the girl. Perhaps I am cured.

Chapter Nine

Magdelaine

The journal fell to the floor.

It could not be, yet it was. She wanted wash her hands, to be cleansed of all contact with the book. Wiped her palms down the front of her dress, stopping when the image of the girl came to her.

Who was this man who dwelt inside the book, as strange and unreal to her as any imagined by the dramatist's hand? She had still held hope that Gallard was mistaken, but for all of Alexandre's folly she had not expected this. That he would record his degeneracy in such a captivating hand, without shame or remorse. As if all he had done was stumble into the girl and they had fallen; a chance incident that became unstoppable. A story to be told and embellished upon while seated among friends.

Now, the lid had indeed been lifted and the jar's contents spilled without hope of recovery; scattering like cockroaches when their nest is disturbed.

She had left the book, the room, the house. First heading to the garden and then further afield when the connection to the girl followed her there. Off towards the stables with all the intention of riding out to nowhere. To some place far from the reach of the book's implications. Before she knew it, she was running, hands hoisting the skirt of her mourning; darting across what passed for a lawn like a flightless crow. Then she tripped and the world spun and she found herself staring up at the sky. High above, a bird circled, its screech akin to a scream, her eyes half blinded by the sun.

A shadow knelt beside her; took a hand, an elbow, helped her to her feet.

She pushed Sandi away, hit him and then hit him again. Shouting things she could not remember as she strode back towards the house, her dress covered in dust and dirt, lace torn away from its hem.

On her return to the study the journal was still there on the floor, like a corpse awaiting collection. She looked over her shoulder, saw no one, and listened for the sounds of the house. The silence that surrounded her, that filled a place which stored so many echoes, felt unnatural, as if the whole household held its breath.

When she closed the door it was with all the delicacy of a child trying to evade discovery, turning the handle and gently pressing it shut.

With book in hand, she sat by the window. The fields were harvest bare, desolate. Everything laid waste by mattock, cane-cutlass and now words. The world stripped bare, not only by promise, but by deed.

If there had been a fireplace she would have thrown the book into it. Yet there was none, and her fingers played with the edges of pages and pushed between cover and flyleaf, as if searching out the next calamity.

Then there came a knock.

And she started, pulling the book to her chest, arms wrapped around it, the disgust she felt for the thing countered by her desire to keep it hidden. By the second knock she was over at the desk, searching for the key. Overwhelmed by the fear that she had lost it, that it now lay discarded on the lawn's rough grass. What would she do if it were lost? Where would she put the journal? It had to be hidden, it must.

All of this in room full of books which might have swallowed up the journal in a wink.

But there it was the key, in a pocket made invisible by the frill of her waistband. The coolness of the key comforting as it turned in the lock.

'Madame,' called a voice from beyond the door, 'Madame.'

The book back in place, under lock and key, she stepped away from the desk and towards the centre of the room.

'Can I not be left in peace?' She called out.

'I have news.'

Whether Sandi had loitered outside the door, she could not say. But if he had she knew it would have been with good reason. And it had been.

For he had made his inquiries, his discreet investigation, and unearthed yet another deception.

*

She had not intended to involve Magdelaine, to expose her plan to untrustworthy ears, but Mme Lousteau had been left with little alternative. 'The girl and the maroon, together,' Sandi told her, 'and the girl carries his child.' There was a kind of malign poetry to it, she supposed; Alexandre's misbegotten lamb and his bête noire. Though, they would take no more from her. Of this she would make sure.

With this news came the possibility that she was not the only one with a plan; that it was not misfortune which had visited la maison de Lousteau but something altogether more sinister. Skulduggery hatched by Alexandre's very own lamb; with his generosity as its inspiration, his death its opening act.

All the things she had been forced to endure, from Alexandre's death to that most damning of journal entries, the result of this pair's conniving.

Out of her despair something new arose. A decision was made.

First the maroon, taking from the girl what she herself had been deprived of, and then the girl. There would be no child.

Magdelaine needed some persuading but Mme Lousteau had made sure to acquire the necessary leverage before asking the favour.

This proved an astute decision.

For at a time when rumours of the freedom seemed likely to become fact, the bribe of affranchisement, alone, provided a less tempting offer to a black.

When summoned, Magdelaine had loitered at the entrance to the drawing room, as if eager to merge with the shadows. She was small and thin, with eyes her skull struggled to contain, and stood there as still as a breezeless night. Too frightened, it seemed, even to breath.

'Vini, Magdelaine, vini,' *Come Magdelaine, come*, Mme Lousteau had said, like one ushering in an old friend.

The woman entered, head bowed, each step no more than a creak of the floorboards. She curtsied before her Mistress.

Mme Lousteau gave a nod in return.

She sat by the window on an old Louis Quinze, brought by her Alexandre from France. The seat had long since surrendered its comfort, the padding stiffened with age and compressed by years of supporting the old man's rump. But she was fond of the old thing. It reminded her of him, even its discomfort. She saw him hunched over a ledger, the Louis pushed back as he balanced on the edge of the cushion, unaware of her eyes. She saw him reclining, elbow on arm rest, the side of his head cupped in his left hand; lids closed, mouth wide open.

She was surprised to alight upon so unsullied a memory.

'Sit,' she said.

Magdelaine made to sit on the floor.

'No, no, please, there are chairs,' Mme Lousteau gave a swirl of the hand, a gesture that seemed to encompass the whole room.

Light from long windows cut slanted rectangles into the shadow, revealing bookcase and settee, cabinet and side table. Magdelaine did not move, herself caught in sunlight, as if she failed to comprehend her mistress's words.

'Allez, fille,' Mme Lousteau said, 'find a chair.'

Magdelaine returned with a footstool and sat down before her mistress, straight backed and pigeon toed, hands lost in the folds of her skirt.

The widow sipped at her tea, looked the woman over. Saw the stockings of dust where Magdelaine's skirt hitched up and feet and ankles that had been washed before entering the house.

Mme Lousteau placed cup and saucer on a side table, and with a handkerchief, dabbed at the corners of her mouth.

'How are you, today, Magdelaine?' She asked.

The woman nodded in return, offered a smile that wavered then was lost.

'Come, come, Magdelaine, you are in no trouble. In fact, I have asked you here in the hope that you might help me.'

Magdelaine's mouth recaptured half of the smile.

'I am— I am well Madame, thank you,' Magdelaine said, flinching, it seemed, at the echo of her voice in that high ceilinged room.

'Good, good. I am well also.'

'Pardon, Madame I— '

'There is no need to apologise, fille. I only wish you to be at ease. Please settle yourself.'

'Thank you, Madame.'

Madame Lousteau waved away the woman's gratitude.

'Now, let us talk. You have a son, Magdelaine, is that right?'

'Yes Madame, Auguste.'

'And Auguste is a good boy?'

'Yes Madame.'

'That is what I hear, healthy and strong, already bundling stalks of sugar cane. A credit to La Belle Horizon. And you still assist the births at the camp, Magdelaine, do you not?'

'I do what I can to help, Madame.'

'Very good, fille. But there are always some you cannot help, I suppose.'

'Some Madame, in the end we are all in God's hands.'

'Indeed, indeed, much responsibility. But do your hands not hold more power than you care to admit?'

'Madame?'

'The losses, those suffered during birth, are not always God's choice.'

Mme Lousteau smiled, watching as Magdelaine shifted on the footstool and twisted her fingers deeper into the fabric of her dress.

'Pardon, Madame but—'

'Is it not true, as mistress of La Belle Horizon everything within this *habitation*, every tree, building, every stalk of cane; every man, woman, *and* child belong to me. Is this not so?' Magdelaine nodded her agreement. 'So, by the same token, in withholding from me even one child, one life, you are taking what is mine. Were you under the misapprehension that you were freeing these mites? That you were somehow saving them from a fate worse than death.'

'Please Madame, please. There is some—'

The widow leaned forward, placing a finger on the woman's lips with such delicacy it could have been a lover's touch.

'We all have our stations, Magdelaine, and you have forgotten yours if you think you have the right to make such decisions about my property. But as I said, I asked you here for your help, not to chastise you. Only, it is important such things are made clear, that our positions remain unambiguous.'

Mme Lousteau stood and walked over to the window, looked out at the fields, at figures who seemed barely to move. It was like looking into a world of mindless things shifting at the mercy of the wind.

'Will you help me, Magdelaine?'

Magdelaine squinted into the sunlight. Mme Lousteau glided from the window into the emptiness of the room, from silhouette to shadow, halting behind the seated figure.

'What... What is it you would have me do?' Magdelaine asked, this time her words were no more than murmurs of their earlier echoes.

The boards behind her sighed.

'I take it you will be attending the labour of Elise?'

'Yes, Madame.'

'Then you must do for me, that, which we both know you are capable.'

'Madame?'

'Come, come, Magdelaine, enough of this deception. We have established that it is not only life you deal in, but death. This is the service I require of you.'

'No.'

'No?'

'No, Madame.'

'Do not be too hasty in your decision, ma fille. I offer you your freedom and not only your own but that of Auguste. And you would do well to remember your son,' Magdelaine shook her head, stared at the darkness between her feet, 'we both know she is sick, shifting between life and death.'

'Then you should wait, Madame.'

'Fate, ma fille, is an unreliable mistress, you are well aware of this,' the widow said, pressing lightly into the flesh of the woman's shoulder, 'and I, Magdelaine, an altogether different dowager, am unwilling to trust in her uncertainties. I approached you in good faith, willing to overlook your past indiscretions. And these are not trivial matters of insolence or sloth. I have besought you more in the guise of an aunt than a mistress, one concerned with the future of you and your child. Yet you remain unwilling to assist me.'

'I cannot do it, Madame, I cannot.'

'You mean you will not, for how different is what I ask from your previous crimes?'

'My mistress you are confused, mistaken.'

She took a breath, a deep inhalation, in whose silence Magdelaine's quiet sobs could be heard. There was an air of abandonment about the house, no sound but the woman's mewling. A presentiment, Mme Lousteau wondered? A likeness to her own abandonment, her own desolation?

As she exhaled she disregarded these thoughts and the anger provoked by the woman's insolence. The hand resting upon Magdelaine's shoulder gave a reassuring pat.

'Auguste will be fine. M. Regnier will take good care of him.'

'Auguste, Madame?' Words Magdelaine choked out as if she were unable to breath.

'He will not be absent for long. We will see to that, now, won't we? A good boy like him always has his uses. But for the moment

I have hired him out to M. Regnier, they are short of hands at *Cascade Tranquille*. He goes through more blacks than one goes through Tea. But I am sure he will show himself more restrained with another's possession.'

The sobbing had stopped and as the widow Mme Lousteau walked from behind Magdelaine to retake her seat what she saw in the woman's face was total capitulation. The helplessness one feels when party to events over which one has no control. It was as if with one touch she would disintegrate into a million tiny pieces. Those large eyes no longer bulged with fear but only stared as at something no other eye could behold. A thing so terrifying that terror itself is nullified, and all that is left is to accept its inexorable clutches. She shook her head, erratic jerks over which it seemed she had no command. Her lips moved and the sounds uttered failed to make it to living ears. A hand was lifted from her lap, wearily as if it were the weight of her heart she raised; palm up, she seemed to pat the air. Then it dropped back to her knees.

'When?' Asked Magdelaine.

The widow could not help but allow the merest of smiles, something that slid onto the face and exited with the same artfulness.

'That, ma fille, is at your discretion. It is you who best know the condition of the woman.'

*

It could be said, there was an inevitability about the happening, Mme Lousteau, in her oversight being fate's co-conspirator. Maybe she had not abandoned the boy to the custody of wolves, but she had certainly sent him to a place where it was likely he would be bitten. Even if it was chance rather than malice that was responsible for his demise.

News of the incident had reached Magdelaine first.

Regnier dispatched his plantation manager to inform Mme Lousteau of the tragedy, and he carried with him the coin his master thought fair compensation – almost the price of a fully mature black. The imbecile, Regnier, had obviously been embarrassed at exceeding even *his* usual ineptitude. She had expressly told him, 'look after the boy, put him on light duties,' but he had been sent to the forest with the lumber team, regardless.

It is true the work he had been assigned, gathering the trimmed and broken branches of felled trees, was the work of a child, but it wasn't only hard work that killed Regnier's *nègres*. It was also the manner in which they went about their duties. Even an ox is taught to pull the till, but the old planter's way was akin to attaching the plough and birching the beast's rump; leaving the thing to run wild about the field. And his turnover of blacks was such that even the most rudimentary safety measures failed to develop among his hands.

Whether the boy, Auguste, had wandered into a zone of falling trees or one such giant had veered off its course into some unexpected area, is unclear. What is certain is that he had been killed instantly, pummelled into the ground like a stake. The body had been squashed and broken beyond recognition. It was, in fact, only those limbs that escaped the path of this behemoth that identified the wreckage as human.

This messenger of Regnier's seemed to have taken the most curious of routes to La Belle Horizon, via the cabin of his mulatto mistress, no doubt, as the widow did not receive notice of the loss of this valuable piece of security until the following day. Even more curious was the state of horse and rider upon arrival, both panting and lathered as if from a gruelling ride. Certainly not what one would expect after taking a day to cover half a day's ride. Maybe it was the night he had spent upon his other chestnut mare that left this rider so depleted, and caused him to race the horse as if he could recapture the lost day.

By this time word had already reached Magdelaine. It came by the way of an old slave named Toussaint; an appellation that stopped the hearts of most planters, but who it is said was named long before that catastrophe in Saint Domingue.

This wretch was a cast-out of old Regnier, living by what wits he had left and the charity of other blacks. He had long taken to wandering the roads from plantation to plantation in search of odd jobs that might bring him a little food or drink, maybe shelter for the night. It so happened he was in the vicinity of woods of the Regnier plantation, a favourite spot of his for poaching cerf and pink pigeon, on that unhappy day. And upon hearing of the calamity he hitched a ride on a passing cart and found himself at La Belle Horizon within hours of the boy's death.

For it was Magdelaine, with an almost filial concern, who gave to the old fellow most generously; who would forgo her own rations that his feeble frame might be fortified when she sent him on his way.

Magdelaine had disappeared from La Belle Horizon before the descending of night's pall.

*

When the shutters of Mme Lousteau's chamber were closed the space assumed a blackness so thick it was at once infinity and a cell. She, herself, and everything in the room lost to nothingness, all existence consumed before the closing of an eye.

The dark did not frighten her, not since her own darkness had made its brash appearance. Around her in the emptiness she saw neither demon nor djin, not even *his* face, but all the possibilities this force might conjure; the dominion of her own hand and the nothingness that her foes would become. This eternity had also soothed a heart beset by misery, replacing it with a thing that could not be broken. Something akin to iron or steel, or some new amalgam, that pumped away the smelted remains of her heart that this new thing might protect her.

And that night it was as if the darkness spoke to her, whispered news of that other breath. She did not open her eyes, but listened for the creak that should not be there and the hiss of breath as she stilled her own.

There it was. A whistle she barely heard for the beating of her heart. A sound one might not notice except in such silence, a faint nasal whine.

'I know you are there,' she said, without a hint of a quiver in her voice, 'speak up, Magdelaine, for it is you, is it not?' Silence. 'Why are you here? Do you think you have it in you to kill your mistress? I am awake now, you know, ma fille, and you have not the guile.'

From the darkness there came no answer.

'I take it you think our agreement null and void. And in truth I admit things have changed. But you know that by returning you have sealed your fate.'

A time that seemed like forever passed before the widow received her reply.

'You killed him.'

'No, no, ma fille, you killed him. There would have been no need for such persuasion if you had just agreed to help me.'

'But he was already gone, you sent him away.'

'He would have been recalled as soon as you gave your assent.'

'But I did, Madame, I did.'

'Only after I had told you about the boy, and you had proved your unwillingness.'

The widow was sure, through the current of darkness, she felt the woman shaking her head.

'You wanted murder.'

'Enough now, Magdelaine. Go, and if you fulfil your promise I might allow you to escape with your life.'

Not even Mme Lousteau heard the door open. There were no footsteps, the floor gave away no secret of the other's approach. There were brief sounds of struggle, muffled words whose indistinctness could not prevent conveying their alarm. With this also came a smell, one that lingered long after the intruder's departure; the musty, floral smell of a soporific – its pungency so acute it even brought sleep to Mme Lousteau's eyes.

'Thank you, Sandi,' Mme Lousteau said before sleep took her, 'let us have no more trouble from this one.'

CHANGE

Chapter Ten

In the Garden

A Reminiscence

How many arpents of land had been lost after emancipation, when the *nègres* fled the fields and harvests were abandoned for lack of hands?

She no longer remembered.

Their plantation had been among the largest on the island, producing abundant crops of sugarcane from before The Battle of Grand Port and the surrender of the colony to the British.

But it was the years between these two upheavals she remembered with the greatest clarity. Memories of those years would often visit her in dreams, and in daydreams induced by the sound of cutlasses hacking through cane.

She remembered the hunt, the feeling of leaves and dirt beneath her feet — her heart beat fast with the recollection.

She stretched out a leg in search of grass at the patio's edge.

It had begun after Alexandre's death. As a consequence of it.

Was it anger or grief that had consumed her? Was it both?

When the men set out for the hills in pursuit of her husband's murderer, she made it clear she would be accompanying them.

'But Madame,' Captain Balteau had said, 'please forgive me, the hunt is no place for a woman. I cannot allow you to put yourself in such danger.'

The slap came as a surprise; as much to her as to Balteau. Yet the evidence was there: the reddening of the gendarme's cheek, her stinging palm.

The voice she heard, her voice, was unwavering and as cold as a winter's morn in *Normandie*.

'Are you my master? Am I your black? Should I curtsy before addressing you?'

The gendarme was silent.

She nodded slowly to herself.

'Then why do you feel it proper to tell me my place, to talk to me as if I ask your permission?'

He had blustered out the beginnings of a reply but she only held up her hand.

There was, she suspected, more to the man's submission than mere spinelessness. For one did not become a captain in the *gendarmerie* without exhibiting some backbone. But, even fools have influential friends. And what difference was it to her, she had her way.

The hunt thrilled her.

Broken branches, the ashes of abandoned campfires, footprints half hidden in undergrowth; things usually dismissed by the eye, became clear and were registered without a thought. She threw away her shoes and tore at the hem of her dress, shortening it to just below the knee.

In the absence of speech sounds filled the silence, sounds beneath bird song and the flutter of wings. Indications of movement she'd thought below the range of the human hearing. Something carnal was roused in her. She tasted the scent of her quarry in the air.

She had not followed, but lead the gang of gendarmes and blacks; the whole troupe in awe of her. She could not have been what they had expected. They had likely imagined some finely dressed Madame, parasol in hand. What they had not expected was a Jeanne d' Arc, a woman who would take up into the mountains with the vigour of a *nègre*.

This all seemed a life time ago, she could hardly believe fifteen years had passed.

It was during these years, the years following Alexandre's death, that the stamp of *La Marseillaise* finally left her and she truly belonged to the island. Such a thing was bound to happen. Her sojourn as a planter's wife had not been a short one. Yet, it felt like she had spent most of her life as a planter's widow. The only attachment she had been left with was the land, and she would not allow this to be taken from her.

But looking out over the fields she could imagine nothing had changed.

Black figures still toiled in the cane, their scrawny and bowlegged forms appearing to dance in the shimmering heat. The faces no longer *Africain* or *Malgache* but those of Calicut. Limp hair replaced thick wool; muscular physiques gave way to slighter, boyish frames.

And there was still *marronage*, although no more hunting.

When the Malabars ran it was impossible to find them. They disappeared into the camps of their own people and those of the blacks. After that they were lost. For who could tell one from the other and which had failed to serve out the term of his contract? It was not in the nature of these wretches to offer up their absconding countrymen.

If she was to return with a head, that favoured old trophy, in all likelihood there would be a prosecution. And it would be the hunter who was hauled up before the courts and tried.

Yet, for every Indian who ran there were ten more to take his place.

They had never had enough blacks. Now the Malabars spread through the island like cholera. They came in their tens of thousands. More bodies landing in one year, than during ten years of trade in contraband *Zambiques*.

More cane was cut and the furnaces raged day and night. More trees were felled, more land reclaimed, more wood was burned. And despite the house's disrepair the coffers were undeniably full.

What will become of us? We are but a white mote in a vast black iris. What good is money if confronted with an island of insurrectionary hearts?

But first, the boy – it would not be to him that all was lost. The one she had seen on that fine market day. A day in which her heart had first been revived and then found itself in turmoil.

She stood and walked from patio to grass. The sun greeting her as she left the shade, she stopped, feeling the warmth become heat and then a brand upon her skin.

In the days of the chase she had browned and become accustomed to the relentless gaze. Caked in dirt and sweat, she cared little for her appearance, eschewing all propriety and refinement. With time these things had returned to her but marked with the unmistakable stain of island.

In two steps she regained the protection of the shadows.

'Sandi,' she called, her voice bearing an inflection not altogether French, and a raucousness that would not have been out of place in the bazaar.

A servant appeared from among the shadows, as if conjured like a genie from some Arabian tale. He was a tall fellow, his cotton pyjamas hanging loosely from slim shoulders and hips. Their whiteness bestowed a greater glow by the mahogany of his skin. His face bore not one line. With cheeks so polished one might doubt they had ever sprouted hair, if not for his moustache; thick and white bristled

Atop his head, like a crowning minaret, sat the intricate bindings of a turban. Altogether, a figure a little too bright for that haven of shade.

He gave a bow.

'Madame.'

His voice was at once sonorous and no more than whisper, like the voice that talks in one's own head.

'Remplissez encore!' *Refill it*, she said pointing to the pitcher on the iron table, 'J'ai soif,' *I am thirsty*, she added, waving the Malabar away with the flick of a hand.

With a second bow he disappeared back into the shadow.

She ran her hand over the leaf of a banane, savouring the thrill of its smoothness upon her fingertips. It was cool, now shaded from sunlight.

I will be buried in this garden.

Voices from the field were carried on the wind. Their tongue as alien to her as Isle de France had been on first arriving. When that young Flanders girl, whose husband was a little too old and little too portly, took her first step onto island soil. (In fact it had been the black stone of the wharf). Although Alexandre had still born traces of one dashing in his youth; those grey eyes, his shoulders broad, chin and jaw a set of tight angles. As yet no sign of those dog-like jowls.

Where had she landed? Where had that man taken her?

Her first sight of a black had been at the port of Marseilles on the day of her departure. There had been gangs of them mixed with loitering sailors and dock men. And not only blacks, but Indians and Chinamen. It had seemed to her that the whole world docked at that port and she had said the very same to Alexandre; unaware of her own naivety.

'It does,' he'd replied, 'it does.'

And there was his smile. In this smile there was no sense of mockery. There was love in that face. She hugged at his arm, pressing her cheek to the cloth of his jacket, inhaling the scent of serge and tobacco smoke. Excited by the world that surrounded her, excited by the new life that awaited. The adventure they would be taking together.

She watched a bird, such a small and beautiful thing. Its plumage a mixture of greens and reds and blues, all so perfectly assembled. Each colour rendered it seemed by the most delicate hand. To her mind came the diary and all it contained, vignettes of such creatures and oh so much more. Things she thought her heart had long hardened to, but which *gamin's* face had woken with ease.

It fluttered down from a tree onto the grass before her and hopped untroubled by her presence, giving out little cheeps of look at me, look at me.

When it took to the air, she turned to watch the Malabar pouring lemon water into a glass and sieving the slices of citrus with a spoon. He wiped the glass before handing it to her.

'Madame.'

'Merci, Sandi.'

She smiled to herself aware of the uncharacteristic slip in her demeanour.

'Away with you now,' she said, 'you are scaring the birds.'

When she next went to take a sip, she found her glass had never been refilled.

Chapter Eleven

Dominère

'Been sitting down too long,' Ma-Jo said, 'my feet forgot they were kin to the rest of me.'

I nodded, saying nothing.

Her breath had found her, at least, and she seemed to have recovered.

That was the day I realised something was wrong, seeing for the first time signs which had doubtless been long apparent.

Over the years Ma-Jo had gotten heavier. Her figure plumper, accentuated in ways that proved alluring to the eyes of men. But she was always a healthy woman and never what you would call fat. The old aunty who wrestled herself up from our stoop, however, I hardly recognised.

She had been sitting on that step when I returned home, preparing our food. Her legs dangled in the rain, just the way she liked; the pot receiving its fill of rain water. Half a year had passed since the incident at the market and I was working as an apprentice to Old Pierre, the carpenter.

When she asked me to carry the marmit over to the cook fire,

I thought nothing of it. As I had grown stronger it had become a common request.

My arms trembled under the pot's weight, the earth seeming unwilling to release its grip. I thought of the thick hands and forearms of Ma-Jo which had raised the pot untold times – how she carried it with neither shake nor stumble.

I staggered, half stooping like an old man, barely able to lift the thing above the dirt of our courtyard.

A sound I took for laughter came from behind me. I would have laughed, too, had it not taken all my determination to keep moving – my head swollen with effort.

It was not until I reached the old lean-to that I looked back, expecting to see the quiver of Ma-Jo's pipe and the playful shudder of her shoulders. What I saw was an old woman struggling; one hand pushing off from the stoop of our little veranda, the other grasping as if for the aid of some phantom hand. She toppled to her feet and walked stiff-legged towards me. I held my peace, knowing her likely rebuttal.

I put down the marmit and lit the kindling, the sticks snapped and hissed as the fire caught.

On reaching me Ma-Jo placed a hand on my shoulder, giving it a gentle pat and then a squeeze.

'Did I ever tell you the story of Dominère?' She asked.

I smiled, shook my head. At least some things had not changed.

'Maybe now is not the time for stories, Ma,' I said, deciding to risk her irritation, 'You look tired. Rest, let me cook.'

'Ey, mo garçon, what do you mean, eh? You want people to think I don't feed my boy, now he's working? Go get me my stool and maybe I'll let you keep me company,'

She gave me a shove to help me on my way.

I stumbled playfully, yet after what I had seen I couldn't bring myself to laugh. When she lowered herself onto the stool, it was with the studied precision of one who can no longer take the act for granted.

'I was no more than seven years old when he first beat me,' she began, the pot starting to bubble before her, 'mama told me I was lucky it was just his hand. And she was right. Children were seldom whipped, but in those days it wasn't unheard of.

'Mama dragged me to my feet and wiped my eyes. Then she shook me. Shook me 'til the little sense I had returned to the front of my head. She didn't say a word, just shook the tears right out of me. By crying I was just inviting more blows, you see, letting him know he could hurt me. You had to be stronger than that. Show yourself to a man like Dominère and it becomes his sport to see you broken.'

While she spoke Ma-Jo nodded to herself, as if in agreement with her own words; eyes closed, journeying I imagined, to see the world again through that young girl's eyes.

'Mama's only concern was preserving the little innocence I had,' she said, 'and mo garçon, it was not easy to hide a child's eyes from the daily cruelties dealt to our people – and when she could no longer ensure my innocence, she did all she could to keep me alive.'

In this tale it was not only the mother who sought to protect a life. For the child was also her mother's salvation and perhaps the one reason this woman had to live. In their own way both mother and daughter endured for the sake of the other's survival. Though why, during a time of such suffering, they clung so dearly to life, my old guardian could not say.

'It is a wonder any of us made it through that sentence of endless damnation.' She said, adding after something of a pause, 'The slave commander known as Dominère was my father. Though, I didn't know it at the time. And that blow, the first memory I have of his touch. Was he trying to teach me something, maybe, a lesson he thought necessary for the life I was to lead? He too was born into cruelty, so what better way would he have known?'

The chill that overcame me was at odds with our place beside the cook fire. I reached over to take Ma-Jo's hand. She held on but briefly, the tops of our fingers gripping before she let go. It was a wound, I guessed, that had long healed over and ceased to require consolation's balm.

Nevertheless, the time chosen to recount this tale seemed far from coincidental. Beneath its surface lay a less obvious truth.

'Mo garçon,' I remember Ma-Jo saying, 'childhood's end is not always so abrupt. Yet, every child knows they will grow up one day and leave behind their simple world. You are no longer a child, Liberté. Look at you. I see manhood in those shoulders, your hands have grown strong. But your eyes betray your innocence. For you, life has been as it should be, your childhood taking a longer path. The kind of childhood every mother wishes for their child.

'Still, you should not fear pain or misfortune, mo garçon, for they will come. Loss has its lessons to teach. Who knows, through these hardships you may discover places that both story and dream have yet to reveal to you.'

After that day I watched her closely, running home as soon as my work with Old Pierre was done.

I noticed she'd slowed and with this torpor came more weight. But just as quickly the weight was gone. And for a fleeting moment she was the beauty I remembered as child – but only briefly.

O my Ma-Jo.

When not working with Old Pierre I would visit the bazaar to buy provisions or take what little crops we had to be sold. For now she hardly left our yard.

Weeds set up habitation among our furrows and rats, seldom seen in better days, became more courageous without the swish of Ma-Jo's broom.

Her thick hands withered and within a matter of months she seemed to age years. My heart wearied in its task of deceiving my eyes. Her pride waned and settled into a wordless gratitude. A thankfulness evinced by the moistness of her eyes.

She quietened. There were no more stories. I filled the silences with my own voice; with the tales and songs she had once told me – recounted with every cadence of that old voice. I mimicked her rhythms and pauses. She laughed and her smile brought with it hope and recollections of the old Ma-Jo.

I aged too; tempered by the flames of misfortune. I was on the verge of losing yet another thing – the most precious of all. (For, I was not blind.) Through her stories Ma-Jo had taught me of my mother and father, but to me she was both, as well as my Ma-Jo. She was the life that gave life to all those things I had never seen and helped nurture my imagination. I was not from her body but in a way it was she who gave birth to me.

*

And then one evening it happened.

As I stepped through our gate daylight was already losing its grip, colours shrinking back into shadow. Yet there was not the flicker of a candle in the window, no light from the cook-fire to set the yard aglow.

I heard Pirat bark, in breathless yelps that sent me cold on that warm evening.

At the sound of footsteps the old mutt scampered from the rear of the house, chickens scattering in his wake, his feet skidding as if on lose macadam. He headed towards me like he meant to attack and skipped about, brushing around and between my legs, before setting off again towards the rear of our plot where our garden lay. I followed, my heart telling me to run back the way I'd came.

The scene did not bode well and the fear of what I might find lay like a stone in the pit of my stomach. At first I saw nothing just a jumble of twilit shapes: an old wooden bucket, parcels of corn still sheathed in their green wrappings, the twisting roots of a tree, a huddle of black stones.

She sat there, leaning against the low parapet of the well, her mouth agape, eyes open too wide. One leg was caught underneath her, the other extended before her, as if in her last curtsey. She listed slightly to one side. Her pallor a dusty grey; the black lustre faded in the evening light.

I ran to her, but she had gone, left hours before.

The flesh was already losing its tautness, beginning to sag from the bone. Her skin was waxy and a fly crawled across a drying eye. When I held her and carried her to bed, her body stiff and misshapen, she felt lighter than a child. Even her familiar smell had gone, replaced by the reek of emptiness. And as I grasped and pushed my face into her cold bosom the remainder of my own child left me, fleeing like a desperate maroon.

I wept and Pirat whimpered and nuzzled his wet snout into my neck. We slept in a sweat cleaving to the body of our beloved guardian.

In the morning I found a letter I knew she could not have written.

Chapter Twelve

The Letter

Alexandre's Letter to Elise

My dearest Elise,

I spent many an hour contemplating the writing of this letter. For in a way it is our first conversation, all be it a one sided one. The words we have shared, thus far, have commanded little more from you than a curtsy or yes mon maître. On this occasion, however, your answer will require more consideration. At least I hope it will.

What I set forth here may or may not endear me to you. It would be misleading to say I do not wish for the former, but I am under no illusion. What kind of man would treat his only child as I have treated you? This you may rightly ask. My only excuse, dear child, is that I have done only what the world expects of me. I made my mark without concern for the consequences, except if the consequences be injurious to my concerns. To this dictum I have remained true, until now.

Men such as I have been the making of this world. It is for the sake of clarity, and not out hubris, that I say so. Through our endeavour commerce and the seeds of civilisation travelled oceans, landing upon shores whose people had progressed little since man's early history. It is true that hardship has been laid upon many a shoulder, profit made from other men's toil. As unfair as it might seem, my dear, this has always been the way of things. It was Aristotle who observed that from the hour of their birth some men are marked for subjection and others to rule them. In this way progress is brought into the world, my dear, and prosperity to man and nation. Conscience is a luxury the man of commerce can seldom afford, and rightly so, for peon, artisan and official all rely on him for bread.

But you my child should have dwelt outside such considerations. It was my brutishness that created you and adherence to propriety that caused me to maintain my distance. Forgiveness may seem like a churlish thing to ask, but nonetheless, I ask it of you. We often neglect to see those things that mark our true wealth, even though they be right before our eyes. To me you are one such rarity.

Both age and the possibility of losing you have made this clear to me.

Also, it is likely the thought of such loss played a part in my failure to release you from servitude. But it is just as likely that shame dictated my behaviour. You may wonder why I do not make these confessions to you in person. This is indeed down to shame, as well as the fear that you may depart from my presence before ever uttering to me the word papa. I beg you humour an old man's fantasies. I know I hope in vain.

It is because of these considerations, because of the lack in a life that should have contained so much more, that I make an offer to you. No, not an offer but a gift. A bestowal that will no doubt shock and outrage, and very likely cause the only one who has ever loved me to view me with disdain. Not a thing any man wishes upon himself. But I would forfeit my good name and the consideration of that other heart if only it were to go some way in repairing the breach between us, and reversing the injustices you have suffered as an unacknowledged daughter. I know things can never be made right but this should not prevent one from trying.

Elise, my daughter, I pledge to you, to be received on my passing, half of the great estate of La Belle Horizon. As a legacy for you and your children. That the hardship you have endured may not be suffered by your child. Also, I grant you (your manumission papers will be drawn up with great urgency) your freedom. Something, that as my child, you should have always possessed. As I doubt the Madame will agree to your lodging with us at La Maison Blanche (there are concessions that must be made to my venerable wife, who has also had to endure), I will have a residence erected for you within the grounds of the estate and without the camp des noirs. It is indeed a compliment to your character that you have become such a fine young woman, and I firmly believe this despite your present condition, while dwelling among such people. Indeed your current circumstance should be excused due to this very fact.

There are, as you might imagine, certain stipulations with regards to this bequest. Although I believe none of these to be unreasonable.

It is impossible to ignore that you are with child, something that would be celebrated in a slave of your age, but which becomes deplorable when it is your very daughter who is expecting. As I have said I understand that circumstance is very much responsible for this fact. Nonetheless, it has come to my attention that the father of this child is one as degenerate as you are meek. One who is not unfamiliar to me and whose name I refuse write. He is an anathema to me. You are doubtless ignorant of the wretchedness of which he is capable and have fallen under some idolising spell, to which the young are often all too susceptible. I have witnessed the outcome of his actions and do not hesitate to say there is a demon within him. The savageness of his land was never tamed from him.

It is through no accident that he lives a life of wretchedness in the mountains. Those many years ago when I first purchased him I saw the intractableness of his nature and thought this rebellion, this disobedience, a trait that might be re-forged by the right hand. That with a perceptive master and a diligent overseer he might become an oxen who could be yoked with the most terrible loads. A slave, who by his very tenacity, might excite others into the same effort. When I christened him it was not in mockery, but in anticipation of what he might become. I was soon to witness the result of my vanity and that his barbarity was beyond the bounds of what I had imagined.

I realise that you have an attachment to him, whether this developed by the way of coercion of some other means I do not know. It would be wrong, given my own history, to pass judgement. In fact I understand. Without a father what choice did you have but to find one who would stand in his stead, but by accident or design, again I do not know, you have chosen one who would have your father's throat. I said I would not name him but to call him nemesis would neither contradict this oath or be far from the truth.

To ask that you immediately relinquish all contact with him would be too pious a demand for one in my position. But, outlaw as he is, he cannot be allowed to enter the bounds of La Belle Horizon. I will redouble the watch to ensure this brigand be kept at distance from these environs. Let it not be said, however, that I am unreasonable when it comes to dealing with a matter so close to your heart. I will not pursue him beyond the borders of our land, although I refuse to honour him with his freedom, his atrocities make such a thing impossible.

If you must see him it should be away from this place.

Should you marry this man or leave La Belle Horizon to be with him the gift offered to you shall become forfeit. There may be some paltry sum left to you, I have not yet decided, but not the great dowry you would have otherwise received.

To your freedom I attach no such conditions as by right of your birth, as my daughter, this should have been so.

I hope that in time you will come to see that other for what he is and disentangle yourself from him. There are many among the gens du couleur who would make a respectable match for you, those who have already amassed their own small fortunes.

When you come into possession of your inheritance I hope there will be roused a spirit of cooperation between yourself and the Madame with regards to the administration of the estate. For while she lives La Belle Horizon shall not be broken apart. This covenant cannot be infracted. I grant you each your share and once the costs of maintaining the concern have been covered and suitable amount reinvested to ensure its longevity, you will both be left with not an inconsiderable sum at your disposal. More than enough so ensure your lives are comfortable. You shall want for nothing. As long as the estate remains in good order, for you would be surprised how the least misstep brings creditors clawing at your door.

The relationship between the Madame, my wife, and you, my daughter must be approached with much delicacy. No doubt, if a situation were to arise at this very moment that thrust you both together the outcome would not be of the auspicious kind. In all likelihood the Madame would pursue every available avenue to ensure your disenfranchisement. But we are at no such juncture and there is time, many years I hope, for the Madame's heart to be softened and for attachment to be formed, however unlikely this may seem at the present.

You have no doubt tired of my ramblings. If you so wish you may visit La Maison Blanche to talk with me and we can, the two of us, make a belated start at that which should have commenced at your exit from the womb. Ask for me and I will see you.

I do not expect you to rush to my door, when confronted with such revelations, it is of benefit that they are given thought. It is only wise to take to ruminating when one has grave matters to consider. Of this I have great experience. I beg you do not dismiss my plea without first considering all that we both may gain.

Although it may be long overdue, your affectionate father,

M. Alexandre Lousteau

Chapter Thirteen

A Wordless Reply

The necessity of all Mme Lousteau had done could not be called into question, yet fate, it seemed, had a very different plan.

After settling her differences with Balteau and heading out into the wild with his troupe, she was in no doubt of the path to be taken. A course that lead beyond their foray into the forest and encompassed those other problems that required swift resolution: the girl Elise and the legacy Alexandre had bequeathed her.

With Alexandre gone and Mme Lousteau's memory of him sheered of its affection, what did she have but the land around her? What was there to ground her but the very ground beneath her feet – the haven of La Belle Horizon.

Prior to their pursuit of Alexandre's killer, she remembered wondering if the sabre that hung at Captain Balteau's waist was merely ornamental. A question which failed to concern her when they caught the maroon and she took to hacking at the captive's neck. The *nègre* had been shot twice, one lung punctured she guessed by his wheeze, and suffered a fall that left him all but disfigured.

Yet, Mme Lousteau had recognised him and without the least indication reached for the captain's sword.

It turned out the blade was as keen as butcher's knife and after three swings the head was severed from the body. On the first chop the maroon's black eyes opened wide, as one wakened from a dream by a fright. By the second his gaze held nothing but emptiness. With the third his head had turned, falling sideways, as if it peered into the trees below.

But the rest of her plan required more subtlety. Her first action had needed to be decisive, stilling her own hand as well as instilling fear into those around her. It was best to discourage any more renegades and the advances of swindlers who might think her an easy target. She had been more concerned with the latter. For, they often came in the most unlikely of guises, their deceptions undiscovered until it was too late. In the case of the girl at least there had still been time to take action.

The violence of the hunt had put the remainder of her plan somewhat in jeopardy – the danger of Elise taking flight on the news of her paramour's death, being very real. But Mme Lousteau wagered on the girl's condition preventing her from leaving. To whom would Elise run? What chance did a pregnant girl have in the mountains? As it turned out the Madame's suspicion had been well founded. For, the death of the maroon drained the last of the girl's lifeblood and she all but crawled to her hut to die.

The girl had indeed perished as did the child or so Mme Lousteau was told; the midwife, she assumed, subject to a less public burial. And although the pain and distress Mme Lousteau suffered could never be annulled, the opportunity for surprises, such as those surrounding her husband's death, had been; leaving La Belle Horizon safe from usurpation and the Lousteau name unsullied. Even if everything had not gone to plan, it appeared that all accounts were settled. Her slate clean and ready for her to begin life anew.

Yet fifteen years on, the boy had appeared and all the old ghosts were awoken. What she had thought settled only shifted out of sight.

Mme Lousteau called out to Sandi from the drawing room, her voice summoning only an echo of his name. The voice, that of an old woman, was almost unrecognisable to her; she could hardly believe it her own. Years she had kept at bay seemed, all of a sudden, to have overwhelmed her; leaving her feeling brittle right down to the bone. She tried to imagine herself taking to horseback, as she had just months earlier, and her mind replaced the ache felt on dismounting with fractures and contusions. If only she had turned back that day and returned to the estate, the boy's existence would never have been considered.

'Sandi, come to your mother.'

How unlike Sandi it was, not to appear on her calling and when there was so much for him to answer for. He was not one to fear reprimand. There had not even been an echo of a reply when she asked him about the boy and the old woman; Elise's child and the midwife; remnants from a lifetime ago. A silence she could so easily have read as an admission of his guilt. What could he say in his defence? 'You were mistaken, Madame, it could not have been them.' This she knew not to be true, for she had seen. Or he might say, 'I left them for dead.' To this she could only reply: it appears that left for dead is not dead, at all.

The other alternative was that he had lied to her and this brought another pain to bear: the possibility that none of it was true, that his faithfulness had been but a performance and their bond only an imitation of devotion. Well, on his part, for she had felt it— hadn't she? Could it be a chink in her armour had allowed the point of another blade to pierce her? Mme Lousteau saw the nature of man's heart for what it was – betrayal; even though she thought herself immune to the effects of that other sweeter potion.

But her Sandi, her loyal Sandi?

'Sandiman, where are you?' she asked, in a tone so gentle only one close to her might hear it.

And she felt him there, although he did not speak; the hypnotic scent of aloeswood and sandalwood insinuating his presence, like a portent that precedes a ghost. Thirty years he had served her, more than she shared with her husband, Alexandre. Such time creates a bond not easily sundered, which even death's horny fingers might struggle to end.

His silence became a comfort once she knew he was there. But Mme Lousteau did not turn; it was not her place to turn. And Sandi did not confront her, for this was his way.

'I am still waiting, you know, you can't avoid it forever,' she said, a hint of playfulness on those old lips, 'you think you know me too well, which you might do, but I am not too old to surprise. And you, dear Sandiman are not exempt from the tenets of mistress and servant.'

She closed her eyes, nodded, as if listening to a reply. The smile that threatened to break through her steel was without warning, retracted.

'Was I not explicit in my instructions? Did you not understand what I asked? If it were any other I might have believed it, but of you— no. Sandi makes no mistakes. With confidence I would place my life in your hands, and I did, have since on many occasions. Not to mention the fate of the *habitation*...

'Oh Sandi, such brazen talk, I would never have expected it from you. But in answer to your question, yes, I am alive and no, apart from Alexandre nothing was taken from me. What you have failed to answer, though, is how the ghost of my troubles has suddenly reappeared...

'Ha, you know me well enough not question my certainty. What I saw was not glimpsed from the corner of my eye, nor did I fall asleep and dream up the boy...

'Yes, there are many such black boys, but this was not only a boy, no, no, he was a replica of his father. You forget I saw that man die, it was my hand. I know his face. And I could almost forgive the slip up with the boy – the mother dead and no proof of a child being born – but the woman, the midwife, she was in your hands. You knew your responsibility...

'Is that— is that truly the best you can do, feign ignorance?...

'Yes, yes you are, Sandi, and claiming ignorance is no different from lying. So, you are lying to me now. You lie to your mistress, to your— your friend...

'How dare you, I am your friend and mor— and after all we have been through...

'Stop, don't try to apologise, I've had enough. Get out, leave now...

'No, wait, on second thoughts, come back. You have told me nothing, other than I misplaced my trust in you. So many years, Sandi, so many years. What have you done? Where has my Sandi gone...

'No, he has and his replacement is a stranger to me, just a shape of him, a shadow. I don't know him...

'Then tell me, at least tell me...

'Honestly, you are going to repeat the same thing, again...

'Just go, then, I've had enough.'

And with that he was no more. To her next question Mme Lousteau could not even imagine a reply. It did not so much fall upon deaf eyes, as into nothingness – silence deeper than the emptiness that surrounded her. There was not even a creak in the house, no footstep; no whisper or laugh, only the obedient hush of the chastised. This was not a companionable silence, the wordlessness that falls between two friendly old souls. It felt like that bridgeless chasm which death exposes, a place where even a cry leaves no echo; from where nothing returns if it turns back too late. Would it be so with them? She hoped not, but still, she could not allow this evasion to continue. If Sandi insisted on being ignorant of the matter at hand, then so be it, it changed nothing. He had failed to perform his duty. Whether it was ten or fifteen years ago, was irrelevant. When something was incomplete, it was incomplete and had to be attended to. For though the dead may haunt you it is the only the living who can threaten your life and take from you what is rightfully yours. And through his carelessness this had again become possible.

Mme Lousteau sat, overcome by a weariness which visited her more often of late. The certainty of her younger years seemed to have deserted her, leaving a mind that dithered as if presented with a thousand forked paths. In bygone times there would not have been a hint of hesitation in her actions – decisions were considered, consequences foreseen and judgement meted out without mercy. Now it seemed she had become too accommodating.

The weight of the air around Mme Lousteau seemed to push her down, a feather caught beneath stones, the room growing larger as if she shrunk in size. Is this what it meant to have so much life behind her, the decline of reason as the earth readied itself for her return – yet more dust to be forgotten and trampled upon.

What continued to trouble her was that other possibility: that Sandi's own cunning, and not his carelessness, had saved both midwife and child. If one dedicated just an iota of thought to it, Sandi's excuse, his denial, appeared transparent. This, in turn, raised the question of a greater conspiracy, one that might well have included Elise, the midwife and even the maroon. It was all conjecture, of course, but once considered this hypothesis provided a most plausible explanation. One might even say it had a whiff of the definitive. Yet, Sandi had never deserted her. He had remained, helped her rebuild her life; he was the anchor that stemmed the pull of the tide. To her this spoke not of a traitor. No, it could not be true. The business with Elise and the midwife was an outlier, the actions of a man whose conscience had staid his hand – the whole deception governed by the shame of failing his mistress.

Or so she told herself. For, despite all that accompanied the boy's appearance, the disturbance which had consumed her life, there were things meant to be consigned to the past. The saga of the last months had left her fatigued, her mind addled with ghouls she thought long exorcised. They needed to be cast out, the door closed on their moaning. She was no more a young woman and approached those years where death was wont to lurk, waiting to spring its surprise. There was only so much life left to live and be they days, months or years they should not be lived in the past. After all that had been tarnished should something not remain intact?

So she sought to waive the business with Sandi, at least until the greater dilemma was resolved. An idea had come to her, one in fact spurned by an earlier recollection: Balteau. Might he help her close that door?

A creak, a sound that might well have been her own skull straining, woke her. Had she been asleep? No, the questions of dreams are ethereal and open ended, such self-interrogation takes place only in the conscious mind. These were the thoughts that kept one awake, not the demons of nightmares.

'Madame?' A voice asked, quietly as if afraid of waking her.

'Are you still in here? Ah, yes you are. It is getting dark, Madame. Supper is ready.'

Outside blue had turned to mauve and the room had become one great shadow. No longer a collection of separate things but relics caught in the net of darkness. The day had slipped away, leaving her forgotten in her own tribulations. Not so unlike her servant Sandi had done.

A face appeared beside her, familiar, yet unfamiliar; young, too close. Her scent a mix of sweat and spice and anise. Her breath warm, if a little sour. She waved the girl away, her fingertips touching the soft flesh between the girl's neck and chin. So smooth. As smooth as a petal, as the drift of a cloud. The girl moved away two steps, stood up straight, not much taller than the seated old woman.

'I will light the lamps if you want to sit a while longer, Madame.'

'Where is Sandi? Send him back to me. I have an errand for him.'

At first, the girl said nothing, did not even let a breath slip. Her smile a sketch of uncertainty.

'But Madame, Sandi— Sandi is gone.'

'Then, my girl, send someone find to him.'

'But he will not be returning. Do you not remember he is—'

'What I know is that age has only increased his petulance. He will return, where else has he to go? No matter, you will do. Go and find the stable boy. Tell him to send word to Captain Balteau, that the Captain should visit me at his earliest convenience – tomorrow if possible.'

Chapter Fourteen

Au Revoir

I held in my tears, ground my teeth in concentration while my heart thumped against the ribs that surrounded it. The thoughts in my head turned and turned until they made me dizzy, and deaf to the verses of the priest as Ma-Jo was committed to the ground; all the while my face fixed in a grimace I thought worthy of a man.

Old Pierre, one who had lived through *le temps margoze*, those most bitter days of slavery, a man they said could shoulder the bole of a tree, sobbed like a grieving widow, like a mother who has lost her child. His big hands covering his face as his shoulders shook.

This shamed tears from my own eyes and I ran from the graveside before the first earth was thrown.

When I returned home I dug up Ma-Jo's trove of piastres from beneath the tamarind tree, from under the ring of burnt earth where we kept campfire.

I took half the coins and put the other half back in the hole. That night I lit my last fire on the spot and drank until my head toppled to the floor.

My head was still there when I woke in the morning. Even when I stood it felt as if I'd left the thing behind. I threw up on the way to the well, heaving until my guts pushed at the back of my eyeballs; crawled to the spot where Ma-Jo had lain. With my hand I searched out the well bucket finding nothing but stone and air.

There was a laugh, and I kicked at Pirat as he lapped at the spew.

In my head an unfamiliar drum played, pounding on my brain and the inside of my skull as if they were percussion instruments. Had the dog really laughed or had I imagined it?

'Ma?' I called out, my eyes watering; forgetting, in those first moments of consciousness, that we had buried her the day before.

A hand guided mine to the smooth surface of a *calebasse*, I felt the water slosh and its coolness through the wood-like skin. I went cold, and for a moment the beating in my head and heart stopped. Had she come back, had I dreamed it all?

The gate had not squeaked, there were no footsteps, when I turned my head there was nobody there. I had only just discovered the wall of the well when the *calebasse* was placed in my hand.

'Come, garçon,' a voice said, it was deep, but soft, and not without a little mirth.

The hair at the back of my head, which now stood to attention, was stroked and my back rubbed; an arm wrapped around my waist. I was helped to sit on the wall.

The *calebasse* was eased up towards my lips. As my head tipped back and the fuzz of my brain was filled with sunlight, the thumping started again. A foot kicked at the overturned demijohn, it clinked over stones and rolled in a half circle.

'You're almost a man, garçon, but you still have a boy's stomach. Ey, you drink all of that?' The voice asked. Not Ma-Jo's.

'Ai-yee, don't talk so loud.' I said.

There came another peal of laughter.

I groaned, put a hand to my brow to shade my eyes from sunlight and looked up at Old Pierre. He was a dark shape silhouetted by a bright blur; his edges still soft and feathered, his features gradually appearing from the darker mass.

First to come into focus were his teeth, then his lips and lines that framed his smile. The anguish and heartache which had consumed him the day before, appeared to have gone. Only when I saw his eyes, did I see the pain was still there.

I lowered my head to escape the sun, to prevent the contents of my own heart gushing out.

He crouched on his haunches, then, it was him who peered up at me. He tilted his head and hunched his shoulders in order to search out my face. When he caught my eye I began to straighten, as slowly and precisely as an old tortoise.

I lifted the *calebasse* and drank more water.

'Pierre,' I said, adding nothing more, the other words, if there had been any, drowned out by the banging in my head. I shut my eyes and let my skin search for a morning breeze, hoping for some small relief from the pain. I found none.

This man of fifty or so wasn't really so old, he didn't even have a grey hair on his head. He was one of those fellows who never seemed to age and always had a sparkle in his eye. The kind you'd pass in the street and think *isn't that so-and-so*, but then tell yourself *no, it can't be*, for if so he hadn't changed since you were a child. Because of this Old Pierre seemed to have lived forever, with even the old folks calling him old.

He had been Ma-Jo's sometime companion and was also teaching me a trade, a carpenter with large heavy hands and arms carved from ebony wood. He seemed tall, though not much taller than other men, and liked to laugh and hug and clap his hands. He smelled of sweat and sawdust and sometimes tilambik. Or these are the things I remember of him.

'Drink garçon,' Old Pierre said, patting my knee, 'then we'll clean up.'

Pierre inclined his head but I chose not to look at the mess I'd made.

'I'm going,' I said, making the idea of departure seem more real. As if naming it meant it was something I must do.

He nodded. I felt it, as if something in the air had changed.

'Going to help me clear up the mess you made before you go?'

I gave a nod and a shake of the head all in one, and added to this a shrug.

'I don't know where to,' I said, hoping it would prevent further enquiry, only after did I realise there was no need.

'None of us know until we get there,' he said 'and even then we might not have reached it.'

My elbow dug into his ribs, aware that this whimsy, so unlike his usual speech, could so easily have been accompanied by Ma-Jo's mischievous smile.

'Iye,' he said grabbing his side, 'I'm an old man.'

'Yet you talk like an old woman.'

We shared a smile and looked at the empty house; its porch and its rails and the worn step where she loved to sit.

'Garçon,' he said, 'she will never be far from us.'

*

We took an old tablecloth and folded it corner to corner so it likened to a sail. At its centre was placed a shirt and pair of trousers. To these were added six parcels: balls of sackcloth, their necks tied with twine so they resembled onions, each one different in size. They contained rice, cornmeal, salt, salted fish, red peas and dried manioc.

The letter I had found was already in my pocket.

If I ate sensibly, Old Pierre told me, these would last me a week, maybe more. I asked him how I might eat without using my good sense.

He looked at me and chuckled, resting a hand on my shoulder.

'Don't eat too much, garçon,' he said, 'cook enough for one meal, only. Walking is a hungry work and if you cook too much you will eat it all.'

He offered me some tilambik to help me regain my senses. But before filling our cups he poured a measure onto the ground as a libation for the departed. The words he muttered were too quiet for me to hear.

Then he said aloud, 'To your journey. May your feet always find the right grooves and keep you clear of rocks and potholes; may that which is calling you take you on the most auspicious routes; and may the surprises of this world not steal all the innocence from your heart.'

'Merci, ton,' *thank you uncle*, I said, looking away from him before my eyes could fill with water. 'To Ma-Jo,' I said, raising my cup and anointing the earth with my own toast.

Pierre added the quart of tilambik to my bundle.

'This food will not spoil,' he said, gesturing towards the sacks, 'if you can take food elsewhere on your journey, do so, and save this. It will keep. Fish, hunt tang, eat the fruit that's in season and you will fare well, mo garçon.'

Before I departed he took my hand, turning the palm upwards, his hand resting beneath my own, and put in it a folded leaf. It too was fastened by a single piece of twine. There was weight about it that suggested something inside. The silver-grey of a piastre was visible at one corner of the wrapping; dull and cold against the skin of the badamier leaf.

He closed my fingers around the package by closing the fingers of his own hand.

I was unsure if what he had given me was a gris-gris or a gift to help me on my journey. I did not ask.

I left our little house and two arpents of land in the stewardship of Old Pierre. It was with a heavy heart that I waved him goodbye.

After Ma-Jo died, I found myself alone, standing in that purgatory between childhood and manhood. And like most boys of this age I was impatient to become a man.

In those times there were still stories from the land of our forebears, told by those among us who were Malgache or Zambique, whose memories still retained the customs of these places. I recalled tales told of certain rites: traditions that set boys on the pathway to becoming men. I had wished that such a thing existed for me, so I would know where to place my next step. But what I remembered of these rituals seemed strange and disjointed.

Now, whether I realised it or not, I was at the beginning of one such path.

Until then I had followed my own customs and took heed of the things Ma-Jo taught me. I took each sunrise and sunset as a blessing and cherished everything in between.

I am not saying I lived in eternal bliss, but even when I was at my most miserable I knew that happiness had not deserted me; that I would pass some tree or take an unexpected turn and find it there waiting patiently for me. Well, before Ma-Jo passed away, that is.

And after that what had I expected to find, what lay in wait just beyond my line of sight? I could not say, but the thought of it filled me with both hope and fear.

Chapter Fifteen

Liberté Leaves Mahébourg

Pirat skittered along beside me.

I thought I'd bid farewell to that old scoundrel and looked for the last time into those rheumy eyes. His golden coat was no more golden, but a mangy brown. And he brought as a companion a mouldering smell which seemed to follow a couple of paces behind him. His fur had fallen off in patches exposing bits of velvet undercoat.

I'd judged him too long in the tooth to accompany me on my journey. At home he would lay in the shade and chase the occasional rat after sunset – but even this he did half-heartedly, often mustering only a single bark and rarely giving chase.

Twice, at the opening and then the waning of the same season, had the old reprobate taken to heel. As if just as Ma-Jo suggested, he had seen the approach of his life's great adventure. For this, it seemed, he had stored up a lifetime of energy.

At the gate I'd shooed that sniffling nose from my legs and between my feet. But not a hundred yards from home I heard a pattering echo to my footsteps. When I turned, ready to chase him from my shadow, he barked and skipped just like a pup. I hadn't the heart to send him away. So I carried on, the old dog behind me at one moment and then suddenly bounding ahead. He'd stop, rigid with excitement, and cock his head to one side waiting for me to catch up, before again taking flight; his four old legs urging on my two young ones.

I thought he'd follow me to the edge of town, tire, and wander off home. But he was like me, wasn't he? Motherless, fatherless, abandoned. He didn't tire. Determined, I guess, not to lose the one person he had left. I will tell you, when I consider that dog's plight, I feel more than a little ashamed. He was not only an animal, but a friend. And I knew what it was to be alone in the world.

I am relieved that he came chasing after me.

What better fellowship is there for a travelling man than that of a dog? A friend who never tires of either silence or chatter, nor frowns upon the strange things you might do. One who does not care if you've washed in one day or five, as it is by your smell that he best knows you. Who is not afraid when the darkness beyond the campfire becomes more impenetrable than that between the stars, and does not laugh at your fear of what the blackness might hold.

*

It was not unusual to take to the road back then. And it was on foot, or if you had a little money, by donkey that you travelled. You risked being rattled to death in a trap or carriage. Not that we were familiar with such luxuries.

Of course some of us drove old carioles, whose axles shook and spokes bickered in their felloes as they bumped around on that rutted surface. Your teeth would chatter and be almost shaken from your head, and it was a surprise when you dismounted and found your bones in all the right places.

But it was either that or donkey if you had crops that needed taking to the bazaar. And believe it or not, and I know there are some of you who will not, a donkey can only bear so heavy a load.

I think the macadam of the Port Louis—Mahébourg road had begun to be laid, but we were yet to see it. Anyway, it might be good for wheels but macadam burns and cuts the feet of men, and does no favours for a dog's paws. The same might not be true for an old wayfarer's soles, but back then I was yet to earn my calluses.

From my sack of tablecloth hung a small cauldron and under my arm I carried my tambour. Its goat skin was warn and darkened by the oil of much use, for it is well known that the story in every *kreol's* heart is set to music.

On my head I wore a straw hat, a *sapo la paille*, to protect me from the sun. My feet were bare and I had rolled up my trouser legs to just below the knee. My four-legged friend was never far away.

As I said, when hot, macadam burns the feet, but on that day the earth itself was so hot it made the shoeless wish for shoes and those with shoes for a donkey. It was a day for snoozing in the shade or swimming in the sea. Not one for roaming off to who-knows-where, especially when your head and belly have still to catch up with you from the night before.

(Though, I'll let you into a secret: I did know – or at least I thought I knew – where I was heading.)

As is often true on so a stifling day, the air was dusty. It carried those smells, which at first intermingle, and then become distinct as you pass the home of this or that craft; sawdust, brimstone, stone dust and pitch; raffia, indigo and spice, each revealing itself from amidst the odour of the former.

I crossed Rivière des Créoles making my way on that old winding road in the direction of Vieux Grand-Port, and left my little coastal town. I loved Mahébourg, I loved it with all of my heart, but the urge to discover what lay beyond – within the islands interior, its coasts, its plateau, the mountains and remnants of its forest – was more fantastic to me than all the wrecks of Grand Port.

For what use is a garden if you only ever look upon one flower?

There was of course the issue of the letter, and this played no small part in my decision to leave. A matter of months had passed, five maybe six, since the incident at the market. Pirat had been saved from a barrage of hooves and wheels, but in the following months Ma-Jo's health deteriorated. Then she was gone. I could not forget the look on her face or the haste with which she packed away our stall, that day at the market. She offered no explanation until we had safely reached home. The revelation that it was she, the mistress of La Belle Horizon we encountered, was no surprise to me. It was as if the continuation of an unfinished story had been announced, Ma-Jo's characters revived for another instalment. What came next would be anyone's guess.

But she said little more about the meeting than this. The heart of it remained untold – this made so clear by the way she first reacted – and would remain so. The reason for this taciturnity was a mystery to me. Maybe, Ma-Jo sought to underplay the significance of the encounter so as not to frighten me – to protect me. Yet, what could be more terrible than the tales already told? Was the answer perhaps to be found among the pages concealed in her pinafore? Could it be that a woman of so many words was left speechless by what she discovered within? Was it possible that Ma-Jo believed the very utterance of the letter's contents would tempt yet another catastrophe? Or had she merely guessed the pages' importance, them being no more than scribbles to the unlettered eye?

Whichever it might have been, I do not believe it was merely coincidence that she kept the document so close.

'There are eyes,' she said to me one morning, as I swept out our yard, making sure that our dust was just-so, 'watching when they think you cannot see.' When I raised my eyebrows and said, 'eh?' All she told me was to trust in my senses and that I would know.

On yet another occasion, again right out of the blue, she had said, 'remember, garçon, mark my words, that woman's gaze reaches far beyond her own sight.' Well, this utterance left me no less flabbergasted, but this time I managed a nod and gave a frown of feigned comprehension.

There were other instances, after that woman's appearance at the bazaar, when Ma-Jo dropped an adage or two, though their meaning amounted to much the same thing: *garçon*, be on your guard. You might think me the superstitious sort, but I was not one to take my ol' guardian's words lightly – whether I understood them or not. Many a wisdom could be gained from her stories and she rarely left a word misplaced.

What I was able to glean from the letter's contents raised more questions than answers. It did little to put my mind at rest. The next episode of the story, you could say, lay waiting at my feet.

Enough beating about the bush, I hear you grumble, what was in the missive you received? Well, it seemed unlikely the appearance of both letter and *Grande Dame*, only months apart, years after the story's flames seemed extinguished, could be a coincidence. Is it a surprise when after solemn days of heat, wind and rain that the cyclone follows? No, no, no. This is the way of nature and so go the workings of fate. Once events are set in motion one thing shall surely follow another. Perhaps the years between mama's death and the woman's arrival were no more than a pause in the story's telling.

What I found in my possession was a letter to Mama Elise from M. Alexandre Lousteau, the dead husband of the madame we had not long ago bumped into. Oh yes and it was true, as the old story went, the fiend had more than a hand in mama's making. Oh *grand-père*. In the letter he confessed as much and promised reparations, none of which mama lived to see. I think it was then that it began to dawn on me, the danger those folded pages put me in.

So with this epistle a path for me was laid, northwards in the direction of Flacq. Not to say I was on a treasure hunt, as I had already made up my mind to leave. (By my life this is true.) But with M. Lousteau's words bubbling in my head, like a bouillon that threatened to boil over, it seemed I had only two choices: to head towards or away from La Belle Horizon, to flee or embrace my destiny. (So is the impetuousness of youth.) Off I headed along the old Mahébourg coast road, while I considered what the dead man had written.

As I said I had already decided to take to the road. Being a carpenter's hand as well as musical sort, I possessed talents useful for one gone a wandering. Not to mention the repertoire of stories I had at my disposal. From my earliest childhood Ma-Jo fed me a hearty diet of folktales; tall tales, short tales, fat tales, thin tales – dramas whose scope extended way beyond my own family saga. I hoped this trip would mark the beginning of my true calling.

It was with this desire that I attempted to lighten my heart, to chase away sorrow and trepidation both.

Out there, in those places I was yet to see, lived an abundance of new tales and new ears to listen; and *mo frère* this excited me. The stories one woman carried in her heart brought life to things I'd never seen and could have passed away with her. But instead they were in my care and the more they were told the more likely they would be remembered.

And how many more voices recounted by the campfire tales that might never be retold? How many more hearts carried the spirits that history would never remember?

I would find them all, learn them all and retell them in a way that would be remembered. This is what I truly craved and everything else, I tried to persuade myself, was merely an aside.

Tell me, is there anything as enthralling as a story told to music? When an audience is enrapt, not only by words, but by that ancestral heartbeat that impels them to become part of the rhythm; part of the story, themselves.

Faces and bodies lighted by flame. Wood crackles and snaps. The smell of sweat and smoke and *tilambik* fill the air. There is laughter and voices are swollen with excitement. Then the first rap of the tambour, its goat skin still warm from the heat of the fire, brings about a moment of silence. A hand dances across its taut surface. Bodies move close, *van-vané*, the distance no more than a spider's thread. Bodies move in perfect harmony as if they share a single heartbeat. We all share that same heartbeat. Eyes lock together, black irises aflame. Man *criyay*, hands clap. And then above this movement, this joy, this celebration of life, comes that unmistakable voice; *la voix cassé*, the broken voice. It is like a growl; it is rough and yet melodic. Timeless. A voice that revives memories of a history no longer remembered, ancestors never seen and distant lands forever lost to the imagination.

The dancers are now actors, riding the rhythm of the tale, a-flight with each word as it is trusted to the wind.

The voice, the singer-storyteller, is as entranced as all the dancers and hand-clappers. In the clutches of a spell cast by his own lips, hypnotised by the beauty of movement that passes before him. It is no longer just story, but a living memory.

I was as bewitched by this spirit of imagination as much as by the yearning for adventure; and I was determined to follow them both to see where they might lead me.

As I wove along that coastal road, my canine companion in tow, I wondered what papi would make of the world around me. Would he first despair at a son who headed towards the bonds, that as a maroon, he spent his lifetime evading? Or would he perhaps, looking down from the mountains, be distracted by the changes he saw? Many of the trails he had taken, the forests that had given him sanctuary, lost forever. Replaced by patchworks of fields and ever growing plantations; growing like some insatiable beast of folklore, that eats first the earth, then the sky and eventually itself out of gluttony.

But even in papi's day the wildness had begun to retreat, edging closer and closer to the mountainside. Almost all the ebony gone and the rains becoming less frequent without the call of the forests.

The sound of saw and axe and groaning trees that snapped and cracked as they toppled helpless, rootless onto forest floors, becoming as common as birdsong.

There were still wild places, remote, inaccessible, ground deemed unfit for production. But in the time I talk of, the beginning of the end of my childhood, even these were being encroached upon.

It started before the British came, during the time of *les Français*. But it was the British, Ma-Jo told me, who turned our little island into a first-class factory. One thousand-thousand arpents dedicated to the production of cane.

With the end of slavery things changed. It was as if a yoke had been removed. But this time I do not mean from, us, *mo frère*: *lepep noir*, no, I mean from them: *bane blanc, la* – those white people. For them the land is something you take from, they have forgotten that you must give back, and with the arrival of the indentured, they took more and more.

To the planters these arrivals from India were only replacement parts for their stalled machine. Emptied onto the docks boatload after boatload, from misery unto misery they came. Slavery was no more, or so it was said, but as I travelled I saw fields filled with black faces doing the same work we had done; the work we had ran from as soon as we were free.

For who would eat dirt when fish is put before them.

Yet, off I had marched heading for one such juggernaut, one which had, with indifference, ground into the earth my own flesh and blood. Oh papi, I thought, to where do I go?

What would he make of the *malbars* I passed? Wretched figures dressed in the same rags that Ma-Jo described to me, the ones that we had worn; weighed down by the same burdens, their faces baring the same contortions. What was the difference, the few cents that would never rattle idly in a pocket, or find refuge in some hiding place? The journey was their choice, it's true, but sometimes the choices that confront us are little more than no choice at all. Or so experience seemed determined to teach me.

Chapter Sixteen

Balteau

What was striking about Colonel Balteau's appearance, for one who had known him in his heyday, was how completely the weight of a too good life had abandoned him. Age, it seemed had taken everything but his breath, and even that he sucked in fits and gasps.

Nevertheless, he moved with an efficiency that spoke not of a lack of vitality, but rather an effort to preserve what life he had left. As if he possessed but a designated quota that was to be mete out by the day.

His clothes were not ill-fitting but neither did they quite fit. They might have been sewn for the man he had been five pounds before. His collar was a little too loose, his waistcoat hung rather than clung and the taper of his jacket alluded to a waist no longer there.

Altogether a figure who had seen better days.

The Colonel had never been one of Mme Lousteau's favourites. Though, he had for a time been somewhat obsessed with her. One only had to glance in his direction to catch him leering. Alexandre had not been long dead and Balteau, a Captain at the time, was charged with catching her husband's killer. To his credit Balteau had carried this out admirably, not without assistance she might add, yet there lingered a suspicion that she was his prime objective. As if she would have considered such a union, even after observing the appropriate period of mourning. The situation was by no means helped by his tendency to be a little too hands-on. Balteau's tactility might have been acceptable from a beloved's hand, or even that of a close relative, but when employed by an acquaintance such as the Colonel it presumed an intimacy inappropriate to their association.

Any such delusions were soon curtailed. Words were not minced and after a short period of awkwardness things between them resumed their normal course. Normal, that was, in regards to their future relations. Little doubt was left of who would defer to whom.

However, as Balteau tottered into the room Mme Lousteau could not help but feel some fondness towards him. She stood, something she had never done in those bygone years, and had to restrain herself from embracing him. (How efficient time can be at erasing or at least diminishing the annoyances of others, those peculiarities that once proved unbearable.) And she was sure that she saw in those blue eyes a spark of the Colonel's old affection.

On sitting he waved away any attempt to take his cane, which he laid across his lap.

'Sitting is not the problem, but once seated gravity refuses to let me rise. But this old thing,' he said, tapping his cane with his index finger, 'affords me a measure of dignity.'

She wondered about his age, he must have been at least a full decade older than her. That would put him somewhere in his mid-seventies.

Mme Lousteau thought to leave an appropriate pause before her reply: one, two, three heartbeats. Moments during which the silence was not uncomfortable, but rather one the old come to appreciate: the contentment of renewing an old acquaintanceship, no matter how tenuous it had once been.

'And how are you, Madame? It seems time has visited you but fleetingly since we last made acquaintance,' Balteau said, seeming only too keen to fill the silence.

'You flatter me, Colonel. I assure you time has been no stranger to me. In fact the more the years pass the greater I feel its pull.'

'Nonsense, from what I see age has only made you more the handsome.'

Mme Lousteau smiled weakly, unsure whether to pity herself or the old man before her.

They sat at right angles to one another on pair of comfortable old *Chaise a la Reines*, the filigrees and flourishes of the chairs' woodwork dulled and chipped, their red damask cushioning worn and sunken. As if in a gesture of conciliation, she leant over and touched the old man's hand, patting it before shifting back in her seat.

'Forgive me, M. Balteau, if I appear brusque but would you mind if we proceed to the matter at hand. Things have been strained of late and my attentions spread between too many concerns. In fact, I have asked you here in the hope that your expertise might help reduce my anxieties.'

A touch of brightness entered to the old man's face.

'Madame, you can be assured I will do all in my power.' Balteau said, bowing with head and shoulders.

And the Colonel's sincerity made her involving him seem all the more foolish. What could the old geriatric be good for other than reading the newspaper and staring out of his window? Might he assist her in some advisory capacity, was that what she wanted? It was unlikely his post required he perform any formal duties, his title more a sentimental token than practical appointment.

But nonetheless he was a man of some expertise and there was a chance his involvement would prove useful. There were also those he commanded within the *détachement des noirs*, who in this situation might prove to be valuable associates. For, even if years and circumstance had separated them, there was bound to be at least one lasting bond.

Not to forget that in her hands Balteau would be quite malleable.

'I am retired now, of course' the old man added, 'but this only means I will have more time to dedicate to your matters.'

She fought back a sigh.

'Please, old friend, do not commit yourself before you have heard what it is, I ask.'

'There is no need,' he said waving this away, 'I am all but mouldering away. If the challenge doesn't it kill me it will do me good. The life of the emeriti suits me not, waiting for death or heading out to meet it, it's all very much the same to me.'

'Your boldness is commendable, M. Balteau. But you understand your death is not something I wish on my conscience. And anyway, it would do little to alleviate my current predicament.'

M. Balteau gave a short laugh, reaching out, she supposed, to give one of those squeezes of the arm he had been so fond of. Then as if remembering himself he withdrew his hand, adopting the most serious of expressions.

'Madame, do not be fooled by this old frame. I am not yet ready to give up the ghost.'

'Very well,' she said, preparing in her mind the story she had concocted, one the Colonel would find a little less fanciful than the truth, 'as we have established your willingness to help, let us proceed. M. Balteau, I not long ago received an interesting visitor, a boy who claimed to be the son of one Elise: a slave girl who assisted our former Gardener, Narram.'

'The mulâtre girl?'

'Indeed, as you say the mulâtre girl. She died almost fifteen years ago, a difficult childbirth claiming her life and that of her child – a tragedy to which I can sadly testify.

'I do not doubt the Madame's testimony.'

'Quite. So as you see, the boy's story was an obvious fiction. I had him immediately removed from the estate. To imagine that I would be taken in by such a ruse is ridiculous.' Mme Lousteau paused. 'It was only later that I began to question the boy's motives. Why make up such a story? Why make the journey to La Belle Horizon knowing he would likely be turned away?

'Maybe the boy believed otherwise or at least wasn't discouraged by the possibility of failure. He probably heard some story or other about the girl and decided to try his luck.'

'Does it not seem strange to you, though, to attempt such a charade?'

'Of course, but you wouldn't believe half the things these blacks get up to, in order to avoid a day's graft. I've retained a casual informer or two and the stories I hear never fail to surprise me.'

'I am not wholly ignorant of the ways of blacks, M. Balteau,' Mme Lousteau said, with a touch of impatience.

'My apologies, Madame, I didn't mean to suggest—'

'It is not important,' Mme Lousteau said, with a dismissive flourish of the hand, 'However, your theory is not without substance. What if the boy had an older accomplice, one who saw profit in that almost forgotten tragedy?'

'Are you suggesting blackmail, Madame? Not inconceivable, though I think it unlikely.'

'What else would you mean by *trying his luck*? Only now you expressed astonishment at these blacks' ability to surprise you. I dare say your post brought you in contact with many an inventive and unscrupulous soul.'

'You are not far from the mark, Madame and maybe my words, unintentionally, carried deeper implications. But still, what grounds would these scoundrels have for blackmail?'

Mme Lousteau stared at Balteau, looking for any trace of insincerity, on all accounts expecting him to avert his gaze. But all she saw was incomprehension. Could the man she once found so easy to wound now mask his emotions with total expertise? Or was it that age had withered his train of thought?

'You are not unaware of the rumours— about Elise?'

Colonel Balteau reddened, leading Mme Lousteau to believe the latter assumption to be true.

'But— but who would give credence to such preposterous lies?' he stuttered. 'Who would even deign to listen?'

'That is beside the point, Colonel. Is the fact that he had the confidence, the audacity to attempt such a fraud not enough?'

The Colonel peered down at his lap, rolled his cane back and forth on his thighs.

'Could there, and I ask this only for clarity's sake, could there be some truth to the boy's claim?' Balteau again faced Mme Lousteau. 'Perhaps the child was born and somehow ferried away without your knowledge, delivered to his father's people, maybe?'

The anger that welled up inside Mme Lousteau was of course irrational. For the scene being enacted was one of her own design. She wanted to instil a sense of urgency within the Colonel, to steer him towards playing his part in her plan, to convince him that his conclusions were his own. Yet Balteau's speculation had been so close to the truth that she could not help but wonder what he really knew. Had her assumptions about him been in err? Had she lost the ability to read even the simplest of men? Of course Balteau might have stumbled upon this idea in all innocence, but what was the likelihood of that? Was it in fact unlikely at all? Despite her uncertainty, it was important that she remain in control. It was not a time for self doubt, no. It was a time for conviction in one's plan; she could not allow herself to be distracted.

When she spoke her voice was cold, but her anger had subsided.

'M. Balteau, was my earlier remark not clear enough? Or was your belief in my sincerity itself insincere? It seems you are not only familiar with the stories that surrounded Elise, but you are happy to commit to them a new chapter.'

Something akin to a whine crept into old man's voice.

'Madame, please, I was not questioning your honesty. I asked only in the name of thoroughness. As for the rumours about Elise – yes, I knew of them but I never believed.'

Mme Lousteau stared intently at the Colonel, nodding to herself as if she had come to a decision.

'Can I trust in your secrecy, M. Balteau? Can I be assured that what I tell you will go no further than this room?'

'You have my word, Madame, I—'

Mme Lousteau raised her palm halting Balteau's response.

There was not an iota of happiness in her smile, or that was how she had played it, the tentative upturn of her lips describing more pain than tears ever could.

'The rumours were true,' she said after a moment, 'my husband, Alexandre, was the girl's father.'

When Mme Lousteau decided upon her story, the lure that would guarantee Balteau's cooperation, she had been unsure of what he knew of Elise. The one thing of which she could be certain, however, was that it would be hearsay: something akin to the many other stories that circulated about the indiscretions of *Grand Monsieurs*. And for a man of Balteau's creed this was as good as no story at all. What he would require was fact and investigation, testimony from a worthy source, an avowal not unlike her confession regarding Elise or her account of the boy's appearance. Or so she believed.

She was not disappointed.

There had been sincerity in his words, this she decided to be true. His disbelief in the stories not a lie but a truth of which he had convinced himself. In relieving the Colonel of his illusions Mme Lousteau exposed her own vulnerability, an offering she felt certain would secure his allegiance. For as well as inquiring Balteau was a chivalrous sort, a weakness that would leave him duty bound to protect her. Or so he would see it, she was sure. To him their discussion would no longer be a matter of business, but a request of aid from a confidant. Thereafter, she might be more exacting in her demands and the Colonel somewhat freed from the constraints of legality.

'There is one other thing,' she told Balteau, certain now she had secured his devotion, 'but a few days after the boy's visit. I was in the process of writing to Frémont & Vidal, the merchant house – a matter of urgent business. For clarifications sake I found it necessary to consult an earlier correspondence. This letter along with other such documents was kept locked in the drawer of Alexandre's old escritoire. Now, I had not entered Alexandre's study for a week or more. It was always his place and out of habit I have, over the years, used it only when essential. On entering the study I found the desk drawer had been forced, though its contents seemed undisturbed. After closer inspection, however, I found a letter to be missing, one of a most delicate nature. I need not go into specifics, only to say that the missive in question related to the matter of Elise and my husband.' She allowed a momentary pause in her delivery. 'Perhaps now you understand why I suspect the objective here to be blackmail.'

It was natural that Mme Lousteau took the Colonel's grimace to be a consequence of her account. This might well have been true, but shortly after he removed his cane from his lap, using the stick to lever himself to his feet. He did so unsteadily, his eye widening with what was no doubt unvoiced pain.

'Forgive me,' he said, his voice strained, 'I must stand. My legs have a tendency to stiffen if I sit too long. I'm afraid my body has become very particular in old age. It appears it is not only the mind that can become set in its ways.'

The old man traced a circle around the room, his step becoming less stilted as he progressed. Mme Lousteau regarded Balteau's journey. Their meeting had indeed become quite the performance.

'Madame, do you mind my pacing as I talk?' Balteau asked.

'Pray, carry on.'

'Thank you. Where were we? Ah, yes, indeed, the letter stolen from the desk drawer. I understand the reasons for your suspicions and they are not without grounds. But is it not more likely the crime was committed by a member of your own staff? By someone who— oh,' he said, stopping in his tracks 'oh, I see, I see, that does put a different complexion on things.'

He gave his cane a tap on the floor.

'M. Balteau?'

'How foolish of me and how perceptive of you. I think sometimes that age has not only caught up with me, but overtaken and left me behind. You were inferring that the boy had an accomplice within your home. This is indeed more serious. We may well have ourselves a cabal. Do you have your suspicions,' he added in a whisper, 'to who the culprit might be, I mean?'

Mme Lousteau shook her head, for a moment speechless.

Despite all her planning, she was surprised her scheme advanced so effortlessly, that each thread had not frayed but led with ease to the next. It was important that Balteau made his own connections and the story acquired substance beyond her account. A tactic not without its risks, especially since the state of Balteau's intellect had been uncertain. Yet, once the cobwebs had been dusted away and his curiosity piqued, so those old talents were revived and he was off in pursuit of a lead.

She shook her head again.

'I thought all my servants trustworthy. Though drawers are locked, doors are left open. There is not a room in the house that is inaccessible. Foolish, I know but I never dreamt of such affairs at La Belle Horizon.'

Balteau stopped his pacing, walked back over to Mme Lousteau and sat down before her.

'We must begin questioning without delay.' He said, leaning in, his voice subdued. 'Summon your man and have your domestics brought in one-by-one.'

Mme Lousteau herself leaned in, taking a firm grip on Balteau's wrist.

'But M. Balteau,' she said matching his tone, 'should we not proceed with more caution, for what reason would the offender have to confess? Let us bring the boy here. Lure him, if you will, though it might prove necessary to employ other means. Then we could both discover the boy's intentions and use his presence to expose the conspirator in our midst. Even if the boy remains tight lipped his proximity is likely to cause his accomplice to panic. And if all else fails we could bring the servants into the room with him, one by one, and study their reactions.'

The Colonel nodded, though Mme Lousteau could tell by his frown that he was yet to be convinced.

'Madame, you may be right and while I commend your inventiveness, what you describe is not a simple affair. The very fact that abduction may be necessary, for there is every chance the boy will suspect foul play, means this venture should not be rushed into.'

Mme Lousteau released her grip on his wrist and restored the distance between them.

'And what of my danger, M. Balteau, is it to be outweighed by your misgivings?'

Mme Lousteau's voice rose as she spoke, its quiver conveying a sense of urgency.

'Come, come. Madame must realise that I take this matter seriously and will do whatever is necessary to resolve it. But there is much investigating to do, at this point both the boy's identity and whereabouts are a mystery. Also, whether we care to acknowledge it or not, there is a chance the rascal may never be found.'

Mme Lousteau was unable to hide her smile. It escaped before she had time to prevent it. She made it part of her performance, once more inclining towards the Colonel, this time taking his hand in hers. She peered over his shoulder as if looking towards the door.

'On this I may be able to shed some light,' she murmured, 'I have not simply been sitting and waiting for your arrival. I have found someone who claims to have recognised the boy: one of the hands, a woman who is trusted to run errands beyond the estate. There have been occasions when, on market days, she has ventured as far as Mahébourg – she has developed quite the talent for bartering. It was during one such outing that she saw the boy, working for a woman with a stall at the market's entrance – our co-conspirator perhaps. A tender thread, I know, but I believe her. She is adamant and swears to have seen both boy and woman there on several of her visits.'

Again the Colonel nodded.

'It is a good lead, I admit, but as you say her account is tenuous and we should choose our steps cautiously.'

'Do this for me, M. Balteau, Gerard, please?' Mme Lousteau asked, placing her other hand atop his, 'I understand your uncertainty, I do, but there is more to this. I have no doubt. You came to my assistance once before, you did not hesitate, and who is to say this too is not a matter of life or death? Please, find the boy and bring him to me. Afterwards, when he is in our custody, I will follow whatever protocol you deem appropriate.'

Chapter Seventeen

Vier Bolom

I had travelled less than a day when I came upon the old man.

The sun was not yet at its summit and I beheld the world through half screwed eyes. I fanned myself with my hat and on replacing it the bright detail of the countryside appeared before me. The road skirted the side of a mountain. Here and there clots of stone and red earth had crumbled onto the causeway, tree roots pushed through the sheared mountainside.

I left behind the houses of Ville Noir, the avenues of trees planted to shade our old masters on likewise days. I passed fisherman's huts that looked out upon the sea, whose anchored boats rocked with the gentle roll of the tide, but even these dwellings petered out when the headland became steeper.

The old dog no longer scarpered ahead, but ambled by my side in close companionship with my shadow. His tongue lolled, his breath drawing in quick shallow pants.

I stopped and poured a draught of water into the lid of my *calebasse*. Pirat danced as I placed it on the floor in front of him.

Despite the sadness of what I had left behind, I felt happy.

The openness of the world around me pulled me in, towards something new.

It was a strange guilty feeling.

Of course, I missed Ma-Jo. I missed her smell, the shuffle of her footsteps, the look that went deeper than eyes are supposed to see; not to forget her stories. A voice that told as much as any tale.

There was more of her in me than there was of mama and papi.

But a gentle distance grew between us, despite the awe her stories awoke within me; because of it, maybe. As I got bigger so did the world, as did the yearning to see beyond our plot, our town, the mountains. With the call of manhood I still loved her.

My love for her not less, but different.

To my right the earth sloped down to the sea, blue and scintillating; a doorway too vast for my imagination. To my left the mountains. And all about the patchwork of cane fields restlessly creeping into the domain of the trees.

Only the mountains will be spared, she told me.

The air bore the freshness of the sea and the fertile musk of the mountain forest.

There had been none of this joy within me the evening before. The first night of camp brought her ghost gliding about my mind and filling my eyes with tears. All of the day's earlier purpose deserting me; the *tilambik* I swigged dragging me deeper into the gully rather than lightening my heart.

Pirat huddled up and pressed his nose into my belly as I cried.

I told tales to the night air, her tales, in the hope my words might conjure her form from the campfire or the strange dancing shadows shaped by the flames. My voice became louder and louder, but failed to call the dead from their sleep. My throat roughened so I wet it with more drink.

When I sang the sound that emerged was enough to make the dog's jaw drop.

I was a young man, no more than a boy, but the moan I uttered was something much older. A great-grandfather voice. It was like the grinding of two hard edges; of rock against rock, the slow shifting rumble when a mountain talks.

But it was not without its melody.

And as I rapped my tambour I felt the eyes of the night upon me. I heard a zako clap his hands, the rustle of a tang, the cricket's call fall into harmony. They all knew the strange new voice that came from inside.

It was a voice for singing stories. And stories I sang. Stories the tang, the zako and cricket had seen; as if their thoughts had somehow snagged upon my rasping chords.

When I finished the moon was high above. The only sound the gnawing embers of the campfire. There was a peculiar silence to the night as if all the night dwellers sat mute with astonishment.

Then one by one the creatures of the dark resumed their affairs and everything was as it should be.

I collapsed onto my blanket.

In my dreams I talked to Pirat of all we would do now we had left home. He told me these were splendid dreams; indeed they were adventures worthy of a dog. I laughed at this. And he nodded and smiled a sad man's smile.

My voice was my own and his was the rough voice with which I'd been singing.

'So it's your voice,' I said but he only shook his head and said no dog has the voice of a man. This one had been lent to him so that we could talk together. He could not tell me from whom the voice came.

On rousing, the next morning, I thought I'd awoken as a child.

I felt so light. My sadness had been left by the firelight. In my head were none of the yesterday's fears. I had not forgotten them, but I felt as if I had just stepped from an embrace and been told not to worry about a thing. I did not know if it was the sleep that refreshed me or if some other force was at work.

Was it her, maybe?

Despite this feeling I dared not speak or sing for fear of what I might hear. Although, I was not sure I trusted my memory.

Was it all a drunken reverie?

Yes, I had liked the old voice and its magical ways but it seemed a curse to be laden with the croak of an old man. Could I live with such an aged voice? How long before my words became no words at all? What powers would I be left with when I was speechless?

I cleared my throat, listened for that ancient gruffness, feeling for the scratching of my gauze. It was not there. I whistled away a few moments before starting to hum; this sounded a little rougher. So I decided to wait before making another sound.

The road widened, the mountain slope glided away, making room upon the flat for a border of trees and bush. Their shade tempting me toward the side of the road.

My first thought was that I saw a root or a fallen branch. The thing protruded out into the roadway, coloured the same dusty yellow, and looked as if it had long been part of the scenery. Bent and crooked with its end splayed out like a foot.

It was as if the sun pressed upon my shoulders with all its might, my legs carried double that of before. My feet did little more than scuff the ground. I halted. The dog barked as we both stared at the space where the leg emerged from the trees. I saw nothing of a body, only bushes. The foot was turned to one side, little toe almost touching the floor. Its owner, I thought, far from living.

There'd been too few days since my last vision of death and I wanted none of this unhappy omen.

A light wind blew from the sea bringing with it the salubrious balm of the ocean. I stood no less than twenty feet from the object, wondering if the scent of the dead was strong enough to drift against the breeze. I shifted to the leeward side of the road.

'Ene dimoun mort,' *a dead body*, I said in a whisper; spying the frayed britches, an elbow, then a shoulder, all coloured the same hue as the road.

I no longer listened for the croak in my voice.

But what if he is not dead? The question came from nowhere, from somewhere inside. Then there is no reason to disturb him, was the reply. But this did not satisfy the questioner. Would she leave one in distress? The voice asked. Maybe he is only sleeping, came the answer.

I scuttled further along the roadside craning my neck, in order to get a better view.

The rest of the body was in among the trees and nothing more could be seen without moving closer. I shook my head. But my legs had already begun to take me across the road. With slow-footed steps I walked. Nostrils flared, searching out any uncommon odour.

There was indeed something unsavoury upon the air, a body unwashed for many days, the stink of a latrine. But as much as I wanted to plug my nose right up to the eyeballs, I did not know if it was the smell of the living or the dead.

What I found upon reaching the tree line was an old man. His chest bare, his head between the roots of a tree. With all the dust that covered him, the splayed legs, the one arm across his body and the other dug into pile of leaves, he looked like some grotesque fruit long fallen from its branch.

After taking pains to stay away from the body I suddenly found I could not tear my eyes from it. The folds of skin encrusted with dirt, the matted hair crowned with earth and leaves. Even the stink had become part of the strange attraction.

I held my breath and knelt down beside him. There was no movement, no rise and fall of his chest. Certain that all life had left him I touched his arm. It was warm. Would a dead man heat up in the sun? Maybe, I did not know. Where my fingers brushed its surface yellow dust came away to reveal a shade as blue-black as the night sky. Against it the reddish-brown of my own hand was but a blemish in the heartwood of ebony.

His body shuddered and I fell back onto my behind. I scrambled into the road, kicking and grasping at the dirt.

Once on my feet, standing three-four-five feet way, I called out to him.

'Ey papa levé,' *ey papa wake up*. I noticed that my young voice had returned to me.

He said nothing.

From the road I picked up a small stone and tossed it towards the old man. When it struck his belly he let out a groan, though I saw no movement of his lips.

Again I edged forward. When before him, I bent over, hands resting upon my knees.

'Ey pa to soif? Mo ene delo,' *ey papa you thirsty? I have water.*

This time his mouth opened exposing yellow teeth, and breath sour enough to call up my eyewater.

He was trying to speak.

I got closer, crouching, my ear close to his mouth.

His words were like the moaning wind through cracked clapboard.

'Mo nepli capav santer,' he said, *I can no longer sing.*

There was no reason for me to think I would sing with that old voice again. But I wondered if it was his that I had taken.

I did not want him to hear me sing.

Pirat's feet scratched the road behind me. He seemed uncertain, unwilling, to venture past my shoulder. The old man had said nothing more, but I could smell his breathing. I lowered myself down beside him, folded my legs; rested one elbow upon a knee and my chin on my palm. My fingertips drummed my cheek. I picked at the dirt beneath my big toenail; breathed through my mouth.

I looked the old man over from head to foot.

Better you'd found a dead man, said the voice inside. And after the thing the old man had said, I did not want him to wake.

Still, there I sat.

What am I supposed to do with you, *bolom*, ey, carry you on my back?

Leave him.

I reached out and took his hand. A leathern thing without callus or corn, stranger to both mattock and cane cutlass. Limp as the hand of the dead. Not all who lived through *letemps margoze*, the bitter times, had worked the fields, but what black hand was left untouched by travail?

The hand squeezed my own and again I jumped. The old man let out a moaning breath.

His eyes blinked open. With each flutter, the crust which had sealed them, crumbled away.

Their whites were as yellow as his teeth. Threads of red shot from his eye-corners and there were tiny clouds of the very same scarlet. I saw cut-outs of the sky and leaves in their round black hearts.

I gave him water. He spluttered, coughing up what looked like wet clay. After wiping his lips I tried again. He drank small sips. Water leaked from the side of his mouth and puddled on the earth.

Nothing but his eyelids moved. Their blinks slow and few. The dark centres of his eyes always still.

Was he blind?

I leant forward and pulled faces at him for as long as I could stand his breath; baring every grimace I remembered from childhood.

'What are you doing?' He asked, very clearly. Not at all in the parched scratches I'd expected.

'You can see?' I said.

'I can see the forty faces of a fool all rolled into one.'

And he gave a laugh that seemed to stop almost as suddenly as it started. A laugh that made me unsure of the smile that had crept onto my own face.

His head bowed forward as he tried to get up onto his elbows.

'Papa atane,' *papa wait*, I said, placing a hand on his shoulder. This he pushed away and grabbed at my upper arm in an attempt to pull himself up. I caught him by the elbow.

'I've lain here too long,' he said, in a desperate voice, as if late for a pressing appointment.

His grip was strong but it was my hands that did the lifting. There was little of him. Once sitting, he shuffled backwards on his behind to rest against a tree.

'How long have you been here?'

'How far back do you remember?' He replied, as he scratched his bellybutton.

'Ayoo papa,' I said under my breath, 'another one who talks in riddles.'

'It's all gone.'

'What are you talking about, papa? What's all gone?'

'Bolom,' *old man*, he said, 'that's all I remember.'

Now, I had a dog and a madman.

'What old man? You? All you remember is that you're an old man?'

'Vier Bolom,' he said, a little louder, stretching out each word as if he thought me the fool, all the time rapping the knuckles of his left hand against his chest.

'Ayoo,' I said, shaking my head.

This was indeed a madman.

'Me, Vier Bolom is my name.'

I laughed, just a splutter, I couldn't help it.

'*Vier Bolom* your name, papa,' I said, he did look as old as a skeleton coughed up by the grave, older enough to be the mountain's grandfather's grandfather, 'maybe they call you that, your people, but that's only a *nom gater*, a nickname, not a real name. Whose mama would call them old man?'

'Boy, you know nothing of names' He said, spitting the words out at me, 'I know, you hear? Wisdom is the brother of the aged,' and weak headedness its twin, the voice in my head countered, 'and you think me stupid – I know.'

I looked at the old fellow through one eye and then the other, as quick as a wink, uncertain of what sat before me. I saw the same man with each glimpse; nothing more, nothing less. Not demon or angel or some other unearthly beast. Though, I could not help thinking: was it I who found him, or he who found me?

'So you remember nothing, papa?' *and your brother wisdom has no clue,* I thought, wondering if he could indeed read minds.

'More water,' was all he said, though.

I handed him my *calebasse*. He glugged until water no longer spilled down his face, held the flask above his mouth until it surrendered its last drop. He sucked like a *moustik* drawing blood. The hand that held the *calebasse* fell to his lap. And I loosed it from between his fingers.

'Forgive me,' he said, after a pause as long as three bars of a cricket's song, 'it is the heat, the dust, this old head of mine. I'm not usually so disagreeable, I'm sure. I've been asleep so long. At my age dreams take longer to recede and I'm not so willing to leave them behind.' He chuckled. 'It's not this old thing I dream of, you know,' he said, pinching the loose skin of his arm, 'you have food?'

The smile he gave, weary and half formed, deepened the lines upon his face. In these grooves I saw the stories of smiles and frowns, things passed never to be seen again. Love and sorrow too painful to remember. Things wished out of memory but unforgotten by the flesh. More memories forgotten than things I had seen.

From my sack I took a guava, sliced it and scraped out its seeds. It squelched out juice, as the old man bit into it. The juice wove its way through his tangled beard and gathered at the end of the hair like dew. He gnawed down to the fruit's rind scraping off each and every piece of flesh; leaving the inside almost as smooth as the out. It took less than five minutes for him to devour the whole thing. No lie.

On completing his vittles he licked round his mouth with a cow-like tongue, that seemed a little too long for a man's, and smacked his lips.

'You going to cut more?' He asked, nodding at the knife.

I was squatting, elbows on knees; knife in my right hand, its tip pointed towards the old man. I wondered what I was thinking. I dropped the knife so the tip dug into the earth.

'All gone, papa,' I said, with a shrug of the shoulders and a smile, turning up empty palms.

'Where are we going?' He asked.

This made me laugh.

To escape the sun's heat I shifted further into the shadow of the trees. I sat opposite the old man and Pirat lay down beside me. The old man's skin, although much darker than the tree, seemed to blend into the bark. Then a blink would bring him back again, features appearing from the tree's grey skin. Just a trick of sun and shadow? Sun blindness brought on by delinquent rays that pierced the canopy, dazzling my eyes.

'So you don't remember where you were headed?' I said.

He doodled shapes in the earth with his fingertips, winding paths and mountains and stick-like trees. Every so often he would halt in his drawing, scratch his head, count his fingers and mutter to himself as if making some calculation. Then he messed the dirt with the wave of a hand and the map disappeared. On looking up he flashed that mischievous smile of his.

'The question, garçon, is do you? Now, help me to my feet.'

When Vier Bolom stood, his crown of dirt and leaves reached no higher than my shoulder. I was sure I saw a movement in that unruly nest – something creeping and maybe a wriggle. He shook his head, rubbed his hands back and forth through his hair revealing patches of pure white, some of grey. I stepped back, out of the storm of debris that followed. I stifled a cough, closing my eyes to the dust; turned away.

As swift as a scorpion's strike a hand caught my wrist, not only halting me but pulling me back. Like the tug of a child but with a stonemason's grip.

'Don't go yet,' the old man said, 'wait for me.'

You see, whispered the doubting voice, you should have left the old sack of bones where you found him, beneath the tree. Now you'll never be rid of him.

He is only an old man, I replied, as much to convince myself as to silence the annoying murmur.

I placed my hand atop his.

'Where can I take you, papa?'

After a squeeze and a pat of the old man's hand, his grip loosened.

Then he let go altogether. But his hand continued to hover about my wrist, as if ready to grab should I make a run for it.

He looked me over with an appraising stare. Eyes squinting – although, this might have been because of the sun – as he studied me from toe to nose-tip then back down again. While his tongue wandered over his gums, as if searching out a last morsel of guava meat.

Then he started off along the mountain road.

All this time Pirat had kept his distance from Vier Bolom. His dog nose offended, no doubt, by the old man's whiff. But now Pirat trotted off behind him, my dog's betrayal leaving me no choice but to tag along.

Well, it was not as if I was heading in the opposite direction, was it? And I had set out on the road for adventure, what kind of adventurer would I be if I baulked at the first sign of mystery? Whether I should have been taking lead from a fool, that, was another question. Good or bad there was something about this old fellow and it seemed easier just to follow.

Was it really mere happenstance that lead our paths to cross?

And how could I leave such a disorientated creature out there on the road by himself? After submitting to compassion, I couldn't very well retract the hand of friendship, no matter what the inner voice said. Who knows what might have happened to him. I knew what Ma-Jo would have done, and it wouldn't have involved leaving the old fool to fend for himself.

I sighed and pushed on, though, I couldn't help but smile, for I imagined her smiling too.

By this time Vier Bolom had built up quite a stride, this was no knock-kneed shuffle, and he was muttering to himself, again. Or so I realised once I caught up with the two old reprobates, dog and dogged old fellow perfectly in step. What he was saying I couldn't quite make out; his voice just loud enough to insinuate words, but not loud enough that I could fathom them. He nodded, too, as if confirming his own suspicions. Every once in a while tapping a finger on his lips or digging into that matted bonnet of his, as if answers were hidden within all that hair.

Occasionally, he would stop and look right, out towards the sea. Either that or he'd stare mountainward, eyeing each dark ingress that gave entry to the forest

'You like the sea, papa?' I asked, by way of conversation as he gazed out over the water. His hand held in a loose fist so he might look out through its centre. 'You see something out there?'

He turned and looked at me through his make-believe telescope, flinching as if I appeared too close.

'Looking for the other side,' he said, though there was no land, not even an island, in sight. Then he took off again, Pirat skipping along beside him.

Chapter Eighteen

The Tales of Vier Bolom

Vier Bolom's feet were as sure as deer's among rock and root and bush. Hidden things, surprises beneath leaves, cones that pricked my feet and left me hopping onto the next ankle-twister, stayed clear of him. That foundered wreck I'd discovered earlier in the day replaced by a forest sprite.

When I looked up at the sky, through breaks in the trees, I saw the blue darkening. The forest's breath, that sweet smell of green and mouldering yellow-browns, cooler than when we first broke from the road.

It had been the old man's idea to leave the track that wound the coast and gave full view of the sea. Where I could look out and see the sails of fishing boats and coasters, and further still what looked to be the edge of the world.

'Vini garçon,' he said, 'I know a place,' pointing to the trees and pulling the sleeve of my shirt with a hand I had just seen scratching, I shall not say where.

Who knows those wild places, I thought. Then remembered his crown of dirt and leaves, and a smell that belonged in the bush; that shabby figure lying by the wayside like some discarded idol of old.

'The sun is not two-thirds across the sky,' I said.

By then, however, he was already on his way to the forest, traipsing across an open field with two trees at its centre, Pirat jaunting along beside him. 'Leave him,' the inner voice said, 'you wanted rid of him,' though it lacked the force of its earlier goading.

So I followed, leaving the afternoon's heat for the shade of the woods.

We travelled up through a landscape that recalled older times, when the island belonged to wood and beast, and man was yet to be imagined. Trees huddled together like conspirators; trunks twisted to spy over shoulders, branches hushing their whispering leaves. The in-between spaces were filled with ferns and vacoa, trees shape shifted by half-light into forms of ancient mystics. Roots twisted like vines, vines plaited like braids of Malgache hair; and all about the emerald green fragments of fallen sunlight.

In the deeper shadows, behind trunk and bush, I imagined forest spirits. Iridescent eyes watching as I pushed on through this forgotten part of time. In their cubbies they lurked not sure if I was friend or foe. But one by one they materialised. Were they there or not? I can only say, it is still a mystery to me.

There was the ghost of M. Doderson that most plump and trusting of birds; fat, uncomely, with scimitar beak and wings too small to fly. I'd heard legend of this foolish fowl, meat enough to fill a squad of men, but he seemed overall an inoffensive fellow. Only he never learnt to run away from man.

The likeness of a parrot nested in the hollow of a tree. Grey feathered, hooked beaked and silent, no more solid than the wind. This bird had suffered a similar fate to old Dodo, its squawk long-forgotten, no longer calling its brothers to fill the nets of Nederlanders.

Night-birds swooped and then returned to their eternal night even though the sun had not yet set. There were crawling, flying and scuttling things – tame and welcoming as so many had been – creatures no longer seen by men though the forest still remembered. Shadows, faint in the failing light, moved in ways that made them impossible to be those of leaves. At first swaying like branches then all of sudden moving off in a way that suggested a life independent of boughs.

'E-e-ey Papa,' I said, 'w-where you taking me?'

The old man just chuckled waving an arm half real, half shadow above his head.

'Up,' was his reply.

When he disappeared before my eyes, along with Pirat – the dog had ran alongside Vier Bolom from the moment the old fellow joined us on our journey – all light appeared to abandon the forest. I found it was not only in dreams that fear steals your words and makes running an impossibility.

I tripped, scrambled up, searched out any foothold to push myself forward; grabbed onto vines that roped tree to tree, waited for something to pull me into the darkness between the trunks.

The climb was too steep for the old man, wasn't it? But I had seen him ahead of me, struggled in vain to follow his steps before the shadow swallowed him.

And then I found it – a blackness as profound as the forest's lost souls.

From somewhere beyond this emptiness came a laugh. *Le Diable* himself has tricked me, I thought, lead me to his lair and fallen into a fit over my stupidity. My body was rigid, my arms and legs as stiff as branches. What a fool, lead to his end within a day of setting out from home.

I screwed my eyes shut and readied myself, preferring the black I already knew.

Pirat's bark saved me from my imagined fate. Not a yelp of fear but a hearty hello in the tongue of dogs.

A spark, a crackle, a dance of shadows and the heart of the blackness dissolved. What emerged was the entrance to a cave, its floor at least, and at its centre the unmistakable silhouette of the old man, Vier Bolom, the beginnings of a fire before him.

'You're not funny, papa,' I said to him, my anger echoing in the cave, 'anything could have happened, leaving me out there in the dark. Not that I'm afraid of the dark, of course I'm not afraid of the dark,' I repeated, trying to sound self-assured, 'but I could have tripped and fell, walked into tree, or wandered off to who knows where. You're not funny, papa, you know that?'

The old trickster, only laughed some more; Pirat yapped, making it sound as if he was partaking in the old man's mockery.

'Enough laughter, old man, enough,' I said, my voice rising. Yet for all my bluster I could not stop my voice shaking.

But the laughter stopped, though there was no apology, and the old man began to speak.

'It was not always a cavern, this cavern,' Vier Bolom began, his words made grave and sonorous by that hollow place, 'nor did it start as a dip burrowed out by hand or rain. Neither did a crack in the earth split the mountainside, revealing a grotto within. No, it was a sheer wall, as solid and impenetrable as those either side of us,' he gestured to each wall with a nod of the head and a shifting of the eyes. 'It is said that a pair of maroons were chased through the forest and up into these mountains – in fact to this very spot. Or rather to that ledge just outside,' he added, pointing forward with a jut of his chin. 'Behind them a captain of the *maréchaussée* followed, with his detachment of men in tow. Unlike many whites this captain was undeterred by the forest, had no fear of what was rumoured to lurk beyond its dark borders. For neither landowner nor planter had sort to chop down these trees, and affected disinterest in claiming the land. And everyone knows it takes some powerful magic to keep those types at bay when there's a piastre of profit to be made.

'This fearlessness proved infectious, every man and dog that followed the captain entering the wood without hesitation. They flowed between the trees like the sea between rocks, churning the ground into mist. Such a barrage of stomping sent birds to the wing and beasts up into trees.

'Oh what a hubbub, this rumbling didn't go unnoticed by the forest. It knew the intruders to be those ebony eaters and makak choppers who had commandeered the island. And wondered, had the day finally arrived when its bark would be turned into dust,' maybe it was the light from the fire, but Vier Bolom's eyes seemed fixed on the very site, 'it also recognised the footfalls of those being pursued. Yes, they were of that disagreeable race called man, but to the old creaking forest they were no strangers. You see, these runaways were not so different from the lost creatures it remembered and in all likelihood, would share the same fate. So, it was no surprise that the forest did them this favour.'

I was captivated.

Kindling cracked as young flames caught and wove between the sticks above. Hands and arms and chest were lighted and finally the old man's face. Vier Bolom's words seemed to come not from his throat but from all around us, as if the cave itself were recounting the tale. I found my hand at my throat as if searching for the vibrations of speech, for I heard in the old man's tone an echo of the voice I had sang with the night before.

On the old man went.

'The crab has his hole, the bird its nest, the bat its tree and cave, but for these maroons each day brought a different hideaway. As meticulous as a maid who works in La Grande Maison, they would remove every trace of their camp before vamoosing. Not even a sniff of their cinders would linger; not even a whiff of their piss would remain. Yet they were only men and not immune to men's foolish ways. The night before these renegades ended up out there on the ledge, they raided the storehouse of a local estate. Emboldened by the ease with which they gained their plunder one maroon went off in search of something more. Ene ti koson, *a little pig*, to go with their chicken, patat and manioc. But this little pig escaped its sack before the maroons had time to flee. Why the pork-snatcher hadn't already snuffed his wriggling parcel is a mystery. It squealed out an alarm alerting the overseer – who slept with one eye open and an ear to the ground, although what his other eye missed and his other ear did not hear was usually enough to keep a crafty belly full – and in two trots of a piggy's hoof their troubles were doubled, then tripled.

'This is when the captain took chase of our two rascals. He and his detachment heard the cries of the overseer while on the search for some other foe. Of course, they headed straight for the estate, thinking the trail which had gone cold was now reheated like yesterday's rice.

'By daybreak the maroons found themselves driven up to heights from where there appeared no escape. The captain and his men spread out and flanked them, though they could not yet be seen. From every direction came the shouts of men and the snarling yelps of dogs. Such a confusion of sound meant the first attack might come from anywhere. Soon they would not be faced with rocky mountainside but a fusillade of shot.

'Their fate was sealed, it seemed.

'They stood waiting for death or capture, between a rock and a hard place indeed. Would it be a mauling, a hacking, a shot to the chest? My boy, these fellows would have taken any such end before submitting to a life chains. But as they waited on that shelf of rock for death's eye to appear, there came a shuddering, a rumbling; a cracking, a shaking and the wall behind them was no longer there. Now our two marauders had their backs against the wall and fell into a place that a breath ago had not existed. Before them the light of the forest receded, to a dot in the black of nowhere. By the time they'd come to their senses and took off towards that last glimpse of light, there was nothing there, not even a flicker, only emptiness as thick as eternal sleep. So, it appeared that instead of being gnawed by dogs they'd been swallowed whole by the mountain.

'Better the devil you know, they say, but maybe not...'

Outside our cave, the light fast fading, each trunk and leaf at first became less distinct and finally was no longer there. Only the light from our fire, which crept out beyond the cave mouth, kept this encroaching darkness at bay. It was not what dwelt outside the cave that scared me, it was where I sat that fed my fear.

'I see what you are thinking,' Vier Bolom said, and at that moment it would not have surprised me to meet him nosing about among my thoughts, 'nightfall without fire would make this a frightening place. You see the perfect explanation for this magic, there before you. For such accidents of nature are the making of stories... are they not? but remember, garçon, our tale takes place in daylight hours when all outside is clear. It was no night eyed illusion. No. And this cave is not so deep that you can get lost and not see daylight. You see? And what of their keen-eyed pursuers, would not one of them have stumbled upon this lair?

'So, just as the cave swallowed all light so too was the maroon's wakefulness taken. Down they fell into the emptiness until there was nothing left of them but their breath. Of where they went they did not remember, and we can but speculate. It might be that to save them from escalating fright they were lulled into a dreamless sleep. Or it could be, of course, that what they saw was beyond their minds' comprehension. So instead of remembering something for which there may not be words, they remembered nothing, and remained blissfully unaware. What they did recall, however, were the currents of the place, like the calm of a placid sea – always moving, swirling and finally leading them to the shore. And it was the brush of dry land against their skin that caused them to awake once more. A misty daylight filtered by the way of the trees into their retreat. The chirps of the marten and the zwazo banan beckoning them from the cave. They flinched at the sight of each other, wondered at being alive. Pinching themselves, then one another, the maroons crept to the entrance of the cave. Instead of a gunpower crack or a cutlass slash they found, just trees and more trees – the forest seeming to whisper "It is safe, my friends, have no fear you're free to make your escape."

'Outside of their rocky refuge another miracle became clear. It was not the slope they'd climbed before them, but a vista of mountains and trees. Through the mountain they must have passed and out to its other side. The way the forest presented for them perfect for escape. So, off they trotted along the mountain ridge and out into the trees, to be lost among the wilderness for blue eyes never to see.

'And of the captain his men, well, they lived to kill another day – but not these two maroons. I told you I knew a place.'

So he did.

'And what of after?' I asked, in the hope of him carrying on.

'After? Well, we sleep of course.'

I pressed him no further. He knew what I meant, but what had I expected?

There we crouched two vagrants in the palsied firelight, Vier Bolom already on his way to sleep. In our hollow there was no sound but the snap of wood under gnawing flames, and the wheeze of the old fellow as he followed his maroons into the dark. The night noises silenced as if in reverence to old man's tale. The peace that of a shrine or sacred place. The silence of a story told; words taken to heart, dismissed or forgotten. Could it have been true, that we had stumbled into the magic of the forest's forgotten past? An idea not beyond the realm of possibility. No matter. For all Vier Bolom's foibles he had gifted me a story. A tale to add to my fledgling collection. So, maybe wandering off into the unknown with a madman hadn't been such a mistake. It was a thought that earlier would have coaxed out that other inner voice, so disdainful of old Vier Bolom. But it too failed to appear, silenced perhaps by the old man's yarn.

I had never seen a man fall asleep on his haunches, it seemed a posture impossible to maintain overnight. So, I lay him down and placed my blanket beneath his head. He did not stir nor skip a breath, only pressed his face deeper into the pillow. I could well imagine he belonged to that other place, and was left by the roadside for me to find.

But if so, to what end?

Pirat wandered over and curled against the old man's back, Vier Bolom himself now sleeping with his knees tucked into his chest, like a frightened child or a tang balled up at the scent a foe. On his face, though, sat a smile that belayed any fear. What a strange creature, mad man and teller of tales. Two selves as distinct as earth and water. But no, that was not true. For what is more familiar than the loon whose rambling contains moments of perfect lucidity? Wisdoms that lay forgotten when he reverts to his common tongue.

Cock-a-doodle-do.

The morning broke, the sun escaped the night's dusky clutches. Orange embers glowed in the remnants of the fire, its heat disguised by ashes. With eyes on Vier Bolom I sought the letter I'd folded until it could fold no more, hidden in a hideaway pocket. As the old man was still sleeping I chanced a look at the pages, barely visible in the cave's morning gloom. Their words not unlike the catechisms taught to us at the mission school and in language, and at times, just as baffling. An appeal for clemency. A soul unclean seeking atonement. So many words to say I'm sorry, please forgive me. Mama's papers, describing a legacy that would never be; La Belle Horizon.

So yes, you might say, just like the instructions from which the missionaries who had taught us to read.

And it was a magical sight that greeted me, when I took those papers to read up above the cave's mouth; the morning mist rising like the exhalation of the trees; the sun's creep across the waters, its surface a mirror of silver and gold and blue.

'Elise, my daughter, I pledge to you...' and 'Also I grant you your freedom...' These were phrases I could comprehend, their meaning not open to interpretation. In them first the confirmation of an identity that had been alluded to only in tales. My *grand-père* the master of La Belle Horizon and not the overseer, on whom there had only ever been a passing suspicion. This was no reflection on the overseer's good character, mind you, for few would have offered a hand if he were drowning. Rather, no one had ever doubted it was the master who had brutalised then failed to exit before letting off his shot. An admission of guilt never to be expected.

And that second thing, her freedom, this was something granted to mama only by death.

To my eyes and heart mysteries were solved and more questions emerged, upon reading that epistle. 'My daughter...', 'freedom...' then death. '...half of the great estate of La Belle Horizon.' Questions that would not allow me to sit still, that forced me into an indigent life; fleeing a world I felt had abandoned me. Oh Ma-Jo, your death and then this. Why keep the letter in the pocket of your piny, why not burn it? Did you know what it held? If so who read you its words? Did you keep it there all those years for me or was it only on feeling the cloak of death that you kept it near? What was I to do but leave? A man-child searching, for what he did not know? Answers, but answers to what? A story I thought had finished when the last word was told.

What was I to do?

I had felt drawn away, tugged from my bed, our garden, our home. A place empty without a voice, a foot-creak, a fart, or a laugh from you, Ma-Jo. From a world of certainty, where all things were known and our habits established as if by decree. A sleepy existence, maybe, but not idle or devoid of its own little dramas. Our hands dirty and calloused and strong from working our cropland. While with Old Pierre my muscles were shaped by hammer and adze and saw. Without you I was shaken awake by the world and by the letter pushed out of the door.

So out I went.

Birds scattered from the treetops then flocked together, weaving messages upon the sky that I could not understand. The early morning heat trailed the rising sun.

And Elise, mama, it was heartbreak that made you follow papi to the grave, that was what the story told. With the child you bore sealing your fate – a life for a life. But there in my hands was some other yarn. Not always understandable, but with a meaning, make no mistake. And upon its conclusion I always heard the words, *I see, I see*, repeating in my head. An inkling of a suspicion of something wrong – something not quite right. That your ending marked not the end but the beginning of another question. Why did you really die, mama?

All these things overwhelmed me.

A light wind, almost unnoticeable upon the skin, ruffled the paper and I wondered if I let go would the breeze be enough to carry the pages away. Over the trees to some other forgotten place where they would light and moulder among the fallen leaves. Would I then be rid of those harrying thoughts? But my fingers held their grip.

Up high, a *manze-poule* hovered as if resting on the winds, looking down on me like prey. To my wave it gave out its falcon screech.

What of the old man, Vier Bolom? What was his place in my misbegotten tale? Trickster, madman and storyteller all, who I'd found fallen from the sky. Was there any harm in him? Maybe not, maybe not. He had been a distraction, a different conundrum, as unreadable as a word I did not understand; a diversion from my misery. For it was only that morning, after rereading the letter, that I again, felt the sorrow of loss. Wondered what was I doing on the road. Not even a road.

Was he only there to alleviate my pain?

Story upon story was layering and from them I could make nothing new – I could make nothing at all. Was this right or was it only that I didn't know what to do with all the pieces? For all my moves forward was I only moving not to stay still, fearing that when I stopped I would be lost?

The tap of stone upon a metal cup drew me from my thoughts and pulled me back down into the cave.

'Tea,' the old man said, my pot blackening among reignited ashes. Some old herby brew, I guessed. The kind of bitter concoction that would cure any ailment but be unbearable after only one sip. My stomach churned and felt hollow. To my surprise, though, it was Indian tea; brown and sweet with an after-draw of leaves from which an old woman might tell us our futures. There had been none in my pack and he had carried little more than his old bones and the dirt upon them. Already, so early in our time together, there seemed nothing unusual about this.

Upon leaving Vier Bolom removed any trace of our camp, like a maroon from his story might have. The fire buried and ground swept with a frond of vacoa, swooshing the ground as we backed out of the cave.

'We must leave it how we found it, that is part of its magic.' I nodded. 'Now, it's time we were gone,' he said, and we stepped out, just as the old man's maroons, onto the other side of the mountain; to a view of forests, ravines and more mountains. It was my turn to pinch myself. I blinked and stuttered out a handful of words that came to nothing. Waited for my voice to return. I don't know why I was surprised.

'We're—,' was all I managed, the crest behind me; the sea further beyond that.

I was afraid.

The ocean was still there, though, I could hear its familiar shush, only it seemed to have moved while my back was turned. We climbed a path that took us up further still to where the mountaintop was covered with trees. If I looked straight ahead or either side I could image us the only three travellers on the isle. Survivors of some schooner taken by the reef.

And excited.

Over my right shoulder was the view I'd looked upon just that morning; the sea, the trees and fields carved into shapes like the patches on old clothes. Expanses whose size could be judged only by the white pebbles that were houses and the black motes of mill chimneys.

'Where—' I began to ask, before losing the will to speak.

The old man shrugged.

'This is your story not mine,' he said.

'Huh,' I replied.

Pirat ran off into the trees with Vier Bolom following at almost a skip.

Maybe it was my story. But just like my old dog, Pirat, I had long since lost control of it and it scrambled off on at a similar speed. Only now is the story mine for the telling.

'Look,' I said doing my best to catch up, 'I was going somewhere.'

'Even the lost and the dead are going somewhere,' he replied.

I shook my head.

'This isn't the way I was heading.'

Then he was away into the woods, as well. Again, I straggled along behind them.

Pirat and Vier Bolom, two creatures who looked as likely to chase their own tails as trek through nowhere towards I know not where. Unlikely adventurers, both, but how very much of the time. A time when the novelty of freedom had not lost its shine and many were happy to live by their wits; relieved to shrug off bonds that tied them to one place or another. This same beautiful freedom allowed me to walk away from my town and not look back, taking not even peak; allowed old dog and old man to move effortlessly with life's ebb and flow. Without a care for where they were going, happy to be moving at all.

How far had I travelled since slamming shut the gate to our yard and sauntering away? Not much further than just up the road, it seemed. And as unwelcome as I convinced myself Vier Bolom's appearance had been, I was happy for the distraction from my troubles. Why ever else would I allow myself to be towed along like a cow to market, putting up little or no resistance to being led to an uncertain fate. Not that fate is a thing that is ever certain, except maybe when glanced by a sibyl's eyes.

From the moment I found my beloved Ma-Jo dead in our garden, everything became unfamiliar. Set adrift in the world with no rudder to steer, it was to providence I turned to fill my sails and off I was taken, trusting uncharted currents. We have some sense of direction when we leave the shore and safe harbour might still be seen. But when we have journeyed out further and there are no landmarks to follow, the heart can become unsettled. Without the lights of your shore, Ma-Jo, every way appeared the same direction; every step one into the unknown.

It is not always the path most walked that leads you to what you seek, or what you do not know you seek, often a stumble or push do just as good. To fall onto the path of some hidden trail, or even the rhythms of a story whose unsought memory takes you from one place to another you never dreamed existed.

I looked out towards a range of mountains, all as green as the island's heart, wondering if I would see anything but trees ever again and why if I was thinking such a thing would I be going that way at all. But I knew, must have known, somewhere inside, that my destiny lay not along the coastal roads. Precipitous paths and hidden footways would mark my route.

'What do you see,' Vier Bolom shouted from beyond the treeline, Pirat barked as if waiting to hear my response.

'Trees,' I said, 'lots of trees.'

Chapter Nineteen

Again the Hunt

Mme Lousteau was surprised by Colonel Balteau's arrival. It was mere days since their first meeting and she had reckoned upon a week or more passing before his return.

Could he really have apprehended the boy, so quickly?

When Balteau entered the room Mme Lousteau hurried to meet him. He fumbled with her hand but she did not allow him to kiss it. Instead she held it fast, shaking it firmly before ushering him to a chair by the window.

'What news?' Mme Lousteau asked.

'Well, Madame—'

'Have you found him?'

'Yes, but—'

'Is he here?'

'Please, Madame—'

'Stop floundering man, out with it!'

The thump of the Colonel's cane echoed around the room, its suddenness causing Mme Lousteau to jump. For a moment she only stared at him, her mouth agape, as her visitor continued to press down on his cane as if attempting to pierce the floor. It was Balteau's fit of temper that roused her, helped her to curb her excitement. She leaned back in her chair, turned her head to the side and gave a flourish of her right hand, deciding to forgive the Colonel his outburst.

'Carry on,' Mme Lousteau said.

Balteau nodded, his face glowing with the remnant of his frustration.

'Thank you, Madame, I apologise for my intrusion and please forgive my lack of preamble. I will be candid. I had some misgivings regarding your plan to apprehend the boy, or rather the haste with which you sought to accomplish it. However, it appears that your vigilance might well have been justified, for he has left Mahébourg and makes his way in the direction of La Belle Horizon. There could, of course, be a dozen or more reasons for his departure, but for safety's sake I think it best to intercept him. Please do not fret, Madame, there is no cause for alarm. I have stationed a man on the road and will leave my best agent here to guard you. I, myself, plan to travel back along the coast road.'

'Would it not be better to send your man to intervene and remain here yourself as my guard? The boy is a spritely thing and you, my dear Colonel, are far from it. Candidly speaking, of course,' she said finding the snipe impossible to resist.

Balteau harrumphed and spluttered out a few incomprehensible words, though he carried on his exposition regardless.

On first hearing the news she had been vexed. For, what could have alerted the boy but Balteau's careless snooping? The man had clearly lost his knack; either that or his men had been indiscreet. But what was to be expected when one employed old men to play the games of their youth?

Nonetheless, it took Mme Lousteau but a few moments to

overcome her annoyance. The boy's flight vindicated her operation, which in turn had put an end to Balteau's constant wavering. Could she have wished for a more auspicious set of circumstances? With a carriage at their disposal it would be easy to accost the boy. Although, according to the Colonel's report it seemed the boy was not such a boy, but a youth on the cusp of manhood. This she found hard to believe, being at odds as it was, with her own recollection. Yet, she could not but think that a young man would make for better sport.

What also came to light was the original purpose of Balteau's visit. He had been on his way to inform Mme Lousteau of the initial findings of his investigation. The Colonel's men had had little difficulty locating the boy, Mahébourg being a small town, with many a tongue prone to wagging. Yet, Balteau's sources were unable to confirm the youth's provenance, though word surfaced that the boy's guardian had hailed from the vicinity of La Belle Horizon. The woman had not long passed away, a situation that made the boy's leaving all the more curious. For, he had inherited a house and small piece of land, and abandoned both to undertake his trek.

By the by, it was while journeying from Grand Port to La Belle Horizon that word of the boy's departure reached Colonel Balteau. As Mme Lousteau understood it, the barer of this report had been the very agent the Colonel wished to station outside her door: the captain of the old man's network and a veteran of the *détachement des noirs*. 'A man with whom I have been through many a scrape,' Balteau had said, 'and to whom I owe my life twice over.' This aide had been readying to leave for La Belle Horizon when he received notice from Mahébourg, causing him to charge off in pursuit of Colonel's transport.

Yet Mme Lousteau would not be dictated to, whether Balteau

felt these latest developments serious or not. The suggestion that she remain behind was preposterous. She refused to stay shuttered in her home like some old maid, under the watchful eye of Balteau's brute. She wanted to be present when they confronted the boy, or maybe she hoped he would try to run. For something in her was awoken. The possibility of such a chase brought with it a kind of freedom; the affirmation that life was not a thing designated to the past, a past which of late had all but overwhelmed her. It was as if in the house at La Belle Horizon, as grand as it might have been, she was suffocated by the fumes of earlier misjudgements. Fresh air and adventure being the much needed panacea.

It came as no surprise that Colonel Balteau was of a different opinion – that her presence on the trip was unnecessary, that she would only endanger herself. She did not doubt Balteau's solicitude, but she had to question whether his judgement had been impaired. He seemed determined to lead the expedition, prompted she suspected, by the need to prove his own virility. Yet, he did not press the matter, made cautious, maybe, by the memory of that earlier stinging cheek. This digression proved to be but a minor one, with any and all debate being halted by Mme Lousteau's utterance of the word *no*.

In fact, as in those latter days, it was Mme Lousteau who led their party along the coast road, followed by the carriage and then Balteau's man. This veteran of the *détachement des noirs*, Celestine, had by Balteau's account been present during the hunt for her maroon and it was alleged, responsible for the kill. Her own part in the matter being conveniently omitted. She could not remember him, however, and why should she have, for he had been but a black among other blacks. She thought his bearing a little too haughty for one of his kind and that upon his mount he looked as incongruous as dog upon a roost. Though, Mme Lousteau could not deny his skill as a horseman. Between horse and rider their existed an obvious bond, the kind which arises only after long acquaintance. This observation put foul Balteau's claim: that the horse was his own and this Celestine only conducted the beast in the event his master should need it. A laughable notion indeed for there seemed little chance of the old man riding in his condition. How the Colonel proposed to mount the horse was a mystery, it being about sixteen hands, as boarding the carriage had been trouble enough for him. Perhaps Balteau imagined being hoisted upon Celestine's shoulders and then transferred to the saddle. Who knows, maybe this unceremonious operation had been performed before?

They travelled less than three miles along the coast road before a waving figure bade them stop.

For the most part the road had been macadamed, but the arteries which lead to this highway were often no more than cart tracks. Despite the Colonel's carriage being of sprung and sturdy construction, one that barely left him in his seat for jouncing, it developed a problem with the rear axle. The driver maintained the fault was not critical, but as a precaution he proceeded at a trot for a mile or two. If it were not for this ambling pace Mme Lousteau would likely have run over the brigand in the road, or at least sped past him. For if there was something civilised about Celestine, the black who flagged them down was his opposite. So much so that running him over would likely have been an act of charity. He was altogether too wretched to be a road agent: short and rather skinny, his shirt undone exposing a sunken chest and pot belly. He was barefoot; the cuffs of his trousers were frayed and looked to be made for a child. They were too short, too tight and would not fasten at the waist. It was but a few buttons that saved his dignity, if he possessed such a thing. Mme Lousteau doubted the oaf did more with his life than daydream and watch the world pass him by. How many lashes, she wondered, would it have taken to get such an imbecile to break a sweat?

Celestine, however, pulled up beside the man, fairly springing down from his horse. Their greeting was enthusiastic, all smiles and shoulder clapping, words gushing from the short one's mouth like water from a sluice. He pointed away from the road out into the trees. Celestine nodded, his every question answered with yet another story.

'What is all this?' She asked Balteau, whose head poked out from the carriage window.

'Nearly eight miles on, Madame' Celestine said, 'they left the road and made off into the trees.'

'They?'

'The boy is apparently in the company of an old man and a dog.'

At this Mme Lousteau could not help but laugh, for was she not accompanied by two erstwhile companions?

'This other fellow,' Colonel Balteau asked, 'do we know who he was?'

'Did your boy, here, not pass them on the way to La Belle Horizon?' Mme Lousteau interrupted, with a nod towards Celestine, 'I thought your intelligence more reliable, Colonel.'

'Madame, I travelled from—' Celestine began.

'Hold your tongue. You will speak only when addressed,' Mme Lousteau snapped.

'M. Balteau,' Celestine said, turning towards his employer, 'if we make haste we might—'

With a movement surprisingly quick for one her age, Mme Lousteau lashed out with her riding crop. It was only Celestine's own swift reflexes that saved him from being struck across the face, the blow instead landing upon his shoulder.

Whatever reaction Mme Lousteau expected, it was not the one that followed. For Celestine did not cower. Mme Lousteau had barely time to withdraw the crop before he snatched it from her hands. When he raised the crop against her, she almost toppled from her horse. It was only grabbing for the reins that saved her, the tug on the horse's bit causing the roan to pull back and right Mme Lousteau in her saddle. For the first time in years she feared for her life. What she saw in those black eyes was the promise of death's agent, his scythe poised and ready to reap.

'Celestine, stop!' Balteau cried, the sound of the Colonel's voice halting the crop in its backward arc.

Mme Lousteau backed her horse, the unnatural movement feeling all too slow. But with distance came composure and the look of fear she suspected her face had betrayed, was replaced by the cold stare of authority.

'Shoot him,' Mme Lousteau said, 'Colonel Balteau, I order you to shoot him. Shoot him, I say!'

But Balteau only shook his head. She was surprised at his defiance, the old man displaying none of his usual acquiescence. If not for the circumstances she might have found it admirable. He stared at her unblinking, as if with the slightest movement his courage would fail.

Dissension is a contagious thing, she thought, and if not arrested spells nothing but catastrophe.

'Pass me your weapon, if you are too spineless to act,' Mme Lousteau said, her horse stepping towards the carriage, 'surrender it or I head off after the boy by myself.'

'There— there is no better tracker than Celestine, Madame,' Balteau blurted out, 'If you wish to catch the boy, discover his intentions, you will need Celestine.'

'I did not ask for a report of his capabilities, M. Balteau, I asked for your gun.'

At that moment Mme Lousteau could not say what she was thinking. She had not lost control, no, there was nothing of the madwoman about her. She was overcome by a single mindedness that refused to allow her to relent. Somewhere within her the seed of bloodlust had again sprouted, its tendrils burrowing through bone and sinew. She was the one who must take lead. She was the only one who could halt the menace that threatened to encroach upon her life. It was she who needed to instil discipline among her retinue. This was what the binding threads told her.

'Madame, please be reasonable. It was a misunderstanding. An overreaction brought on by the suddenness of your out— of your chastisement. Celestine will apologise.'

'Give me the gun!'

To her surprise it was Celestine who carried out the command.

Without a word he circled the carriage, opening the door opposite to the Colonel. Mme Lousteau manoeuvred her roan to follow Celestine's course and watched open mouthed as he removed the gun from its mounting at the rear of the box. The swiftness of these events left the Colonel unable to react, though there was little chance of him overpowering his subordinate. As Celestine alighted Mme Lousteau was quelled of all anger, thinking of nothing but flight. Yet she could not move, her blood running as cold as mercury.

Celestine offered Mme Lousteau the weapon, silent, holding her gaze. The gun was cocked and ready for firing.

The question of whether the rifle was loaded never occurred to her; she checked for no percussion cap, only turned the gun on Celestine and pulled the trigger. Then cocked and pulled again, then again.

There was no report, the whole world silent but for the snap of the hammer.

Mme Lousteau regarded the gun with incomprehension and then the man who stood unharmed before her. When Celestine extended a hand she freely surrendered the weapon, a fact she later found difficult to fathom. He in turn returned the gun to its place – the whole scene taking place in the space of minutes.

The crop he never returned.

The wretch who had flagged them down stared on in amazement. Balteau himself, watched slack jawed. Before mounting his horse Celestine clapped his itinerant companion on the shoulder, and then was off again in the direction of Grand Port; the carriage driver shucking the reigns and following close behind.

As the carriage departed – Balteau still regarding her, his head poking through its open window – Mme Lousteau realised she was laughing, her eyes full of tears and her body shaking. For the life of her she could not decide why she was laughing – whether out of fear or relief. But then what was one to do in such situations other than laugh or cry. The impatience brought on by the journey's vapid pace and her apprehension at confronting the boy had disappeared, replaced by something altogether much colder.

So, off she took in pursuit of the carriage, their destination as likely to be imaginary as it was to be real. She wondered at her own folly, following a brute and a fogy on the word of a fool. Remembered the oath within her, that she swore to take lead and she would, yes she would.

On a stretch of road whose eastern side curved out towards the sea, they found it: a plot of uncultivated grassland with two solitary trees standing almost at its centre. Beyond these two sentries lay the forest. There seemed to be no pathway through the field. If indeed their informant was telling the truth, both the boy and his companion had crossed it without leaving a trace. Only on closer inspection did she see the line of tousled grass, a faint corridor that lead from the roadside, between the trees and up to the forest's edge.

She took a deep breath, tasted the sea upon her lips and again felt the ocean breeze that quelled the sunlight's unforgiving stare. It was as if she was savouring her last moments before stepping into the breach.

*

The voices seemed distant, muffled like sounds heard from beneath the sea. It was as if in stepping over the forest's threshold she had passed from one world into another. Not only from a world of daylight to one of gloom, but into a region whose differences were bound to something more than just the trees. Of course, Mme Lousteau was not superstitious and certainly not the type to endow such a place with mystical properties. For, if these powers did indeed exist they had proved ineffective. They had done nothing to prevent the forests being razed and creating the landscape that was her island. Nevertheless, something tugged at her, daring her to delve deeper into the woodland's interior. A force, she reasoned, that was as likely to have come from within her, as it was from without. But she resisted, waiting just within the forest's boundary for the Colonel and Celestine to appear.

Celestine took the lead, the old man at his arm. Mme Lousteau was irked by the black's initiative, yet she could not deny her own unsuitability for the task. Just as with the field that preceded it, there seemed to be no clear path through the woodland. The patches of sparse undergrowth looked to be nothing more than that and failed to consolidate into anything like a trail. She kept close watch of Celestine's twists and turns, movements that appeared to be quite random. Yet, there was a purposefulness to his decisions that convinced Mme Lousteau that they were not without motive. Only after they had penetrated deeper into the forest did she begin to see the signs, hints that alluded to human passage: a broken branch here, a parting of ferns and bushes there, a scratch upon the trunk of a tree. It was such guide marks that she stored ready for when she would again take the fore.

They had not travelled far before Colonel Balteau began to tire, each fall of foot or cane seeming more a struggle. It will not be long before he is riding upon his man's back, she thought.

'Colonel Balteau,' Mme Lousteau called out, 'would it not be wiser for you to go back to the carriage and await our return?'

Only after its utterance did she realise the consequences of her statement. For if the Colonel did indeed return she would have to continue the journey alone or in the company of Celestine. Neither of which seemed appealing at that moment.

'He will not listen, Madame,' Celestine replied.

A reply Mme Lousteau chose not to register.

'There is no need for concern,' Balteau called out between puffs, 'I shall be fine.'

She could not tell whether what she felt was disappointment or relief, though there was no doubting the old man's resilience – or foolishness, maybe.

Those first hours moved at little more than a crawl, and Mme Lousteau imagined the boy's lead to be constantly on the increase. She could only hope the *gamin* was similarly hindered by his own straggling bag of bones.

The haze at the edge of her vision had begun to spread, of late, and it was unclear whether she suffered from a loss of sight or mind. She suspected it was due to a loss of faith in her own judgement. A reasonable supposition given she was gallivanting about the forest with a geriatric and his flunky. Was there really any need for her to be out there? Would it not have been easier to let Balteau and Celestine catch the boy and deliver him to La Belle Horizon? No, that was ridiculous; she had neither the patience nor the inclination. From planter's wife to planter and guardian of her own domain, life had allowed her little respite and still she was assailed by its difficulties. It was time to re-write this refrain. With each of her recent excursions the world around her had seemed clearer. The further Mme Lousteau travelled from La Belle Horizon the more of its dust she cast off. Now she was giving chase, unwilling to concede even a fraction of what she and Alexandre had built. Whether she was pursuing a ghost, the restoration of Sandi's honour or genuine threat to her dominion, Mme Lousteau was determined to prevail by her own hand.

When night came upon them it was with a suddenness that surprised them all, the encroaching shadows seeming to snuff out the last rays of sunlight. Silhouette and gloom gave way to a darkness that made navigating the woodland a treacherous task, with Mme Lousteau reduced to clutching onto Celestine's shirttail. They arrived at a small clearing, the party almost collapsing on its discovery. A fire was lit, bread and cheese eaten, a carafe of wine produced to wash it all down. It was not long before Mme Lousteau was overcome by her own darkness, the fatigue of the day only increased by the weight of a sated stomach.

When she awoke – head upon a blanket, a cloak wrapped around her for warmth – the faint light of morning could be seen in glimpses through the forest canopy. Her body felt bound to the earth and she was visited by the aches and pains that age had made familiar. She found Celestine sitting with Colonel Balteau's head rested upon his lap. The old man's face was pale and covered in sweat, his eyes darting beneath the lids; his febrile murmurings impossible to comprehend.

'We must go back,' Celestine said, without looking up, 'the Colonel is sick. You must help me.'

Mme Lousteau said nothing. There was no question of Balteau continuing, but equally she was unwilling to turn back – she could not. She shook her head, struggling to her feet.

'We will lose the boy. He cannot be allowed to escape.'

'Madame, the Colonel is in no state to—'

'I will go on alone.'

'Madame, that is impossible, who will guide you? There are no—'

But she turned away, the rest of his words lost to her. She packed what little she had: took bread and water, the last of the wine and slung the rifle across her back.

'The ammunition,' she demanded.

'You have it. It's there in the haversack.'

She nodded.

'Which way?' Mme Lousteau asked.

Celestine indicated to his left with a tilt of his chin and Mme Lousteau made off without so much as a farewell.

Now that it was daylight, she saw that their campsite was at the bottom of an incline, likely the base of a mountain or steep hill. It took only an hour's climb for her to question Celestine's guidance. Had she not imagined he might send her to her death? If she could only get to higher ground, to a place with fewer trees, so that she might be afforded a greater view of her surroundings. But the trees thinned little as she travelled, her path seeming no more than a series of arbitrary steps. She saw none of the signs that had become apparent to her during Celestine's lead. It had not occurred to her that Celestine's own process might have been much the same; allowing the path of least resistance to dictate his route. Half way through the second hour, however, woodland gave way to scrub and scrubland gradually changed to earth and rock.

It was not long until the slope led her to one of the mountain's lower crests. Behind her she could see all the way to the coast road, which from that height seemed almost close enough to touch. While over the ridge was a wooded valley and beyond further mountain peaks. It was a moment in which hopes were both raised and dashed, like the survivor of a wreck spotting land only to be thrust upon the rocks. How likely was it that she might stumble upon the boy in such a vast intractable land? The road was not far, if she turned back she would get there before sunset. In that other direction was there anything waiting but death? Yet, this bout of melancholy was short lived. The swashbuckler within her made sure of that. Find the boy, it said, find the boy or die trying. She replied with a smile; ate some bread, took a swig of wine and was off into the valley below.

Chapter Twenty

The Fall

When Mme Lousteau fell, it seemed bravado had sealed her fate. 'Find the boy or die trying,' had been her mantra. But what use was this pursuit if her death handed him what might never have been his? Nothing would have been saved, and who, in all truth, knew the *gamin's* real intentions? Not her, nor would she ever know it seemed.

One misstep, a stumble, her footing lost in the midst of excitement, and down she went the world swirling round about her. Then there had been dark, then light, then pain.

That morning she had proceeded down into the valley, roused by the venturousness which had seemed the cure to all her anxieties. Those aches which all but debilitated her upon waking, lessened with each hour of her trek. In their wake was left an increase in strength and she no longer felt the need to take each step with such conscious consideration. Her feet found the safe spots, avoiding root and stone and lichen covered log taking her deep into the heart of the forest. If she had been the sort to believe in such things, she might have thought herself driven by some otherworldly spirit. The smell of that place, a fecund mix of life and death; the denseness of green and shadow; the filtered light; the air cooled to a temperature more conducive to walking, all played their part in this change of disposition. The task of locating the boy in the vastness of the forest was no longer so overwhelming. She just went on, the undertaking itself, enough. It was a hunt and if she remained sharp eyed and vigilant her prey would reveal itself.

What alerted her she could not say. The forest is place of rustlings and flutters, the calls of all kinds of beast of foot and wing. Shadow and light move in ways that do not always seem natural, but something that is not part of the place will always reveal itself. Her attention was drawn to a distant section of trees like a doe, by instinct, is drawn to signs of danger. At first, she saw nothing. She stood still, focused on the spaces between the trunks, which at that distance were filled with nothing more than daubs of colour. There was a movement, it was impossible to determine its nature with any certainty, but she felt sure it was the movement of a man. Then it was gone. Mme Lousteau closed her eyes, opened them, searched off into that greater distance but there was nothing. Still, her intuition sent her off in that direction.

It was maybe another half-an-hour before she spotted the movement again. This time it was closer, not by much, but enough to see it was indeed a man – or the boy she hoped. It felt as if her blood ran at a constant gush, she could feel her cheeks flushing and was overcome by the urge to run. But she resisted; moving quicker, yes, though not so much as to endanger or reveal herself. They had almost reached the valley floor by the time she caught up with him. No more than a few hundred yards separated them and the individual's identity was clear. There was no mistaking him. He looked more man than boy, though, as if the intervening months had in fact been years. In a crouch she sighted him with her rifle, this time its chamber was not empty. But before she had the chance to shoot the boy moved into the light of a clearing. The glare beyond the forest's edge leaving him as no more than dissolving silhouette. She lowered the barrel. The shot when it came should be decisive.

Dipped down, she followed with a predator's stealth, holding back in the wood a few feet from the tree line. For the first time she saw the boy's companion, a thing more wretched than the reprobate they had met by the road. His clothes were torn, there were no buttons on his shirt and his trousers were held up with rope. The hair on his head was not so much unkempt as it was a midden ready for burning – full of twigs and leaves and who knows what else. He was like something death had swallowed and coughed back up in disgust. With them was a yellow mongrel, its fur patchy and greying, a most fitting escort for the pair.

There was a stream not far from the wood's end. They bathed, the old man emerged looking less bedraggled, the water seeming to rinse some of the dust from his bones. His appearance, however, still could not be described as anything but miserable. She watched, rifle across her knees, unsure of why she resisted firing. There was a clear sightline to the boy and the pair were oblivious to any danger the world might pose. Even the dog seemed to have suspended its canine intuition to frolic in the waters of the stream. The young black was without a doubt the maroon's son, but she saw in him the mother too. Was this why she held fire, perhaps? Some mote of affection she once held for the girl; an attachment that existed only in the fiction of memory. The scene before her had become quite fascinating, though, like watching beasts perform in their natural habitat.

On the opposite side of the stream, there was an acre of grassland then forest began again. She allowed the group to reach the further tree line then left her hiding place. First taking water, splashing her face and after crossing the tract of land.

The boy seemed to be continuously playing catch up; either that or he preferred to lag behind. It was strange to see the youngster trailing those two woebegone souls. Shouldn't he have been out front struggling not to lose them? Was it really that he valued his own solitude or did he perhaps sense he was being followed? She had taken care, though; kept her distance, ensured she travelled without a sound. No, the boy seemed no less at ease than he had by the water's edge. The situation played to her advantage, having only the boy to contend with. If he maintained the same pace the others would soon be ahead by some distance. Indeed, that was how it went, with boy's companions becoming lost in the further reaches of the forest.

At this point Mme Lousteau began to move with more haste, knowing full well she might only have one shot. Who knew how long circumstances would remain so favourable? When close enough, she set herself, the boy being fully within her sights. She followed his movement, tracking his progress through an area of the forest where the trees were less dense. Her shoulders relaxed, she took a deep breath, exhaled, continued to pivot unaware of the precariousness of her position; paused to take a shot.

When she came to, but was not yet fully conscious, she thought it had all been a dream. That she still lay in her bed at La Belle Horizon, Sandi close by and the whole episode with the boy concocted by her imagination. This was more than just a momentary lapse, it seemed to linger too long to be a remnant of sleep. That it was gloom and not sunlight which greeted her upon opening her eyes, served to prolong the fiction. But pain soon cured Mme Lousteau of such illusions, as if her body had been the recipient of a thousand and one blows.

Yet, things still made no sense. She was outside, yes, she could tell by the current of the air, the smell of it: a scent that would be alien inside a house – well unless the house had fallen into ruin. The smell of green and of composting earth. It did not occur to her that what she had perceived to be a dream might indeed be true. The route to such logic being somehow blocked.

There was a presence nearby, a dark shape among other dark shapes.

'Sandi,' she said, 'Sandi, is that you?'

But her enquiry was greeted by nothing but the sound of wind in the trees, the silence of bated breath.

She was wrapped in something, a blanket. A course thing, that smelled of man and dog and made her itch. But it was warm and helped ward off the chill of the ground. It could not have been cold, because she was sweating, the coldness instead coming from inside.

'Sandi', she called out again, suddenly afraid, 'Sandi, please hold my hand.'

And a hand did indeed find hers, though not the one she expected. The palm was calloused, but also possessed the softness of youth. She squeezed the hand with all her might, as if seeking to keep a firmer grip on life.

'Where am I?' She asked. 'It is dark.'

Her trauma lingered, yet to give way to deception. Which it inevitably would.

'You fell,' a voice said, in a French course with Creole tones.

In part it returned to her: the slip, the point at which her turn left much of her right foot without support. She had relaxed into the shot, at that moment blissfully unaware. Then the world had pulled her down into a deeper place, its path steep, fraught with root and stone. Then there was nothing. But this memory was enough to jolt open further doors and the pursuit of the boy, at least, became real.

'Will you die?' The voice asked, with an innocence that bordered on imbecilic, but also held a curiosity that hinted at just the opposite.

Mme Lousteau struggled to move, to lever herself from the ground, aware she was in a position of much vulnerability. But a hand held her down, and the push though gentle was enough to foil any attempt at rising.

'Wait, you are hurt. I will make a fire.'

And she remembered Balteau and Celestine, and how she had abandoned them only to find herself as helpless as the Colonel.

'Is anything broken?' The voice she now knew to be the boy's asked. It was not like the mother's; the father's she did not know. It was deep and strong, the voice of larger man and should not have been the possession of such a child. Its calmness and sobriety scared her.

Once the fire was lighted her surroundings began to make more sense. Mme Lousteau lay at the bottom of the gully into which she had fallen. In all likelihood in the very same spot where she had come to rest. These observations were made surreptitiously, through squinting eyes when the boy was not looking. At all other times she kept her eyes closed. She said nothing. The boy fed her some gruel, cornmeal seasoned with nutmeg and cinnamon and sweetened with honey. She opened her mouth as if by reflex, doing her best not betray any sense of enjoyment. The food was warming and in her weakened state she could swear she felt its restorative powers taking effect.

To begin with she had been scared to move. Her fear not on account of the boy, or even the pain she might feel, but because she might truly have been incapacitated. It was the chance of escape that allowed Mme Lousteau to subdue those other anxieties. The boy seemed to pose no immediate threat, his behaviour making her question whether he recognised her. An uncertainty which in time would be answered. She intended to wait and make off when the boy was asleep. But this strategy depended on her being able to move.

The process of examination had begun with her hands – her fingers to be exact. With care she flexed each digit, rotated and bent her wrists, making her way up each arm and around her whole body in this same fashion. Her movements were subtle, easily disguised as the jostling of a fevered body. To her surprise, though she encountered pain, she found nothing like the all-consuming scream of a break.

It was from this methodical search that sprung the seeds of her deception. For Mme Lousteau knew she was capable of escape.

When the boy washed her face, wiping its contours with a cloth and warm water, it was with a tenderness one reserves for the dead. Not once did her lips taste silt's grimy run-off, nor did water build up in the hollows of her eyes. It was easy to imagine herself as already passed, awaiting passage to that other place and the relief such repose would bring. To allow one's troubles to drift away, or maybe just ceasing to be; to spend eternity in weightless submission. Where time or timelessness flowed over you washing your soul into the sea of some other being.

For a long time, no words were spoken and she could feel herself drifting back into sleep.

'Are you her?' Asked a voice close to her ear, in a whisper that might have belonged to an arbiter of the divine. 'You are her, aren't you?'

Mme Lousteau did her best not to stiffen, to maintain the

appearance of unconsciousness. She moaned not by way of reply, but out of the same deception she had employed since waking.

'Are you a witch? What spell did you cast to find me? Are you only silent so you can steal my soul when I sleep?'

The boy no longer whispered in her ear. Rather than questioning her he seemed to talk to himself – voicing suspicions to which he expected no answer. She chanced a look, half opened an eye and saw him staring off into the dark.

'Are you still here, or have you travelled to another place, to another body?' He asked. 'And if you are not here can you still hear me? What distance can you travel? Do you need to return to claim the body you've forsaken? In this light, I can see you were once a beauty, but evil too can have a pretty face.' He rummaged in his pocket, pulling out a small white rectangle which he unfolded to reveal three or four sheets of paper. 'What does this mean?' He asked, waving the sheets, 'and what did you do so they might disappear?'

When he turned to her she still had one eye open, though it was only for but a second there was no doubt he had seen. Through shuttered eyes she could feel him smiling.

'I know,' he said, 'I know this is something. I know you are someone, but are you real in the here and now, or should all this be left to the stories. Why are you following me and why was I heading to you, ey? You are awake or you are not, you hear me or you do not, does it matter? And anyway, would your words be sincere or lies? Would I even be able to tell? Perhaps, perhaps not.' It was the silence that followed more than his queries that seemed to beckon her to speak. When he spoke again it was with composure, in those same hushed tones of his first questions. 'Did you kill Ma-Jo? Was that your white magic, or did you employ some other agent?'

And Mme Lousteau realised that even if she had wanted to speak, she was unsure how to answer this question; could not be certain she was not somehow involved. Is this where her Sandi had been and why he had been so coy about correcting his mistake? Was there a chance he was on a path similar to her own?

'What good are you, anyway, ey?' Continued the boy, 'I gave you food and aid but still you won't talk. Maybe I should smother you with my shirt and be done with it. Save all of this hot air.'

Mme Lousteau doubted the boy's words were anything but bluster. Yet, in light of her position it seemed foolish to leave such a thing to chance.

'D-duh,' she croaked, 'do not hurt me— please.'

'Aiy, so you speak, ey.'

'Don't hurt me.'

'Me, hurt you— you had the gun. Or will you tell me it was here when you fell?'

She noticed the gun behind him. There was no chance of her reaching it before the boy.

'I am an old woman—'

'You are her, that's who you are. Old or not. What were you planning, ey, to shoot me? Kill me like you did mama and papi? You'd have my blood if I turned my back.'

'I don't understand— water, please.'

The boy poured water into the lid of his gourde, tipped this carefully into the mouth of Mme Lousteau. Despite all that had happened, this act of kindness somehow did not seem out of place.

'I'm speaking your tongue, you understand me.'

'I've killed no one, please—'

'How did you do it, ey? Poison the well water? Is that it? With some potion that works only on the old, or was I supposed to die too? Yes, that makes more sense.'

'I do not understand. What are you—'

'You understand.'

'Where am I? And who are you? You are not my Sandi.'

'Aiy, not this. I know a trickster, black or white. What you say is only monkey chatter. It means nothing, or it means just the opposite. I saw you and you were scared. Was it because of this.' again the boy waved the papers, 'you want me to read, ey, is that it?'

And by his smile Mme Lousteau guessed the boy had seen something. Some giveaway or tell that betrayed her intentions.

'You do,' he said, with a raise of his eyebrows, 'you don't know what's in it, maybe, but you want it, anyway. That's it, ey? You want me dead, as well, or is this here enough?' He said with another flourish.

But this time she remained silent, her face a mask of bewilderment.

'I'll read a piece, then. This man,' he said, brandishing the letter, 'your husband, yes? Well, he talks and talks before he says anything, uses many words to say the simplest of things. But listen, you'll like this, it'll interest you. Ahem. "Elise, my daughter," was she your daughter, too? Should I call you grand-mère, then? No, no, too much, we've only just met, "I pledge to you, to be received on my passing, half of the great estate of La Belle Horizon." Interesting, ey? As simple as I am, not even I can misinterpret that. "As a legacy for you and your children. That the hardship you have endured may not be suffered by your child." Huh, who knew all this time I'd been living like a *Grand Blanc*. But wait, listen up,' the boy said ruffling through the sheets, 'ah here, this is even better, "The relationship between the Madame, my wife, and you, my daughter must be approached with much delicacy. No doubt, if a situation were to arise at this very moment that thrust you both together the outcome would not be of the auspicious kind." Well, who wants to find out their old man had been so careless when diddling a slave, ey? "In all likelihood the Madame would pursue every available avenue to ensure your disenfranchisement.'"

He stopped, stroked his jaw in mock contemplation, still nary a hair on his chin. Mme Lousteau, meanwhile, saw her own hand raised; heard the words leave her mouth before, it seemed, the thought had entered her mind.

'Let me see?' She asked, her voice shedding its former frailty, 'Give it here.'

The boy shook his head, folded the papers and put them back in his pocket, wagged his finger.

'At mission school,' he said, 'we were taught only simple French, but our master, Père Bernard, said I was a smart boy and could learn much more. He took it upon himself to teach me outside of lessons. He made me read many things I didn't understand: passages from books and newspapers, a document or two, much of it in the jargon you whites use to hide the meaning of your words. I soon got bored, though, and anyway there was no time for it. Ma-Jo needed me and Ol' Pierre wanted me as his apprentice. It wasn't all lost on me, though, the learning. The more I pondered the line I've just read the clearer its meaning became. I didn't even have to think about it, it sort of worked itself out. Funny, ey? When I left my home, my town and started walking I didn't know why, I only knew something was wrong. That was before I realised, you see. It wasn't the thought that I could have been an heir, I was already an heir to all I wanted, Ma-Jo gave me this. I'd heard of you, witch, but you weren't real – only words, a tragic story. Then I saw you in the market and your evil eye recognised me – I saw it, saw the fear that overtook Ma-Jo; saw her withered by your poison. She died, you took the last thing from me and all I was left with was this paper. It was that last line that told me it was all true. Everything I'd heard, all I suspected. But it took me until now, to fully realise. You were hunting me long before today, weren't you, even before I was born?'

To say Mme Lousteau was unaffected by the boy's homily would have been untrue. He had about him a simple charm. She might have found him endearing if their situation had not dictated otherwise. In a way he was Mme Lousteau's only family; the last living trace of her Alexandre. Yes, there was La Belle Horizon, but it was hers now and had long ceased to harbour her husband's ghost. But just as Alexandre was the road on which their paths met, Alexandre's death was a gulf that would forever separate them. There was no way to traverse its depths and any attempt might have brought about a fall more damaging than the one she had already suffered.

She did not fear the boy physically, no. What aggression he had shown she saw as a plea, an appeal to help him make sense of the world. For though mature in physique he was still a child, yet to outgrow fairy tales and supernatural beings. But what the boy desired could never be allowed. The resolutions each of their worlds required would always be in conflict.

What the boy asked – to be told the truth concerning the fate of his mother and how it might reconcile the missive he had held in his hands – she could never reveal. How could the mind of this man-child comprehend the motives behind her actions? How could she explain the chain of events to one who had not lived her life? Would an admission not suppose regret and how could one regret securing one's very survival? Would this in turn not call into question all she had achieved in the passing years?

Even to those closest to her, she had spoken only in the vaguest terms about the events surrounding Alexandre's death; everything had been cloaked in hint and suggestion. The explicit was never uttered, all was inference; there was nothing to be confirmed or denied.

No, all that was left was to decide how she would escape and in what way her performance needed adapting. It made no sense to deviate from the role she was playing, even if the boy had become suspicious. How were the concussed supposed to act if not with inconsistency? A bump on the brain could lead to the most curious of doings. It would, however, be necessary to feed the boy some morsels of information. The garbled ramblings of a confused old woman, maybe, but with just the right balance of sense and nonsense to leave him a wondering.

She had an idea.

'Help me to sit,' she said, smiling what she hoped was a pitying smile. And as the boy helped rest her back against the foot of tree, she added a wince that was not altogether for effect.

Mme Lousteau touched the boy's cheek, a stroke with the knuckles of her fingers, before he had a chance to withdraw. The skin so soft and smooth that it was a pleasure. The boy flinched, pulled away. She allowed her hand to hang for a moment as if to caress the memory of his face. Then let it drop to her thigh. To her side he knelt, hands upon his own knees, as if in waiting.

'Do you have a drink, boy? Something that might help revive my senses?'

Without standing he moved over to his bindle, which seemed no more than an old flour sack. After a rummage he pulled out small demijohn and crawled back over to where she sat. He tipped a draught into the lid of his water gourde, passing it to her with a roughness at odds with the care he had showed in its pouring.

Her hands shook with the palsy that sometimes affects the old and the newly awakened. She sipped, coughed, swallowed.

'Be careful with that, witch,' the boy said, 'you won't be getting any more.'

The liquor burnt her throat and its heat spread through her body like a warming of the blood. With the first sip she felt revived, with the second her confidence returned. She offered the cup to the boy.

'Share with me,' she said. The boy eyed her as if the liquid was poisoned by her lips. 'Please,' she added.

He took the cup, his swallow draining the rest of its contents.

'Just a little more,' the boy shook his head, 'for the pain, please.'

And again, he poured a draught, she sipped and passed him the remainder. It was important she gauge her consumption carefully, for she did not want to lose what acuity she had regained.

The next measure he poured without her asking. Mme Lousteau wanted no more liquor but neither did she want to refuse. The boy's eyes shined with the early glimmer of intoxication and she began to feel a lightness to her own body.

'Where did you find that letter?' She asked, as the boy poured one more.

'Why— why should I tell you when you tell me nothing?' He said, handing her the drink.

'What can I tell you?' She waved a hand indicating no particular direction, 'I slipped and fell into a gully. Look at me, I am an old woman lucky to be alive.'

'You were hunting me when you fell,' he said nodding towards the gun, 'maybe I'm the one who should feel lucky.'

'I was hunting cerf. Do you not know whose land this is?'

'An old white woman out here on her own?'

'I travelled with companions. One became sick and I decided to proceed on my own. There was no use in my own sport being spoilt by another's misfortune.'

'A fine witch, you are.'

'Why do you insist on call me a witch?'

'I call a witch a witch.'

'You are saying nothing.'

'I say what I mean.'

Mme Lousteau said nothing for a moment, listening to the crackle of the fire.

'What are you doing out here in the middle of the forest?'

'Hunting cerf.'

She smiled.

'I really don't know anything about your letter,' she said, 'it sounds like a fascinating story. All you tell, I mean. If it is true.'

'Of course, it's true. You know it's true. Do you think me a fool? Don't you play your games with me witch, I won't be enchanted.'

'Whoever you think I am, you are mistaken.'

'I know you. I saw you,' he said, moving in so close she could smell the rum on his breath, 'and eventually your tongue will grow loose and betray you.'

It was then Mme Lousteau struck the boy.

She had felt the stone while still laying on her back. It dug into her forearm. When Mme Lousteau made that initial investigation of her body's condition, the stone moved with minimal force. At the time she had thought nothing of it, just that she would suffer from one less source of pain. It was only when searching out the gun that she remembered it. Thoughts of concussion and a bump on her own brain being the deed's inspiration. The stone fit perfectly into her palm, protruding enough to provide a good source of contact. She caught hold of it when the boy dragged her to the tree, pressing the stone close to her thigh and concealing it while the boy was distracted. There it stayed beneath her leg, as she worked on dulling the boy's reflexes.

The blow was swift, her aim and reactions better than expected. She knelt over him and hit him once more for luck.

The boy was alive: his breathing regular; he looked to be peacefully asleep. Of course, she could not rule out phrenitis. Who knew how the blow might affect the workings of his brain? There was every chance he might die and to be honest Mme Lousteau was unsure how she felt about it. After all, had the boy's intervention not saved her? Had he not given her aid despite his misgivings? But there was no time for procrastination nor was it the moment for her to forget her purpose. Anyway, the boy's actions had come with their own motives. It was not as if he had acted out of concern. She removed the papers from the boy's pocket, folded them and put them in her own hideaway. Then she checked his pockets for any other documents, finding only a few piastres, an old brass tinderbox with flint and firesteel and few yards of balled twine. Next, she searched his bindle. In here she found only provisions and another set of clothes. With the cord she tied his hands and feet, taking a shirt from among his belongings and tearing it to fashion a gag.

The night was clear and through breaks in the forest's canopy the moon could be seen. Beneath its leafy rafters, however, darkness held sway and there were still many hours before dawn. To wait until daybreak, to wait any longer than necessity required, was to delay the fulfilment of her plan and it felt urgent that the matter be resolved. What she at last possessed meant the end to almost a year's anxiety. It was a time during which memories, both mislaid and abandoned, had been stirred from their silty depths and attempted to drag her down to their place of rest. If she paused and waited until sunrise, she ran the risk of stalling her excitement; allowing the surge of energy which had driven her on, to recede. What then: the onset of lethargy, the awareness of her intoxication, the return of pain, of fear, of remorse?

But carelessness had already seen her tumble to near doom, what greater perils awaited in the darkness where danger could not be seen?

From amidst the firewood, the boy had gathered, Mme Lousteau found a good thick branch. She wound the remaining cord tightly around one end, its tautness stretching and thinning the strands. After wrapping the layers of twine around the stick's head she forced the last piece of cord under this binding with a knife. She then soaked the cord with boy's liquor and dipped the head of the branch into the fire. With this torch she struck out into a darkness that would have made the stoutest of hearts quail.

Chapter Twenty-One

The White Witch

I was plagued by a strange sensation, like the feeling of being followed when there's nobody there. Or maybe there was someone but in possession of no body. I looked up the slope and into the trees but saw nothing, listened but heard only the murmur of the forest. I felt not the breath of a pursuer at my neck, no earth or stone tumbled dislodged by the fall of heavy feet.

This fancy I ascribed to an overactive imagination. (Though, what other kind of imagination would a storyteller have, ey?) Distraction seemed to me the perfect remedy. I considered the direction of our journey: why we headed down the mountain instead of along its level ridge. If we kept to the highland, it would take but a brief detour before we were moving north again, back in the direction we'd first been travelling. What this elevated trail added in distance, would be made up for in level terrain. And let's face it if there'd been any hurry, we'd have stuck to the coast road.

Suffice to say, I struggle to understand the old man's reasoning.

As we moved further down the mountainside the trees thinned to reveal a gully, at its bottom a trickling stream. There was a short bank on the far side of the water, leading up to a meadow, beyond which the mountains rose again.

It was hard to believe that during the wetter months the stream before us became the Grande Rivière du Sud, its torrents muscling their way to the sea. The water was clear and paved with pebbles and slick roots that seemed to slither out from the bank and delve into the shallows. At the water's edge we stopped to bathe and quench our thirst, before climbing the opposite bank. To my surprise the old man looked younger, a dip in the stream seeming to wash away the years – his white hair becoming the chief mark of his age. Even Pirat splashed about like a pup, rejuvenated by the waters.

Past the grassland more trees awaited, Pirat and Vier Bolom headed straight for their border. Me, I sauntered along behind, walking my unhurried walk, whistling a tune; all the time keeping them in sight. I'd spent too many hours in the forest's gloom to be in a rush to leave the open sky. I imagined lying in the sun and falling asleep, dreaming the day away and wondered why I was doing the very opposite. I wondered what it was that drove those two adventurers on and left them happy to leave the grassy expanse behind. It was only when the pair disappeared into the woods that I thought I'd better make haste.

I took a last wistful glance at the meadow, fearing I would never again see the breadth of the sky.

It was while taking that last glance, that something caught my eye: a movement in the grass, a ripple travelling opposite to the wind. I closed my eyes, opened them; blinked two-three times, concentrating on the area where I'd seen the disturbance. I held my breath, stood as still as deer in fright: nothing. A trick of the light, I thought, or a whirl in the currents of the breeze. I shook my head and moved off into the forest.

Some of us are adaptable by nature, able to adjust to the world no matter the challenges it brings. That was not me, or so I'd believed. I'd lived a settled life, rife with routine, happy with my rote existence. Any change had been gradual, like the change of seasons or the passage of time; like the drip from leaf to pool. That was until Ma-Jo's passing, for despite Ma-Jo wilting before my eyes, her death had come as a shock; the emptiness where her presence had been too great to ever be filled. Thereafter, I was cast out into a world full of the unexpected; on a journey as strange as a myth. And it was not only the world that surprised me; I found in myself undiscovered things. I'd assumed it was loss that made me a take to the road, that I was curious by necessity rather than choice. Yet in those woods, as the light receded to mere flashes between the trees, I realised change had not overwhelmed me and I was able to cope with the unpredictability of things; that each trial I'd faced I'd done so without fear. And if not without fear, then without apprehension. And if I'd been apprehensive, I'd carried on regardless.

So, with only shadow and leaf for company and my companions far ahead, I strove to forget the glare of the outside world and forged deep into the wooded country.

The cry was somewhere between a scream and a howl. I couldn't tell if it came from man or beast, whether it was a cry of distress or a lament to some ancient god. That I headed towards it, instead of bolting off in the opposite direction, was tribute to how much I'd changed. (Though, it could easily be marked down as a bout of temporary insanity.)

I peeked from behind bush and tree, moving with predatory stealth; uncertain and a little scared of what I might find. I searched the pits and troughs of the landscape; beneath shrubs and toppled tree boles slippery with lichen; in the hollows of crumbling banks and the depths of deserted dens. Yet, for all this snooping I discovered nothing, well, apart from one particular fact: I had become lost.

Here, I almost came a cropper.

After walking in so many circles every direction looked the same. I saw myself wandering the woods for eternity, a lost soul forever trapped in his arboreal prison. The world around me seemed to spin and I was unsure if the movement came from my feet or my brain. Despite this I wanted to run, fear it seemed, demanded it, panic getting the better of my senses. But I forced myself to stop; I gave my arm a pinch, took a few deep breaths (as Ma-Jo had taught me) to help my mind and body reconvene. When I went to take my next step, still shaking but the world now back in sight, I realised the place I was about to step wasn't there. I stood at the edge of a hollow, poised to go head-over-heels. Back I shuffled, lucky to have avoided such a pitfall.

Where the forest floor should have been, the ground fell away, as if scooped up by a giant's paw. (The wood had its natural undulations but this dip was really quite a drop.) The lip where I stood plunged into a run of roots and bushes, with who knows what hidden in between. That I'd so narrowly avoided a fall made me come out in a sweat. While reflecting upon the consequences of such a dive, I saw it. At the bottom of the trench lay what looked like a body. Was I seeing there before me the shape of things that might have been?

I descended the slope, steadying myself with trunk and tree branch, digging in my heels in an attempt not to slip. The body lay face down in the dirt, one arm flung out to the side, the other hidden beneath its torso. It was a woman, or so it seemed: barefoot, her hair wild with dirt and leaves, exposed skin glowing against the forest hues. If it wasn't for her being white, she could have been ol' Vier Bolom's spouse. (Indeed, like the old man this *femme blanche* might have fallen from the sky – though as it turned out her tumble was strictly an earth-bound affair.)

The woman's back rose and fell with an ease of rhythm, as if she'd fallen asleep on the spot. I gave her shoulder a tentative poke. There was no reaction, not even a flinch. With care I rolled her onto her back and almost keeled over in surprise. My mouth hung open in disbelief, an obscenity caught in my throat. What I saw before me, made me wish I'd left her staring into the mud. For there, amidst the muck and the leaves, lay the woman whose buggy had almost flattened me at the bazaar. Dirtier and more bedraggled, indeed, but there was no doubt it was her. Much had happened since the day I'd saved Pirat and Ma-Jo took off in fright, but this face I would never forget.

Her hair was redder than I remembered and liberally streaked with silver strands. Though lined and sullied by dirt, there was in her face a kind of faded beauty. A quality often lost, I supposed, beneath her mask of cold refinement. Maybe it was only during the innocence of sleep, that this comeliness returned; that the woman she'd once been was able to shed the woman she'd become.

She began to shake. I took a blanket from my pack and covered her. By all rights I should have left the woman for dead the moment I recognised her, this bearer of ill fortune, this albatross, for what could come of such a meeting but more of the same?

When she grabbed my wrist, I jumped. (I tell you, it's a miracle I didn't piss myself then and there.) When she murmured, 'Hold my hand,' her words clearer this time, I held on more out of fright than compassion. Her lips moved, but the rest of her seemed lost in dreamland. Like the mind had woken but forgot to rouse the skin and bones. It was an eerie sight. There's more to this woman than meets the eye, I thought. (And who could blame me, ey, after the other ol' reprobate I'd picked up by the wayside. The collecting of antiques was beginning to become quite a habit.)

'Where am I?' she croaked, awake but still not awake. 'Why is it so dark?'

(No surprise here, mo frer, for her eyes remained firmly shut.)

'Tone tombé,' *you fell*, I replied, and a breath later her torso jerked up as if to sit, 'aye, seigner, poupette la pe levé,' *my god, the doll is alive*, I spluttered, sticking out my hands to keep her at arm's length.

What was happening?

I averted my gaze just in case her eyes had opened, for who knew what terrors they might bear; what devilry a single glance might bestow. Truth be told, it was probably more a twitch than a jolt. But I had the right to be a little jumpy, for my woodland jaunt had proved capable in springing the odd surprise or two.

Gently, I eased the woman back down.

'R-r-r-rest,' I said, still a little shaky, 'you might be hurt.'

Light was fast fading and the shadows drawing in, and no doubt fatigue was feeding my fears. So, I searched for kindling to make us a fire and rustled up a bit of grub, quick-time. In the underbrush, not far from the woman, I found the rifle: a strange thing made of rich brown wood and a metal that looked a lot like brass. It was smooth and oiled and well maintained, the muck on its surface easily displaced. I stopped there in those last throes of sunlight and peeked over my shoulder to check the woman was still there. I'm no expert on firearms (who would have guessed, ey) but I could see this was no long forgotten relic. The appearance of the thing seemed no coincidence – the woman behind me had been out on a hunt.

After we'd eaten, I bathed the woman's face, cleaning a nasty cut I'd noticed just above her hairline. It was deep and jagged and clotted with dirt, an invite for infection to turn her blood bad. I gathered some herbs and made a poultice, using my shirt to bandage the wound.

Why all this trouble, ey, you might ask me? Why not let the poison find its way to that rotten heart? Wasn't it bad blood what ran through her veins, anyway? What difference would a little more make?

Mama, papa; mo ser and *mo frer*, I can't claim to find sense in my actions. Perhaps, in those days, I had the purest of intentions and couldn't bear to see even a devil in pain. That might be stretching the truth a little too far, though, don't you think? Just a day earlier, if not for the thought of Ma-Jo, I would have snuck past an unconscious Vier Bolom. And I can guarantee you, that there in the woods, I felt not the pang of Ma-Jo's scruples.

But what I did have was a captured she-wolf, one who'd been on my scent since who-knows-when. (Now, maybe this clue brings us a little closer to the truth.) This woman was the root of my family's misfortune, the one who'd profited most from mama's death. What use would I have for the white woman's ghost? What could a body tell me if there was no spirit there? Ma-Jo's stories had taught me my history, but mama's letter told me there was more to discover. It seemed no accident that the woman appeared when she did, so soon after I'd come into possession of those papers. Had she been drawn to the letter or sensed its reappearance, just as the document seemed to be steering me to her? When I began my journey, I knew not where it would take me. Whether I ever expected to confront this woman, I'm unsure. It was just as likely that my empty home drove me to flee and the letter and its contents were an excuse for me to leave. But whatever the truth, I would have been a fool to dismiss a living connection to mama's death.

And I swear I could feel the deepest secrets of the woman before me, trying to escape her sleep.

'Are you there?' I whispered into the woman's ear, inquiring of her in that other realm, 'You are her, aren't you?'

The woman ceased to murmur, her jitters stopped and she stiffened like a thief caught with his hand in a pocket.

'Are you a witch?' I asked.

Twice this woman had appeared in my life and neither as the bearer of good fortune. (And I would've forgone even the greatest of fortunes for the return of my simple life and those lost to me.) The first meeting could be chalked up to coincidence, but of the second what were chances that she'd be there?

I felt like shaking the woman awake and asking her what sorcery had delivered her to those backwoods. Why she was there – well, with my discovery of the gun this seemed no great mystery – but why choose a gun and not a spell to do me in? Was I, perhaps, on the wrong track with this witchy business, it being no more than the hocus-pocus of my imagination? Wasn't it more plausible that the ol' girl was all about the hunt, that whatever our connection, I was just an excuse for a little recreational shooting? What was more frightening, I wondered, meeting your end by incantation or by gun?

I concluded that I wished for neither.

It had taken only a glance from the woman to seed Ma-Jo's sickness, or so I'd believed. Mama and papi died not long after the witch's spouse gave up the ghost. In mama's letter, this same old patriarch confessed to being her father and alluded to mama being with child. Words written not long before the trio were snuffed out. Let us not forget, this storyteller here was never supposed to have made it out alive, the only one left standing should've been the old snow queen.

It was all as bloody, incestuous and murky as history tends to be; too interconnected to be put down to chance, with too many coincidences for the supernatural to be ruled out.

So, there I was, an aside to the woman's story, a lose end she couldn't afford to let be. In her story The End would certainly spell my end and my own tragedy had drawn me helplessly towards her. No, there was no need to ask her why she pursued me, only for her to help me fill in the blanks.

My hand was drawn to my pocket, I stroked the folded pages it concealed. Could it be that harm had come to so many over something so small; over words whose greatest distinction was that they had been written down? Frozen like only the manmade can be, the passages of this epistle existed in a place where no amount of imagination could change them. So unlike a story, which might evolve in the telling, be adapted to your audience, and gain new flourishes and embellishments when passed between raconteurs.

I withdrew the letter, unfolded it, gave it a snap or three to loosen its creases. I cleared my throat, ahem, (just in case my audience was unaware I was about to begin) and then to my surprise: gotcha! She couldn't help herself. There she was getting an eyeful of the goods – leaving me no doubt as to where her interests lie. When she saw that I'd seen her peepers snapped shut. But she'd seen what she'd saw and for her that was impossible to unsee.

The hook was now well and truly baited. Her coma looked to have been an act.

Of course, I didn't want to reveal the letter's contents too soon. Instead, I let her believe I was unprepared. (That this was true is neither here nor there.) I acted all a fluster, blurting out a raft of questions and accusations, in the hope I would catch her off guard. The result, however: not even a nibble. It seemed that after her first slip, she'd wised up to my plan.

'What good are you, anyway, ey,' I said, unable to contain my frustration, 'if you won't talk? I'm not stupid, I know you're awake. Pah, I should have smothered you with my shirt when I found you and put us both out of our misery.'

Only after this did she deem it necessary to reply.

Not the most sophisticated method of interrogation, I admit – I was young and impudent and unschooled in the ways of deception, and still not particularly proud of my threat – though it appeared to have the desired effect.

'Don't hurt me,' she mumbled, all innocent eyed, eyes I was sure had sited the gun just behind me.

'You're the hunter, not me,' I said, giving the rifle a blind tap, for good measure, 'though it seems you've underestimated your prey.'

'Where am I? I— I don't understand,' the old woman said, feigning incomprehension, her squint one of the more devious kind. She proved to be as cunning as, well, an old maid: evading my questions as efficiently with words as she had with her silence.

She wet her lips and with creaking joints propped herself up on her elbows.

'Water,' she said, adding the hint of a rasp to her plea, 'please young man, I'm thirsty.'

The woman cannot speak with a dusty gorge, I thought, so I poured her a draught and helped her to drink. It might have been my imagination but I'm sure I saw a softening around her eyes – a flash of curiosity where lines of deception had been. At that moment I might have wondered who this woman really was and how different she was from the role that I'd cast for her. (I'm not denying her pedigree for such a part, only that I doubt this identity existed in solitude. Who among us has only one 'I' dwelling inside them? Which of us isn't in a constant battle with that other self?) Instead, I avoided this line of thought. Maybe, out of naivety, it never even crossed my mind. Or maybe it was necessary that she remained the villain to me. Who can say whether this was the wrong tactic to follow? When the shoe fits, you likely have the right foot. Anyway, it was during this brief interlude that I decided it was time to draw my trump card. (Or trump letter, you might say.)

I began to hum to myself, made an exhibition of studying the letter as if in search of its juiciest excerpts.

'This is what you want, ey?' I said, looking up from the papers, flourishing them like a gentleman's hankie, 'let me read you a piece, just a portion to whet your appetite.'

The woman made a grab for the letter, a feeble movement, no more than a snatch at thin air.

I gave her a disapproving look, then returned to the papers.

'Mr Dearest Elise,' I began.

To be honest I felt the teeniest, tiniest pang of guilt. (Yes, you can even feel pity for one of Beelzebub's kin, especially if they flash you their vulnerable side.) I was exposing the ol' girl to her husband's intimate reflections, words written for a woman who clearly wasn't her. That they were for his daughter, I imagine, was of little consolation and perhaps this made it a touch worse. Then there was my presence. I wasn't only the narrator of this exposé, but also witness to her humiliation, far from an outsider to the whole sordid affair.

'I pledge to you, to be received on my passing, half of the great estate of La Belle Horizon.'

Ouch, it might not have been a shock but I'm sure I saw the ol' buzzard flinch. Anyway, the gist of the letter was clear: the woman's husband had become so overwhelmed with love for his daughter, that he was willing to sacrifice anything to heal the rift that he'd caused. (Well, anything within the scope of his own dictated terms. And let's be honest, what more could be expected from an old slaveholding white?)

Yet, when I came to the line, 'In all likelihood the Madame would pursue every available avenue to ensure your disenfranchisement...' all remorse seemed to flee from my soul.

Was this not a clear indictment of my suspicions? Could there be any doubt to lengths to which she had in fact gone?

'Let me see that?' the woman said. 'Give it here!'

To this I shook my head and made a show of stowing the letter away. (An act of needless ostentation, I know.) At this point I began to wonder: are the powerful ever humbled when helpless, or do they only wait to regain the upper hand?

I guess we will see.

'At mission school,' I said, 'we were taught only simple French, but our master, Père Bernard, told me I was a smart boy and could learn much more.'

From this point I began to lay it on thick. I added a pinch of biography and a sprinkle of vitriol into a bouillon of facts and suspicions. (What more is anyone's truth, anyway, ey? Though don't think what I said wasn't heartfelt.)

'Then I saw you in the market and your evil eye recognised me – I saw it, saw the fear that overtook Ma-Jo; saw her withered by the poison of your soul. She died, you took the last thing I had from me and all I was left with was this paper,' I said, tapping my pocket, 'and here it will stay.'

I had no great strategy to net the old broad, things just happened to turn out the way they did. Maybe, blurting out everything I knew in the hope she would confess, wasn't the brightest of all plans. Though, let's not forget I was making up my plan as I went along.

'You were hunting me long before today,' I said, 'weren't you, ey? Since before I was born.'

It was true, I have no doubt. The same thorn had been lodged in her side since *grand-mère* suffered her less than immaculate conception. That this thorn took on a different shape, from time to time, might have been something the woman failed even to see. Who knows? As far as her thoughts went, my imagination only stretched so far. But her being there with me, that very moment, told me she would do anything to retain what was hers. And from the practiced evasion of her replies, this applied especially to the secrets she held.

'Help me to sit,' she said.

'Phhfff, you're not easy, old woman,' was my reply.

I couldn't help myself. I wasn't sure I had the strength to continue the interrogation.

She put her arms around my neck, as I leaned her against a tree for support.

Was I surprised that my latest oration had so little effect? No, of course not, what else should I have expected? Each time the woman's façade slipped, a moment later she raised it again. Each lapse just a stumble of a convalescing mind: exceptions rather than the rule.

What I hadn't expected, however, was the touch to my cheek.

I pulled away, shocked at the gentleness of her caress. Her hand, itself, was as hard and dry as bone – but the sentiment it betrayed was something much softer. An aberration I could not place, or maybe didn't want to. The way the gesture was left hanging, her hand suspended in the air, I imagined a murmured incantation. Was it that or just the sound of the wind between the leaves? Or was it something I invented to hide the unexplained tenderness, to halt any further inquiry into what it might mean. Did her eyes softened or had I imagined it? Was there, at the corners of her mouth, the beginnings of smile? I couldn't trust myself to say. I couldn't afford any such notion to be true.

'Do you have a drink, boy?' She asked. 'Something that might help revive my senses.'

I shook my head in an attempt to clear my thoughts, this the woman took as a sign that I refused. She asked again.

What harm would a little drink do other than loosen her tongue? She could hardly become any less cooperative. So, I rustled up a cup of *tilambik* and of course, out of courtesy, I joined her in a sip.

There was another drink and another and maybe one more, and surprise, surprise, I began to loosen my grip. After her fourth drink the woman seemed no less sober than after her first, needless to say, I was more than a little worse for wear. Shouldn't I have been able to out-drink the old woman, what was this crone compared to a virile young scamp like me? As it inflated my ego, so the liquor simultaneously shrank my brain.

Now, my final miscalculation came when she summoned me close, so she could whisper a little something in my ear. With my good sense suspended by yet another drink, this request appeared perfectly reasonable, despite there being no one about who could hear.

Darkness curled in around us. The night was warm, with just the hint of a breeze breaching the forest's palisade. Somewhere in the dark the spirits of yesterday, watched with interest our little game.

I leaned in and turned my ear to her whisper.

'Thank you,' was all she said and then a blackness akin to that which took those fleeing maroons, swallowed me up in a single gulp.

AND SO...

Chapter Twenty-Two

The Village of Pas-Cousin

When the light was blown out, I felt no pain, so sudden did the darkness take me. But upon waking, I wished for a quick and painless death. My head rang like a bell, like the shuddering reverberations after the clapper has struck. It seemed like there'd be no end to these agonising tremors. A situation far from improved when I began retching up my guts.

My blubbering was silent, or at least it had been from inside my head. There was no room for any sound but the ringing. I drooled sick and bile, pleading for my agony to cease.

What I saw, on opening my eyes, described nothing of any sense: my left eye refused to open; my right was just a field of blinding light. Rather than an escape from misery, sight seemed only the doorway to more suffering. Though, closing my eye again didn't change a thing. I wanted to wipe them; to shade them from the glare; to find out whether I'd been blinded or if something obscured my sightless eye. But I couldn't move my arms, I couldn't find them. Even after my hands had been freed it was an effort to move them. I had to think too hard, to battle against the torture that ruled inside my head.

At the time I didn't know I'd been freed; didn't know I'd been bound or that someone had shaken me awake. The urgency with which I was roused I only learnt later, when I could understand again, from the relief on the old man's face. He treated me with a tenderness at odds with our earlier interactions. Gone was the trickster, the storyteller, the cantankerous fiend, in his place a more avuncular soul.

It was evening by the time they realised they'd lost me. They had come searching only for darkness to drive them back to camp. They'd been calling out, so old Vier Bolom said, my name cast to the wind. That I hadn't heard it, surprised him. I'd wandered a mile out of my way, but in the silence of those woods distance mattered little. It surprised me more that I hadn't once thought of the old man or Pirat, while I was— while I was what? Of the night before, I drew a blank. The last thing I remembered was reaching the stream.

'I wasn't worried,' Vier Bolom said, laying a hand on my shoulder, its gentleness a shadow of something I couldn't recall, 'but the dog, he didn't get a wink of sleep. It seems this old man no longer has the sense of an animal.'

Towards the end his voice caught as he struggled out the words. I wanted to hug the old man but I didn't yet have the strength to console him.

Some time passed and I might have drifted off. I found myself up on my feet, supported by a body on either side. There must have been a shallow side to the pit, because I couldn't remember the struggle of climbing out. On top of this, I appeared to have regained the sight in both my eyes. Yet, despite this, the ache in my head still raged on.

'Steady, mo garçon,' Vier Bolom said, as my legs gave way beneath me, my aides unable to do more than drag me along. It was at this time, before the stretcher came and I was hoisted above the heads of its bearers, that I saw the first uncanny shapes. Such figments made from the darkness between trees, were unsurprising given my condition. My vision was no more than a series of variegated blurs; that shadows seemed to move and accompany us on our way, was not beyond the realms of the expected. Thereafter, lofted above the ground, and drifting in and out of consciousness, all that was visible was the puzzle work of the canopy; its missing pieces revealing glimpses of the sky.

The change came with the sudden loss of the trees. I found myself at the mercy of the unbroken blue, its field so vast and bright that I squeezed my eyes closed. Never had the day appeared so dazzling, the glare only abating when a hand covered my shuttered eyes.

Along with a clear view of the sky, came sounds, a hubbub strange to me after so many days among the trees. There was a clink, then another, a series of knocks, a tumult of chattering tongues; a cock-a-doodle-do, a long barrage of laughter, and what I was sure to be the bleat of a goat. A settlement, I wondered, out here among the trees?

There had been other sounds – murmurs that sidled me as I drifted among the trees – but these I took to be the fading screams of my mind. For when I was laid upon the stretcher, a compress placed on my head, the pain had seemed to draw away. Its remnants stored somewhere distant and closed off. With the advent of these new village sounds, those earlier whispers took on new meaning. No longer were they the mumblings of a distressed mind, but voices from the world outside. My rescue had required more than a dog and an old man: there had, of course, been others. To any reasonable mind this would have been clear. Two had been required to prop me up, and two or more to heft me to wherever it was I'd arrived. The wagging tongues belonged to those who carried me, I supposed, or maybe members of a search party at large. How had Vier Bolom managed to roust such a band of Samaritans?

Again, I passed out and it was another day before I came to.

In my dreams I wandered the forest, unable to escape no matter what direction I took. I saw shapes among the trees, too human to be mere shadows, too ethereal for beings of the flesh. They would appear in the corner of an eye, teetering at the edge of my vision, when I turned there would be nothing there; disappearing like a child playing hide and seek. Despite the fear that overtook me, I couldn't stop walking. And so deep in the forest where could I go to escape? In front of me, or to the side was always the promise of freedom. A light just beyond the trees: bright enough to keep hope alive, but far enough for that hope never to be real. I wanted to break down and weep, to fall down and die, but my feet they wouldn't let me.

On waking, I felt so tired that every dream mile I'd walked might have been real. I wasn't sure if I'd escaped sleep, or whether I'd dreamed at all. The air around me was cool, my skin so damp I thought I must have broken a fever. A fact that seemed confirmed when I tried to get to my feet. It was like a premonition of what old age would bring: a spirit willing to rise but a body unable to comply. It took me three attempts to lever myself from that bed, an act which drained me of almost all the energy I possessed.

I'd woken in the dark, slithers of light cast about the floor like remnants of the forgotten day. It wasn't the intense black of night that surrounded me. The walls glowed with an almost orange tinge, giving shape and boundary to the darkness. A doorway was lined in a fainter hue and motes of dust roiled in the filtered light. After

I'd struggled to the door and opened it, there was the rest of the day: a whole to the pieces I'd found.

Whether the clearing was natural or man-made, I couldn't say. I had to adjust to the light before I could understand what I was seeing. I took two steps out of the doorway, looked to my left and to my right; took another step and wheeled around to see what I could see. My head still being out of kilter I almost lost my feet.

I was in a street made up of two rows of houses, bounded by a perimeter of trees. Some of these homes had walls of plank with roofs of latanier leaves; while others were made using only bundles of these same leaves. Each home was finely constructed in a fashion that would've made Old Pierre proud: not a caved ridge or crooked hip in sight. This was no knocked together shanty, no indeed.

Between these two rows ran a thoroughfare wide enough for two carts to pass side by side. Well, if it were not for a fat trunked mapou sitting in the middle of the street. It was the only large tree that grew within the clearing; almost thirty feet high and fifteen at the base from root to root. As small as this hamlet might have been, there was little chance of stumbling out your door and over your neighbour's threshold. Though late at night with a belly full of arak anything is possible. Who hasn't heard the cry *'what, you mean this isn't my bed?'* used for such misadventures, even when the culprit's house is a whole street away.

To the right of where I stood, past the old mapou and to the end of the avenue, a field of maize could be seen. Beyond that who could say, there was a quite a break between the crop and the opposite treeline. At that moment a child darted from between two houses, naked, in pursuit of a flapping hen. The boy laughed amid cries of 'poule, poule,' his arms outstretched ready to embrace. The chicken, well it flapped careful to keep two leaps away from the child's clutches.

In front of one of the houses sat a group of half-a-dozen women, shaded by a bough of the great tree. Each had a basket at their side. Their chatter so fast it seemed more rhythm than words, their laughter always on the verge of escape. They sat on stools or flat rocks, in a rough semi-circle, around a pile of yellow-green husks. Without so much as a dropped word they stripped cobs of corn and tossed them into the baskets beside them.

Further on, a group of men worked on the frame of a house. One sawed, one measured, one held a board while another hammered, their cheerful banter echoing within the arena of the trees. What a haven this was, silent to the world beyond its borders. At everything I looked twice, three times, wondering by what magic such a place came to be.

Yet, all seemed oblivious to my presence; so much so I pinched my arm to make sure I was there.

It was from the direction of these denizens, to the far side of the tree, that I saw the pair approaching: Vier Bolom and a woman with whom he walked in perfect stride.

The smile on the old man's face outshone his usual grin; unencumbered by that ever-present artful air. His embrace was so tight my tender noggin began to pulse and he pressed his head to my chest as to hear the beat within. When he released me, he took a step back, holding me at arm's length.

'Mo garçon,' was all he could say.

The woman beside Vier Bolom looked older than he, her golden-brown skin as wrinkled as long discarded shirt. Her smile was broad, her teeth few, her brown eyes watery and dotted with flecks of grey. It was a face lined with a lifetime of stories. In height she was no more than a child with a frame that promised just as much mischief. Without a word of introduction, she took my face in her hands, pulling me down to give me a kiss – a smack on both cheeks. The old girl seemed oblivious to my grimace of pain. Her lips were a young girl's, her hands a pion's. When she let go, she left a hand on one cheek. She looked deep into my eyes as if searching out something glimpsed but not quite seen. I held my breath; feeling again the brush of some forgotten thread, expecting what I did not know. Then back came the smile and she gave my cheek a tap before falling in beside Vier Bolom. The hands of the two geriatrics lightly touching, with the tentativeness of those young and in love.

'Pas-Cousin,' the old woman said with a grin.

'Ey?' I said, confused by this non sequitur and feeling more than a little overwhelmed.

Did she mean we weren't cousins? Sure enough that was true, or did she perhaps mean herself and Vier Bolom (if they were they were definitely the kissing kind). The *vier fam* chuckled and with a sweep of the arm, gestured to the village around us.

'Ah, *Pas-Cousin*,' I said, matching her smile.

The old man just rolled his eyes, as we wandered over to the shade of the tree.

Now, at seeing the familiarity that these two enjoyed, the flywheel began to spin. Was it possible, maybe so, that we'd always been heading towards Pas-Cousin? And if that was indeed so, how far back did the old man's itinerary stretch? Could it be that when I found him by the side of the road, he'd been waiting there for me? Not the most outlandish of suppositions, considering all that had taken place. Yet, I was unsure if I wanted to know yea or nay.

'Pas-Cousin,' the old woman said once more, before heading off to the group stripping maize.

There was something strange about the language spoken by the villagers. I heard African, Malgache and Creole, yet, it wasn't just a mixture of all three. Rather, it was as if all were voiced simultaneously. Language layered upon language; like rock upon earth and earth upon rock, but even so I was sure I could understand. I remembered tales of those most ancient days when words didn't separate tribe from tribe – all language being one, all people one in the same. Was this distinctive tongue a clue to the village's magical origins, or was it just the result of the clan's hidden life in the forest?

We sat on our haunches between the roots of the trees, Vier Bolom and I, watching village life pass us by. The smiles, the laughter, the wandering children, the animals roaming without pen or leash; the smell so different from the forest: of dung and man and cooking food a musk that said man was about.

'Why are we here?' I asked, settling back against the tree and looking into the knit of branches above; looking for birds, the sky, I knew not what. I let myself slip down so I was sitting on the ground. The old man sat down beside me.

'You're not tired of sleeping among the trees?' Vier Bolom asked in reply.

'You know what I mean.'

The old man patted my shoulder, squeezing it until I turned to look at him.

'Garçon, you want answers but don't even know what question you're asking?'

'Ayo,' I said, shrugging his hand off my shoulder, 'why always the riddles with you, ey papa? For once just take the shortest path?'

'What brought you here, that's a question to ask yourself, don't you think?'

It was my turn to roll my eyes. I should have known.

'You,' I said, 'and them,' gesturing towards some arbitrary villager with my chin. 'This time you saved me.'

'I saved you, you saved me, is that it?'

239

'I was out there dying.'

'Yet here you are, alive and well. A little bruised but unbroken.'

'Unbroken? My head feels like a cracked coconut.'

'And it looks like bruised papaya, but its meat is still intact—mostly,' he said with a grin.

'Ay papa, you're hurting my head.'

He shook his old grey coconut.

'That wasn't me,' he said, all joviality leaving his face, suddenly bowed and slumped as if under some great weight. 'Though, in a way it was. I'm sorry I left you. I was— I was in too much of a rush, forgot, was distracted from the task at hand. I never thought—'

I removed Vier Bolom's hand from my shoulder and took it in my own. It felt cold and leathery, and seemed to bely a strength fitting for so spritely a soul.

'I don't blame you, papa, and maybe I do understand what you meant, before. Because as much as I followed you, I followed my own path here – wound up in my own pit.'

'You remember what happened, now?' The old man asked.

I shook my head, unsure of what I remembered; wondering if perhaps I had fallen into that pit and what I recalled were snatches of a dream.

'The woman, you were walking with,' I said instead, 'she your girlfriend?'

He pulled his hand away. Happy I guessed, to play along.

'As much as she's not a girl, she's a friend.'

'Yeah, she is old,' I said with a nod, struggling to keep a straight face.

'You know I didn't mean that.'

'You two suit each other, though, papa.'

The old man squinted.

'What do you mean?'

'You know: "Pas-Cousin, Pas-Cousin. Welcome to our village, here is our tree, goodbye,"' I said, affecting the cracked voice of the old crone. 'You're both a bit doolal— different, both a bit different.'

'Sorry,' he said.

'I said you're—' I'd barely begun the sentence before he slapped the back of my head. 'Ayi, what's wrong with you, old man? My head.'

'What is wrong with me, uh-uh, no, what is wrong with you, ey? What do you want? You don't know. Where are you going? You don't know. Why are you here? Maybe you know.' The tone of his outburst betrayed, by the twinkle in his eyes. 'No matter, ey. Listen, look, see, and with patience, understand... easy. But no, you're already too wise to—'

'Whoa, papa,' I said with a laugh, 'I apologise. I'm sorry.'

'Visitors are rare, here, you should be grateful. It's an honour.'

I put up and my hands in surrender.

'I am, papa. I am. Very grateful'

'You want to know why this place is called Pas-Cousin?' He asked.

I nodded, miming to the old man that I could not speak.

He paused, head askance, looking at me through half closed eyes. The delay being long enough that I felt obliged to say something.

'Go o—'

'All the land from this side of the river to the foot of the mountain, belongs to the people of Pas-Cousin,' he began, 'as much as the land can belong to anyone.'

I looked at the women, the huts, the naked child; thought of all that land and the humble patch on which they'd settled, could it be true? To take so little when there was so much to have, why stop there? Why not just a little more of the forest for charcoal or crop or to expand their village? Why not a little bit more after that?

Maybe they wanted for nothing, but when you had plantation's worth of land should you not use it?

As I considered this, figures began to emerge from the trees at the end of the street. They wandered into the village. Men, women; straight-backed and bowed; from black to ochre, all with baskets full of *brède*. They talked and joked and ambled, doing all those things folks are prone to do. Were these harvesters of greens among the shadow-like forms that flanked me as I was carried there? Many of them joined us in the mapou's shade, while others went off and then returned with large flat baskets. All of their spoils being tipped onto these platters then divided equally among a greater number of smaller baskets.

We were greeted with smiles and *bonzors*. An older woman who sorted through one such pile of leaves, called out: 'Cozé,' *speak on, continue* and Vier Bolom went on.

'This haven of theirs, with bounty of river and wood and field, was given to them by an old borzoir, M. Cousin, whose *habitation* was no more than a day's stroll from here. Those good folks of Pas-Cousin who are fifteen years old or more, being once this Grand Blanc's possessions. It is said he was neither the best nor worst of masters. His overseer did not spare the whip, but he never beat children, nor the old or decrepit (well, almost never). The old blanc believing the whip should be reserved for those special occasions, when a good lashing was the only recourse. You know serious offences like: murder, attempted murder, marronage; disobedience, indolence, theft; threats towards the master, threats towards the overseer, fighting, dissatisfaction, drunkenness; acts of a venery kind performed during the work day, loose tonguedness; giving the evil eye, giving the indifferent eye, looks that might be misconstrued as the evil eye, the use of magic and potions, and a few other minor infractions.'

'Ti patron esclave la, sa, et pas Cousin la,' *it was the overseer and not Cousin*, an old voice croaked, 'pas Cousin.'

Vier Bolom nodded and smiled, lifting a hand in acknowledgement.

'Be that as it may, this old man who was neither the best nor the worst of masters had either an epiphany or a moment of insanity, depending on how you looked at it – by that I mean through black eyes or through blue. As the years of apprenticeship neared their end (or as they were known to us: still slavery) M. Cousin witnessed first-hand the former slaves of other plantations deserting their masters. And as with all these blancs he felt a little put out by the ungratefulness of his workers (despite the fact his were yet to leave). For he thought himself a father to them and saw their behaviour like that of ungrateful children. The actions of those who made decisions based on emotion and had never considered the consequences to any but themselves. (I know, unbelievable, ey? And I must say, the stripes we received from these *wise* masters bore little resemblance to the gifts they lavished upon their own children.)

'But as I said ol' Cousin had himself a revelation, an idea that might just stay such an exodus. He had already noticed shacks popping up by the roadside; huts built among the bush and held together by no more than a prayer. What greater proof of our idleness was needed than our readiness to make do with so little. So was the white wisdom of the day. It was the sight of these rickety coops, though, that reminded Cousin of the scrub land he owned between the mountains. A tract bought long ago, neglected and probably inhabited by freeloaders and maroons. In the days of our tale when there were barely enough hands to work the plantation, clearing this land would have been an impossibility. Or so the old master first believed...'

Half-a-dozen children joined the audience, soon followed by half-a-dozen more. The hammering stopped, saw and adze were abandoned, as the carpenters strolled to the edge of the tree's shade. Even those bantering womenfolk, hands raw from husking, wandered over once the cook fires had been lighted.

'Here M. Cousin spied his gambit,' said Vier Bolom, 'a chance to kill two birds with one stone.'

'Oui, Vier Cousin habitier manz pizon,' *yes, ol' Cousin loved to eat pigeon*, called out one of the carpenters to much amusement.

'Vrai,' added another, 'mais li pli contan so pizon bien cuit ki cri,' *but he preferred his pigeon well-cooked more than rare*, inciting more laughter and the shaking of a few of those multi-hued heads.

Even Vier Bolom had himself a chuckle.

'Maybe,' he said, 'maybe, but this time it was another scheme that excited Cousin: the chance to clear his land and while holding onto his soon-to-be-free slaves (Well, for a little longer, at least. Long enough for him to rustle up some other unfortunates to sweat for his profit). So, this generous old soul gathered his workers five minutes before sunset – because, you know, what better way to butter up your peons than by letting them off early – and made them an offer. He stood upon an upturned washtub and cleared his throat, assuming a pose he thought befitting a great orator, just so,' with this Vier Bolom pushed away from the tree and gazed at some invisible point before him. One arm he stretched out; his hand not-quite cupped. The other hand he placed upon his heart. He continued, 'then Cousin remembered his audience and decided hands on hips and would do.'

'Lucky for you,' one spectator heckled, 'I thought you'd summoned the old blanc's ghost. I was about to call for a (s)witch.'

There was more laughter; a mumble of agreement among the crowd, a few *ouis* and an *allez-allez*.

'I am not a fool,' the old man began again, at which point the tittering started and I must say I was not least among the culprits. Vier Bolom for his part ignored it, carrying on with deaf ears, '"I am not a fool," M. Cousin said to those gathered before him. "I know in but a few months many of you will have fled the safety of my wing, a decision you will no doubt come to regret. No matter, I am here to tell you this need not be the way. You need not desert your master and consign yourselves to certain destitution." Despite sounding quite convincing, if he did say so himself, he could see he was losing his audience; eyes rolled lighting on more interesting subjects such as the setting sun, any old rock or the dirt stuck beneath a fingernail; there were those who inched away like clandestine crabs, their shuffling sidesteps fooling no one; others looked dead on their feet, not even five minutes grace saving them from fatigue. "Land," Cousin blurted out, in a boom that couldn't help but catch the ear, surprising himself as much as those in attendance, "I'll give you all land, good land, I will, yonder between the mountains. It will be yours. Not to rent, you'll pay nothing." Now, this did grab their attention, though after they'd heard his proposition, many were not so keen. For who among them hadn't felt the sting of that *rarely* used whip? Who among them had an ounce of fat on their bones? What his words told them their experience refuted. There were enough, though, twenty or more who were intrigued by his offer."

Vier Bolom's crowd too had settled down, pipes chuffed as the shadows drew in; elbows rested on knees; bodies reclined, legs out before them; children wandered, sat, wandered again. A few left to tend fires and put on their stews but each returned once their chores were completed. There was in the air now, the heady aroma of garlic, coriander and thyme; the sizzle of fish and bubble of bouillon; umpteen mouths watered stayed only by the captivating account.

There was in that pliable old face, that storyteller's face, a delight that shone from the eyes; a happiness that replaced the mischief and madness. I too, rapt by the tale, rested my head on the mapou's trunk like the shoulder of a sweetheart; watched and listened. And when he looked at me, I saw those things, the story dancing in his eyes, the pleasure of capturing imaginations, an excitement his aged flesh could hardly contain. And I felt a wetness on my own cheek.

He went on.

'Among those interested was a spry ol' poule, a milatress who though no spring chicken, was as handsome as a game hen and just as feisty. In fact, despite her threescore years, she looked not a day or so over forty. And when you have lived as many years as me, you know those middling years are when a woman is at her most vivacious.' This he said with a wink at the golden skinned aunty who had escorted us to our spot beneath the tree, she having now re-joined the gathering. Her response, a theatrical roll of the eyes.

'When the crowd had dwindled,' Vier Bolom continued, 'each missier and madame wandering off to cook and sleep and sing, and you know, dance their secret dances, she approached Cousin. He for his part knew not what to make of his bondservants' response. As they at one point seemed rallied with excitement only to turn and leave without a word. Well, all except for our poule d'or. She gave the master a smile, a little curtsey, and without a stutter came straight out with it. "Thank you kindly, M. Cousin, sir, you certainly are the most generous of all masters," she said in a tone whose honey was just a little too sweet, "You who are like a father to us, dear master, we will gladly help in your time of need. "Now this did befuddle ol' Cousin for he was sure it was he doing the favour. (Because as with all such deceptions the conniver ends up believing his own lie.) Cousin didn't know if he should frown or smile and instead took on a kind of constipated look, the two expressions struggling for the upper hand.

'Our doyenne, meanwhile, flashed her perfect white teeth – such a contrast to the master's vinous old chompers – and said, "if you could just do one little thing for us, we'll get right down to it." And would you believe her smile grew? "What?" Cousin replied, whether in question or exclamation, who knows? I don't think he knew, himself. "Well," said our heroine, giving him no time to consider this conundrum, "if we could just have all that in writing we'll make a start. Not that we don't trust you, dear master, oh no," she added, "but a wise man like you knows a deal is not a deal until it's in ink?"

'Now, as insolent as Cousin found the ol' poule's demands, he couldn't help but admire her spirit. What harm would it do to scribble down a few lines, he reasoned, it wasn't like any of those peons could read and anyhoo he'd just deny all knowledge once the work was done. Which was about as likely to happen as a baby being born fully clothed. You see, what Cousin proposed was to give a patch of land to those who cleared the terrain between the mountains. A job to be done in those idling hours when they weren't performing their usual grind (namely Sundays and the few hours they had to sleep). There were few among the slaves who reckoned the scale of the task, even fewer sure of what they'd see in return. Or maybe they weren't so naive and thought, ah what the hell. A plot of land all of their own, wasn't such a reward worth the risk? Coz when you have nothing what is there to lose? Along with the promise to clear the land, Cousin required one other thing: that they remain in his service until the work was done. Even if this meant staying beyond the date that marked the end of apprenticeship. (Which it undoubtedly would. For with so little time to do the work and only a couple dozen pairs of hands, they were looking at an endless task).

'So here were the birds that ol' Cousin sought to fell with his one stone: labour enough for those tricky years after the extension to slavery expired; and a fine acreage for planting – if by some miracle his shackleless slaves managed to clear it. The second being but a boon once the first was achieved. You see Cousin was not the only one to put pen to paper in this deal, oh no, the old blanc made sure his apprentices marked their clause with an X, too. (And you can guarantee this section of the deed wouldn't be a-disappearing.) Not so rosy for those brothers and sisters, then ey, no-no.

'Now, before you get rowdy and tell me I've given you indigestion before you've even spied the good eating, let me say, all was not lost. For it turned out, ol' M. Cousin would never witness his land being cleared nor the days when his ex-slaves were set free. For, he found himself as dead as the heart of a merchant less than a year after the said contract was writ.

'Oh, the hand of fate is a mysterious thing,' Vier Bolom said, hands held together in mock entreaty as he looked to the heavens with a pitiable stare. A rakish grin snuck onto his face and placing a foot on a jutting mapou root, he leaned in towards his crowd with a conspiratorial mien, 'there's no telling when you might find it grasping your throat or some other place, indeed. As the ol' master keeled over, one hot summer's eve, while trying to acquaint a young poule noir with his old cock bird. The old master's cock bird being struck down by his own stone, you might say. Who knew there were such dangers in rearing a fowl.'

At this he chuckled, shoulders shaking, and even those serious mouths hidden behind hands could not contain their mirth.

'And you know what they found in the pocket of the old master's corpse?' the storyteller inquired, and every head shook despite the answer being no surprise, 'a deed that granted to M. Cousin's onetime slaves, not scrap of scraggy good-for-nothing dirt, oh no, but all the land between the mountains (on the advent of his death, of course). What a surprise to find such a note on his person. Signed, sealed and delivered, oh yes, its courier none other than destiny's hand. Who can fathom what persuaded him to include such a clause. Or what took hold of his heart (or some other vital place) to inspire this act of generosity.

'Now, here at the conclusion of this tale I must add one final thing: a key to this place's curious name. Cousin's papers insisted this was no family bequest but the gift of (ahem) a generous heart. Those recipients of his benevolence were like children to him but never to be considered his flesh (for God forbid anyone suspect their many hues were any of his doing), and therefore should not be allowed to assume his family name. What the papers actually said was that they were *pas Cousin*, and whether by error or judgement this statement was taken to heart. And from that day forth the village and its inhabitants were called after the same. I could say the end, but really, it's just the end of the beginning.

'What more can I say my friends other than manze,' *eat*, Vier Bolom said taking an exaggerated bow, his right arm sweeping before him and his left, behind his back.

And as if by mention of the word food was distributed among the gathering: woven platters of roasted corn, cauldrons of bouillon, fish fry straight from the pan; rice and bread, a giant pot of rougaille and another of caripoule; let's not forget the demijohns of tilambik that did the rounds, filling cups, coconut shells and yes, the occasional glass. Aromas that rivalled the enchantment of Vier Bolom's tale. Enticement enough to summon saliva to the mouth and rumbles to the belly. Would it be conceited to believe that these festivities were in honour of our arrival or was it just good luck that we'd turned up? Had we, by some happy accident, stumbled into the village on a festival day or did they feast like this every night? For who says that folks can't keep their own *fêtes* and celebrate what endeavour or good fortune has brought them. I say it is just the opposite.

The faint smells of cooking I'd sniffed out earlier hadn't hinted at such concoctions, I'd never dreamed of such a spread. I was in danger of drooling and to be honest I couldn't be sure I was not. After two or three days of just enough and barely staving off hunger, I welcomed eating little bit more on top.

The chatter which had enveloped the crowd after the story's end, the cries of *reconter encore* and *en joli l'istoire* and the one or two of *ne pas vrai*, were soon quieted by the chewing of food. The only sounds uttered a mish-mash of syllables and slurps, vowels and consonants chomped, gnawed and nibbled, and morsels sputtered out by mistake.

As is the tradition in stories told, and indeed my friends in life too, journeys like the one I'd undertaken are as much about their adventures as their destinations. And of course, the transformative power of these ordeals. So, you'd assume it was me who was doing the changing. You know, something like that usual staple of boyhood to manhood or the enlightening of a rustic mind. And while this was likely true, what struck me was how the old man was a-changing. For, as you know, it is the changes in others rather than those in ourselves that we see. It seemed that the old hermit crab was discarding his cracked shell and donning something a little less shabby – sprucing up that dusty space between his ears. He'd looked a little less dishevelled after a splash in the stream and not quite as ancient as the ancient of days. But it wasn't just a bit of muck and leaves that were washed away, no, more than that some of the craziness, too.

His moments of clarity were becoming more ogles than glimpses. Were those waters indeed the scene of some mystical baptism, freeing the sage from inside the madman? Was the figure he first cut but a disguise and this player now revealed, the true Vier Bolom? Quite the quandary, I think you'd agree. For he'd delivered a tale with a flair uncommon in the broken headed, definitely not the ravings of the crazed. (Unless a bash or two on the head had left me better equipped to decipher such talk.)

Now, I grant you, Vier Bolom told quite a tale two nights before, so good I almost forgave him for the ordeal he first put me through. I'd been enrapt by this fable in the telling. But with only one such example, who was to say that it wasn't dumb luck. A moment of lucidity that by fluke carried on longer than was wont. Now, though, he'd delivered his own minor epic. And there was no chalking this one down as an accident.

Even his voice had changed – something I must say pleased me no end especially after the panic I felt on first hearing it: the twin of that phantom voice with which I'd sung my drunken laments – only adding to his stack of mysteries. Gone was that *voix cassé*, that broken voice, replaced by a pleasanter sound, its tone gliding where the former had rasped. Deep and melodious like the moan of a horn and not without its musical tone. Oh, how the brows of his listeners creased with concentration as he spoke and eyes misted imagining his scenes.

What a transformation over a couple of days. So much so that I questioned my own judgement, being quick as I had to dub the old man a loon. Such hasty verdicts are the bread of the young, though, and by rote forgiven by the old. Maybe it was me who had changed, then, and was seeing the old raconteur through new eyes. Those young peepers of mine looking further than my own sorrow, for the first time since Ma-Jo's passing. Could I have been so blind? No doubt. Very likely we had both changed our differences visible only in the mirror of the other.

So, suffice to say the ol' rascal appeared sharper in body and mind.

Now, by this time bowls had been scraped clean, cups filled and refilled. So, that merriment glowed from bodies and eyes, spreading between folks faster than cholera. And you know this kind of fever is only relieved a good bout of dancing, singing or lovemaking. I myself being no stranger to the mood, felt my inhibitions loosed by the festival air and the desire to sing took me. And not only me, for as with the miracle of the food so the first sounds of music began to appear: the rhythmic clink of spoon against bottle, the rap of hand against goat skin, seeds rattling in a bouquet banane. A bonfire held the early evening shadows at bay, children were ushered to their beds, still others in anticipation of the night's events showed no intention of sleeping. Even Pirat's tail wagged with excitement, eyes bright with the flames of the fire. The old golden skinned woman stood beside Vier Bolom, the space between them only air could negotiate. So are those moments before a *fête* begins.

It was into this air weighted with anticipation that Vier Bolom's companion stepped.

Not looking as frail as she had appeared at our first meeting, gone was that grandmotherly manner. Still as springy as spring, no doubt, but with this was an aura of something else. A quality that held in check all the excitement around her, as if all had been stopped in time. Held back by a look, a smile, not mirthful but the kind one gives when looking in awe upon a child. Eyes drifted towards her, like a frond drifting on the tide, with looks that mirrored the woman's own. Her voice when she spoke was deep for one of her size, in it no crack of age. Not a manly voice but warm like stew and as true as a mother's love.

She nodded, put up a hand, as much out of apology as to still voices it seemed, for it was the only the very young who chattered.

'This old fella,' she said, her head tipping back towards where Vier Bolom stood by the mapou tree, 'is as wise as he is old as he is mad,' her mouth now all a-grin, 'and we are lucky to have him with us. It's not often we see the old wanderer, but when we do, there is no doubt we will be entertained. And today with our own history no less. It is important for us to remember our own beginnings. Don't forget, though, a story is a story and whether the heart of it is true or not, it is as much fun as it is a lesson. There is no denying its truths, but it is more difficult to say what they are. We are family, here, we are one family, "what is for the one is for the all," we say, and this has seen us grow in happiness and seen our bellies filled. We have a life that in days passed was promised to us only in death, for this time, for this moment we have our heaven here. It is a rare thing in the world, and especially for us on this island. Our scars should not be forgotten, no, but neither should we irritate them for if so they will never heal. A salve that might not even grace our children's skin, there will come a time, though. So, remember, whether you believe it is through Old Cousin's generosity or our own art that we gained our portion of earth, such contentions are nothing compared to what we have. To love him or despise him is much the same. Don't let petty differences rule your hearts. And in the likelihood that you do, for we are of flesh are we not, see them for what they are: the things of childish squabbles and that will trouble no heart more than your own. For as much as I remember things a little differently from our friend's tale, I still love the old fool and would not go as far as to say he lies. Only that the truth does not always make for a good story. And in this his telling differs little from any other history: a thing that no two people ever remember the same. That he might not get all he wants tonight because of it, or that he will have to perform a penance or two before he does, well, that is a woman's privilege and between the two of us. I won't deny I'll take pleasure from it, for it won't be heads that will be clashing, don't you worry. Now, I have prattled on enough. Dance and sing and give thanks, and don't forget that what we have is from Cousin, but also that we are Pas-Cousin, too.'

With her last word the festivities recommenced, and the old *poule* was again at the side of Vier Bolom. The two as close as young lovers and making eyes that would have made many a parent cringe. Well, only those from whose hearts the spark of youth had taken flight. In among the celebrants I saw a wealth of pretty faces some smooth with adolescence others framed by lines of age; others still that seemed timeless and might have belonged to any generation. But all had congregated, were in the arms of their amours, or sat in conversation – friends laughed and libations were poured. There stood I, alone, shoulder against that grandfather of a tree, with even ol' Pirat sidled up to a comely she-dog.

Music played, bodies whirled, hips shook and enjoyment spread through face and hand and body-touch and let us not forget through sound. The whole thoroughfare that ran the length of the village filled with bodies, surely more than the enclave could hold. But before melancholy assailed me, I was pulled into the fray. What I first saw were the beautiful feet and the anklet that had made me drop the guava at the bazaar, what seemed like one hundred years ago. Too perfect you might say, an unbelievable coincidence, but true nonetheless. And don't go asking why I was staring at the ground, just then, as you'll spoil my story. On raising my eyes and following a map whose landmarks were all but delightful, I came to a face whose smile made my feet turn to stone. But with that strength of arm peculiar to all country girls she managed to get me moving. And move we did after few stumbles and missteps I fell into the rhythm of the girl's body.

We faced each other, stances overlapping, inside of right leg touching inside of right leg, a brush enough to foster excitement but not enough to make it expel. With the flourish of her skirt bare skin pressed against my trouser leg and I longed to feel its touch. I watched the movements of our bodies close, falling under their hypnotic spell. Only by looking into her eyes could I escape but there I found but another enchantment. Her countenance was one of those younger belles, a mask dark and dramatic by the light of the fire. Eyes round and full, and her lips too; with a nose small and flat and beautiful, a forehead smooth and long with dimpled sides; her slender neck banded with darker rings; a whiff of coconut and vanilla. Then she was gone, drawn into some other embrace. And I, left with another partner, one of no less beauty and whose salaciousness I must say excelled. She was not many years shy of Ma-Jo's age, from what I could tell, but village life had kept her young. Still, over her shoulder I peered, searching for the forest flower stolen from my arms. So, the night went, partner exchanged for partner – some old some young, both beautiful and plain – with the girl never coming to me again. And in all my joy and intoxication I was left wondering whether I had imagined her, a figment woven by the thread of some other memory.

A time came when revellers were called forth to sing, to belt out the ballad that their heart concealed. And there too came a time, when I was pushed forward or called out by a mysterious figure – who else but the old storyteller, himself, Vier Bolom – and with aid of drunken bravado I stumbled forth to take my place. A ravanne appeared in my hands as if I had summoned it; first tapping its frame to mark the beat of the percussion, then beginning to rap a slow rhythm on its skin.

That my voice was that old *voix cassé* of two nights before, mattered little to my clouded mind. But I saw in the faces of those before me the surprise that such a sound gave. I was half way through the first verse before the dancing began again. It was as if they saw me for the first time. There I was one who looked no more than a child with a voice of a life-warn old player. This had the effect of stilling every foot rather than feeding the frenzy. A silence of bated breath broken only by fire crack and bottle tap, a sense of wonder that only spurred me on. As if the emptiness called forth for my song, pulling my heart strings to loose its bonds, and of course, drawing them into my story.

And so went the song; composed word by word, bar by bar as I sang.

Papi was killed by a rifle shot
They cut off his head, a trophy they got
Mama died of grief, giving birth to child
Just a child herself, woman for only a while
But she bore papi a boy, an orphan rescued by love
Who grew up happy, cared for by a woman of grace
But my aunty died, left me with no one but me
Her spirit taking flight, along with the breeze
And I was alone again except for my old dog
So, I took to the road in search of things lost

But I found a girl, her spirit so bold
Then I lost her to the wiles of the world
But I found a girl, and she loved to dance
And she took my heart from the very first glance

On the road I met a man I took for dead
Covered from toe to head in dust
My head told me to leave him where he lay
But these words my soul couldn't trust
The voice of my old aunty showed me the way
Saying show mercy to this old man
What looked like death came alive
I fell back and my old dog ran
When the old man spoke, he made no sense
His breath smelled like nothing living
But he got up and walked with intent
I couldn't help but go along with him

But I found a girl, her spirit so bold
Then I lost her to the wiles of the world
But I found a girl, and she loved to dance
And she took my heart from the very first glance

So off I went following a fool
From the road up into the trees
Into a world that to me seemed unreal
I couldn't believe the things I did see
I heard voices and I heard sounds
Stories of things no longer here
But the deeper we got the more the path wound
The more I was taken by fear
That night I spent in a cave as dark as death
Lit by the magic of the old man's fire
Then a story the old man did tell
Its wit made of me a liar

But I found a girl, her spirit so bold
Then I lost her to the wiles of the world
But I found a girl, and she loved to dance
And she took my heart from the very first glance

So was he mad, I couldn't say
But I followed him out, the very next day
On stepping out from the cave what did I see
But the other side of the mountain where it shouldn't be
Again, down the mountain and into the trees
Across a river and into more trees
Once into those trees I lost my way
The old man couldn't find me, I was lost for a day
Left in a hollow with my head almost shattered
But the old fellow found me and that's all that matters
Then here I appeared as if out of a dream
A place no outsider had for many years seen
And what the old man preceded to say
Was enough to leave me feeling amazed
A history bold, a history clear
That brought to my heart a smile and a tear
A when it was finished a feast they did bring
And after, this song I proceeded to sing

But I found a girl, her spirit so bold
Then I lost her to the wiles of the world
But I found a girl, and she loved to dance
And she took my heart from very the first glance

I finished the song and there she was. What else did I expect?

Chapter Twenty-Three

Mme Lousteau

She woke by the side of the stream, its gentle burble having filled her sleep with visions of rain. The most vivid of these dreams took place in her garden at La Belle Horizon. In the arbour her bench had been replaced by an altar, upon it lay a body that she washed in the rain. The care Mme Lousteau took in cleansing this form was akin to a mother bathing a child, or a lover tending to their fated beau. The gentle stroke of cloth against skin lay in stark contrast to the pummel of the downpour, each splash creating a tiny dimple on the surface of the flesh. She washed from head to toe, following each contour to its conclusion without a hint of shame or embarrassment. And with each pass from foot to crown so the identity of this individual changed: at first Alexandre, then Elise, then the boy – Elise's son and finally Sandi. The change of colour and gender were somehow unapparent until she reached the face. Or maybe it was only on seeing the difference in physiognomy that the physique itself was altered. With the transformation of this person to Sandi, so the location changed. Mme Lousteau found herself in Sandi's chamber; in place of the cloth she held the dying man's hand. Yes, he was dying for there seemed no more life in the man's face than in the marble sepulchre upon which he lay. There was no bed, the room was cold and all the rich brown had drained out of her man servant – her something more. She was still wet from the rain, no, no she was crying, her tears running off the sheets that covered the near cadaver as if it was made from stone. And then she found herself back in that niche where the body had first lain, holding the sculpted fingers of a memorial to the departed. What she saw did not surprise her, although she was well within her rights to be stricken with fear. For now, it was her face, stone smooth with white lifeless eyes; her hair in a spray that framed her face and flowed out to the edges of the tomb's lid. This effigy was carved with an exactness that spoke of a familiar intimacy, compounded by the fact this likeness was as naked as the day. The sound she heard might not even have been a sound at all, for she remembered the silence of the dream; like silence before first word of the litany is chanted. However, she looked up, hand still in sculptured hand, only to see Sandi standing near the hidden entrance to the garden. He was that man of middling years, the one whose comfort she had come to rely on; all his life restored. Beside him, in his shadow, like wards of some great benefactor, were standing Alexandre and Elise. With all her heart Mme Lousteau wanted to go to them, this without a doubt, but she could neither nor rise, nor speak, nor smile. For a moment they waited as if expecting her to join them, only for them to turn and disappear through the hidden way. Alone she had knelt, a statue holding the hand of her own departed self.

Of the other dreams she remembered but one and this only in part: sitting in Alexandre's study, the roof of their great house gone, she unfolded the letter she had stolen. Only, Mme Lousteau did not read the letter, but held it open, letting the rain pour down upon it, waiting for the words to dissolve. A light shone in that dank and stormy room, illuminating the pages in her hands. The source of the light was the letter itself, all else in the sanctum being moss and lichen covered, attired in the gloom of abandonment. Yet the paper did not dampen, nor even the ink feather at its edges. The words and their medium become indelible with time, a memento to the hearts no longer there. Her hands shook. Whether from cold, or rage, or fear she could not remember. Then the letter was gone, sailing on a stream that ran between her feet. There was no other choice, she had to catch it, for who knew what other fingers might retrieve the epistle. Afterwards, she could destroy it by some other means. However, on attempting to rise, she toppled down into the mud, her legs overcome with infirmity. Her head lay on the stream bank, one arm outstretched in a vain attempt at capture; all the while the letter sailed further away, in the shape of child's paper boat.

It stood to reason that Mme Lousteau was suspicious of the world upon waking. Before her succession of rain soaked dreams she had collapsed in the dark beside a stream: a resting place not so different from where she fell in her nightmare. Pain and fatigue had assailed her on escaping the trees and she stumbled as far as her legs would carry her. In the east beyond the mountain, the penumbra of daylight could vaguely be seen. The sun's faint halo making the edifice appear like a piece cut away from the world. Towards this great absence she headed, it was only chance that saw her drop at the water's edge.

When she opened her eyes (closing them immediately against brilliance of the day) it was not only her sight that felt in shock. Every tumble and fall, every mile she had walked seemed to exact its toll that morning. Yes, she had grown old, but she rose like a woman of greater years. Not so unlike those dusty crones who conceal no more than a feeble pulse beneath their shells. It took minutes for her to rise, through a series of motions one might have mistaken for an ancient rite: the transformation from cub, to beast, to woman. Once on her feet she was steadier, though; hands on her knees, taking in deep puffs of air, seeing the world coalesce into something that made sense. Mme Lousteau took her first look at the day and the ascent that lay before her. Then she straightened herself, as if the extra inches might lessen the extent of the climb.

It took but a few seconds for her to notice him, by the tree line on the opposite side of the stream. She wiped her eyes clean of the tears of sleep. Celestine looked not so different from the darkness between the trees. He lifted a hand either in greeting or as proof he was really there.

Mme Lousteau waved back, more a beckon than a greeting.

'Hoy, garçon du Balteau, viens ici,' she called out, hoping for some assistance in crossing the stream. 'Come and help me.'

The stream's bank was shallow, yet steep enough that in her condition she might fall. The black, however, only mimicked her gesture, not moving an inch until she had crossed the water. She did not take kindly to this insolence, especially since her request for help exposed her vulnerability. She waved away his hand as she climbed the streamside, pushed him to the side when he offered her his arm.

'I have been looking for you,' he said, indifferent to her vexations. As she strode on ahead of him, her steps shortened with the gradient's increase.

Less than ten metres passed before she stopped, waiting for Balteau's attendant to catch up. It seemed to take him but a few strides to cross the ground she had struggled to cover.

'The colonel is home, now, resting' he continued.

'The stupid old fool,' she said, glaring at Celestine as she struggled to catch her breath. The man held her gaze without a flinch, as if ignorant of the rules regarding such interactions. In years past such brazenness would have earned him the heat of her riding crop. It occurred to her, however, that she might have already administered that very punishment. A moment of confusion accompanied this bout of déjà vu, which left her unsure of exactly where she was.

She shook her head in an attempt to regain her reason.

'I think maybe he will not recover,' Celestine said, 'I have never seen him so broken. In his heart, I think, he is tired of life.'

'Nonsense,' Mme Lousteau said, already weary of the man's conversation. She planted a hand roughly on his shoulder, 'the old fool will soon be on his feet, again. Now hold you peace and lead on.'

In truth she was not so sure, having herself thought the selfsame thing. Now that she had recovered the letter and possessed the item which had long haunted her, so too a time for self-reflection presented itself; self-reflection that so easily lead to regret.

Regret that she dragged old Balteau into her troubles in full knowledge of the likely outcome. He would try to prove himself of course she had known that, no matter the circumstances, even if it was to his own detriment. Indeed, Mme Lousteau had banked on it, counted on the Colonel's desire to demonstrate that age had not left him impotent – that there was life in the old dog yet. Though but for a glimpse during their first meeting, she had seen nothing but a worn out old man. But she had gladly let him sacrifice that last scrap of vitality in pursuit of her goal.

Something, it seemed, had come loose within her and she was unsure how to set it back in place.

And then there was the boy: lying dead or dying somewhere out among the trees. She had made a decision, at least she thought she had, not to kill him. But when the moment arose she had not hesitated, striking with a volley of blows. Was it two or three times she had struck him? Had she felt his skull give way under her pummelling? Murder had not been her intention, though, had it? Of course not, there had been some measure of premeditation but her goal had been to incapacitate the boy. She was being held captive and had done only what was necessary for her escape. But did she believe that? Or had she just taken what she desired regardless of the cost? No, not desired, but needed. Anyway, there was life enough in the boy, she suspected, to afford his recovery. That was if he was ever found. Every kindness he performed was steeped in motive, this she had to remember. It was not the goodness of his heart that found him at her side, but the desire for something that was not his. Even if it was only the truth about his mother, the past belongs to no one but itself. Who was to say he had any right to it? Who was to say she herself had the right?

With her hand on the black's shoulder she had scaled the mountain, allowing an arm around her waist when the climb was too much to bear. It had been a gruelling task, one she would have performed on hands and knees if it were not for Balteau's man. But, she chose not speak to him, nor did Celestine attempt conversation.

On their descent towards the roadway, she found the woodland possessed a peculiar air. She felt pushed down the path, like a foreign body the forest was trying to expel. The shadow around them ever contracting and seeming to close off the way they had come. It was a sensation absent during her trek up the mountainside, when she travelled with the spirit of adventure in her breast. It would have been no surprise, if on leaving that accursed place the tree line became a palisade – warding off any further intruders.

However, curiosity did not tempt her to look back and see.

Balteau's carriage stood where it had two days before, her own horse nowhere to be seen. This matter bothered her little, as she fell asleep once the carriage door was closed. Not even the rattle and jolt of the post chaise could wake Mme Lousteau from her slumber. It had taken a shaking from her serving girl to rouse the Madame on her arrival.

There was no sight of Celestine.

At La Belle Horizon Mme Lousteau's first instinct was to head for Alexandre's study, not to wash away the grime of her ordeal, as one might have supposed. Informed by paranoia Mme Lousteau closed and then locked the door behind her, shielding her prize from prying eyes that were not there. The haste with which she withdrew the letter caused it to catch in her pocket, making a tear through the centre of each sheet. This urgency came to a halt once the sheets were unfolded before her. Even in the bright light of the room the words seemed clouded by a mist of incomprehension, as if the manner of their acquisition prevented them from being seen. She could not say whether it was fear or fatigue that assailed her, but in time definition returned to these indistinct shapes.

There was in the writing something different from the formality of hand used in the old man's addendum, or the compelling account of his depravity exposed by his journal entries. What Mme Lousteau found were traces of her old Alexandre, the one she had lost to the operations of La Belle Horizon. Unlike in her dream the tears that fell washed away words, cut streaks through whole paragraphs. Embarrassed by her own sentiment she pushed the papers away, wiping her eyes on the grimy fabric of her dress. She was unsure why she was crying: was it for what she had lost or the pain caused by the things she read or even relief that her ordeal was over? Because had she not safeguarded the future of La Belle Horizon? But when she picked up the letter again and began to read she wondered: if so, then for what and for whom?

As she read on an appreciation for Alexandre's courage grew within her. To once again catch a glimpse of that love, a thing almost forgotten, even though she was not the object of this affection, lead Mme Lousteau to smile. She almost believed that by closing her eyes she could fall back into the days of their love. But it was a path she could not bear to follow. She felt the lines of her frown begin to regain ground, although they were not as deeply set as before. She had not forgiven Alexandre his indiscretions, no, of course not, this resentment she would take to the grave. But the humility he had shown in the extending of that first olive branch to Elise, deserved respect. (Had he not done what she, Mme Lousteau had been unable to do: offered and by extension received a hand in atonement? Or was she being unfair to herself? Had she really been afforded such an opportunity? Was she not comparing apples and pears, because what affiliation did she have with the boy? Her husband at least had had an heir. What was he to her this *gamin*, but an urchin, a vagabond... yet also the blood of her Alexandre.)

The letter had been composed many years after the birth of Elise, as many as between the girl's death and Mme Lousteau's first glimpse of the boy. It would have been easier for Alexandre to remain silent about his connection to the girl, to pursue a route more conventional for a man of his standing. (For, there was many a white mistress who might have provided him with an heir; if not legitimate, then at least of a fairer sort.) But no, the old man had waded into the murky waters of succession with his little mulatto girl in hand. Still, who could say whether this infatuation with his daughter was not but a passing phase?

It is easy to say you will do a thing, but to do it takes motivation. That was the difference. That was what had made Alexandre's path the plainer and made what she had begun to consider, a leap towards a bank she could not see. It was true Mme Lousteau had been inspired to do a great many things, but had she ever had the courage to create something new? To raise the rotten timbers so new foundations could be laid? Her decision to kill Elise, and her assault upon the boy, had taken less consideration than what she now pondered. At the time Elise's death had caused her little remorse, with Alexandre's murder and the later revelations being sufficient motivators. What was she to have done, widowed, broken-hearted and besieged, but safeguard all that remained of her life? In the end it was a decision determined by necessity.

Nothing she did could reverse that choice, and by her life she would not want to do so, but what of the future? To whom would she entrust the legacy of La Belle Horizon? This was something that occurred to her only after executing that second act: a crowning she administered with her own fair hands. Now she was left imagining a very different coronation. The letter left her contemplating what had been previously unthinkable; an anathema to all she held dear. Yet there she was imagining how the words before for her might apply to her own situation; leaving her to wonder how different Alexandre's decision was from what she now faced. The spectre of regret weighing heavier than remorse seemed ever to have done. You couldn't take back from death but life, life was always there to remind you of your mistakes.

So how then was she supposed to proceed? By handing over to the boy that which might have been his mother's? Was Mme Lousteau so eager to fulfil a pledge made by her husband a lifetime ago? Should she bequeath the estate to some unknown boy on the strength of few scraps of paper? What was the young *nègre* likely to do but squander it and lead it to ruin. Would it not be better to set fire to the place and be done with it? This was of course but a mere reflexive, though understandable, response. In the case of such a bequest stipulations would be set in place, caveats designed to prevent the boy from committing such gross misadventures. So, had been Alexandre's codicil, so was the form of any good legal document.

In the midst of this rumination she wondered where was her Sandi? Why hadn't she called for him? Was it him she had seen on the far bank of the stream? This time it was not he upon whom she depended, the responsibility of action her burden to bear. His opinion, however, she would have valued; a concession to his importance in her life. They would have discussed it, had they perhaps and she had forgotten, one thing lost among many others? With any certainty she could not say.

There was a long established format for preparing the bequeathed for their future responsibilities. She might start by simply employing the boy. This way she could gauge his suitability for the task, ensure his trustworthiness, his intelligence; school him in the ways of the plantation. So that by pen and by callous his hands might be made ready to receive custody of the estate. No, you could not expect a vagabond to be familiar with the responsibilities of governance, but if the mind was right one could be taught. The girl Elise had not been without her wits and the boy's father, brigand that he was, had had a cunning mind. (Though not cunning enough to escape the bullet, though that was beside the point.) There existed the possibility of fertile ground nonetheless, remote maybe, but not out of the question. And as proved by that newspaper man Ollier and certain *gens du couleur* of the landowning class, blacks could on occasions hold positions of responsibility – but what of this son of a *mulâtre* and a maroon? If, as was likely, it was the white blood of those others that made their works possible, well, at least the *gamin* was one quarter French.

As rare as the occurrence might have been, leaving property to a black was not without precedence – though it would hardly ingratiate her with her neighbours. This made her laugh, for when had she ever cared about the opinions of others, those who often mistook their own arrogance for wisdom. 'Just the sort of thing that Lousteau *dame* would do,' is what they would say; a statement so preposterous that it only proved her point. If there was one who could be trusted to oppose such a thing it was her – what with her history. And yet there was a logic to the doing of it, even a kind of poetry she supposed, albeit one that cast her in the role of villainess. For if a king has no son the crown is passed to the next suitable heir, even if it be a cousin thrice times removed. So it had always been, if a line was to remain unbroken there were often difficult decisions to be made. And to imagine the line of any great house was as pure as it seemed, was folly. Each had a black of some kind or another in its closet, a secret conveniently forgotten. And when the time came if the boy could be persuaded to take a lighter wife, one from a family who could pass almost for white, even this stain might be washed away, eventually.

They might also say she had gone mad with age and this she was not sure if she could dispute.

Only after the boy had been vetted and received the correct tutelage would she make her decision. The boy's capabilities being the measure of what he would receive. He had seemed desperate, though not a fool. Defiant, of course, but curious too; making up for in daring where knowledge might be incomplete. And knowledge could be gained whereas courage often could not. All of this, however, failed to take into account that she had cracked the *gamin's* skull. Could that be why she was considering such an absurd resolution? If the boy was dead what harm was there in flirting with something so outrageous? For all the shock and daring lived nowhere but in her mind. And if for a moment she considered it a serious proposition, and somehow the boy had survived her assault, why would he view her offer with anything but suspicion, contempt even? 'Oh, I apologise for trying to top you like an egg. Please, by way of recompense except a menial position on my estate. I promise if you are good it will one day all be yours.' If the boy accepted such a proposal did it not prove he was too foolish to preside over anything but disaster? And how was she to find the boy? Would it be worth it, expending all that effort, convincing herself of the soundness of her plan, only for the boy to turn up dead? It would be better to do nothing at all. To leave all she had to some forgotten relative back in France? But what would they know of Isle de France, of l'île Maurice? La Belle Horizon would be auctioned off, her only legacy being the profits from its sale. If that were to be the case, why wait for death? Why not sell the estate, all she and Alexandre had worked to achieve, to some outside interest? Let those who had long envied the plantation's magnificence, bid for the right to possess what they themselves had been unable to accomplish?

Was it not too late to diverge from the path she had taken? Had she not travelled too far? If she had begun her moral floundering before attacking the boy, things might have been different. Perhaps, she had stumbled upon some forgotten thread, one that persisted through time waiting to be tugged when its moment arrived? Maybe such skeins existed in every life only most people were too preoccupied to see them? Maybe she had discovered the route to her own redemption; a mission born of self-interest becoming a way to correct her own misjudgements. True, her endowment lacked the compassion of Alexandre's, but his bequest had been to a daughter and carried its own history. Her journey, though connected, was very much her own.

Still, there was a persistent whisper: what if Alexandre's codicil was but a whim fate sort to give permanence, a mistake his death prevented him from recanting? True, her husband's letter to Elise had complicated matters, making his offer difficult to retract. But, if one was determined, not an impossible task – especially for a man of his astuteness. Yes, who was to say he would not have recovered from this bout of madness? Leaving his wishes not his wishes, at all?

For a time it had been locked away – the mess of memories surrounding Alexandre's death, the revelation of his betrayal – secured in a strongbox, cast into the deep of her mind; full fathom five thy father's lies. That was until the appearance of the *gamin*. With his arrival remembrances began to wash ashore, flotsam and jetsam both. Some broken, some whole, pieces of the lost and the intentionally forgotten, at one moment beached and another taken back out to sea. She could not say they were only memories, so easily did she fall into them. Maybe they were shards of time, moments so important, that they broke from life's mirror remaining free to visit during times of joy or despair. Here she now rested, on an island besieged by her past, her decisions determined by the wishes of the dead and their imaginary hearts.

Oh, her Sandi where was he. He should have returned.

The room was lighted with stars of candlelight, its corners sucking in the dark. Night and day, came upon her with a swiftness that confused her. Fatigue descended with the weight of a lifetime of sleepless nights. There were candles and then there were not; there was darkness and then there was light. And Alexandre, where was he? for she sat in his study alone. Alone in the silence, in a room full of shadows with pen and paper and ink laid out before her. Alone in a room it was usual for her to enter only after knocking and her husband's permission to come in. What was she doing in there?

She should call Sandi. No, she should leave before Alexandre found her. But instead, she laid her head upon her arms, resting among the sundries of writing that dressed the bureau top. Why she did this, out of fatigue or despair, she could not say. She had wanted to write something, a letter or note. Had it been important? Maybe or maybe not.

Oh, Sandi. She remembered before it was gone.

It was an arm, either in a paroxysm or a dream that knocked the desk lamp to the floor. Oil spread across the boards in a current of liquid fire, the room and all its contents soon ablaze.

Chapter Twenty-Four

Liberté

I watched from a ridge, hidden in the dark of the trees.

It was a night lit by flame and ornamented by dancing shadows. Even from where I stood on the mountainside the crackle of that great campfire could be heard; a pyre whose fingers stretched up so high they almost touched the moon. Amid the snapping of board and beam, the collapsing of ceiling and floor, the roar of a thousand stories could be heard; voices whose blood had long been trodden into the dust and absorbed by the roots of sugar cane.

I felt its heat, as if pushing me away, encouraging me to make my escape. But there I stood mesmerised, as did those souls who had wandered over from the Camp des Malabars. Figures cut from the night by the fires brightness, many of whom looked on in delight if anything was to be reckoned by their clapping hands or dancing feet. Some sat crossed legged in contemplation; others stretched out their arms in front of them, palms up, warming hands. What a night of festival for those black limbs who witnessed and those who had passed on in the days of yore. A great foe vanquished, a devil consumed by its own fire.

No buckets were passed from hand to hand, no attempt made to quell the fire. It was a blaze to appease the dead and give hope to the living. Onlookers one and all seeing nothing worth saving, not even a life.

Pirat stood by my side, in his eyes the burning house. Vier Bolom was no longer with us and I could not say for sure he had ever been. I knew, though, he would be watching; if not in happiness then with the satisfaction that the place was no more. The dead cannot be revived nor rescued from the fates that befell them, but their sleep can be made more restful, the stones swept from beneath their mattresses. So it was with this conflagration, at least a part settlement was made. Not all wronged had been righted, but a few entries would be struck from the ledger.

That morn I had been surprised when Vier Bolom hurried me from my bed, shaking me awake with no regard for where I lay. When I fell asleep there had only been the girl and I, but on waking there were also three children in the room. These little ones curled around us like cubs about their mother, their faces as innocent as cherubims. I had not even a moment to wonder when they had snuck in, before Vier Bolom pulled me from the room; tugging on my arm like a child eager to show its mother a new thing.

I left the girl where she lay still in the midst of her dreams, no time even for a goodbye. Had my liaison with the her been an offence against the village, had our secret dance been a step too far. For what happens in the haze of a night's bacchanal is not always acceptable to the morning's clear sight. Maybe, but we were not the only ones to sneak away from the celebration with desire in our eyes. I was a stranger, though, and not much more than a boy, might that have been the problem? However, we were not chased from the village and those we saw at that early hour greeted us with smiles, *bonzors* and *ki maniers*. Not the usual penalty for such an offence. Vier Bolom gave me little in the way of explanation, conserving his energy, it seemed, for the journey ahead. We left without even so much as a sip of water or a fork full of manioc.

It took almost a day to walk from Pas-Cousin to the ridge that overlooked La Belle Horizon. Again, we travelled through forest and up mountain trails, I thought we would walk forever. But when we reached the top of this particular mountain the plains of Flacq lay before us, and further again, the sea. Below, in a valley that opened onto the coastal flats sat the white house; the fields and outbuildings I had imagined a thousand times. A place whose malignity could not be guessed from this idyllic scene.

There was little smoke at this time, no more than one might expect from a small kitchen fire. Wisps puffed lightly from windows only to be lost in the early evening air. It was on reaching this peak that Vier Bolom spoke. The rest of the day he had mumbled but a handful of words, as if the previous night's storytelling had left him tired of talking. But when he did speak, there on the mountaintop, it was with an unfamiliar gravity. Never once taking his eyes off the estate, as if his words were directed only at that place.

'You were born down there,' he said, pointing at the plantation, his finger shaking, age seeming to have retaken him, 'La Belle Horizon. You know, it has changed little since that time, garçon. It is still a monster, yes, it is. Born of ideas strange to people like you and me, a place imagined by a mind made evil. Not evil because it wanted people to suffer, no, garçon, no, but because suffering meant nothing to it if money could be made. There is no good or bad to a mind like that, all it ever sees is gain.'

Then he made his way off down the mountainside, waiting for no reply.

All I knew of La Belle Horizon I learnt from stories, from the mouths of those who lived what passed for life in that place; who brought with them the stripes and impediments such an existence bequeathed them. Even in those lines M. Lousteau wrote to mama I sensed a belief in the necessity of its cruelty. Who was I to contradict Vier Bolom? What was I to do but accede to wisdom of those who had lived through those times?

I looked down on the *habitation* it had taken me so many days to reach, still wondering why I was there; realising that maybe the why was there before me: to witness that very moment. The smoke a little thicker now, stick figures were emerging from the back door of the house. There was a stillness about the place, an anticipation, all work on the plantation seemed to have ceased, even the wind that ruffled the fields of cane held its breath. I too felt it, the fluttering in my belly, the mixture of fear and excitement that rooted my feet. Then the moment passed and I followed the old man and Pirat on their descent.

About a quarter of the way down the eastern side of the mountain was a shelf and break in the trees. This spot offered a clear view of the valley below. Here I found Pirat and Vier Bolom, their unflinching gazes set on La Belle Horizon. I sat beside them, amazed to see fire where the house had once been. Flames licked the sides of the building; the smoke no longer wisps but black clouds of devil's breath that looked too heavy to take to the sky. Instead of windows I saw the demon's many mouths coughing out the guts of the inferno. The smell of burning wood was so strong it was as if the forest itself was alight, the air about us full of soot. It seemed to have taken mere moments for the house to go up in a blaze, leaving a mansion made of fire in its stead.

There were no shouts and the three of us looked on without a word.

'All over the island we ran from fields like those,' Vier Bolom said, breaking the silence, 'looked for any way to escape. Some made it up into the mountains, others escaped only in death. That was the way of things back then, how we had to live. The souls of those you lost are free, garçon, have flown away to wherever it is they chose to rest. They no longer need to look over their shoulders. They no longer feel the yoke of this place, neither should you,' Vier Bolom again jabbed a finger towards the storm of flames, his hand no longer shaking. 'Look at the fire, don't you realise? They are telling you, *you are free*. That place belongs to the realm of stories, now. Your story, though, continues.'

Here he took a moments breath, as if waiting for his mind to catch up with his words.

'The whole island is yours. You are free to go wherever your feet take you. You have stories and songs, the air you breathe; you have life. Mo garçon, I heard you sing last night, I heard a story-singer – I heard the magic of Tiéga. That is a gift, indeed, a bequest worth more than all the money in the coffers of the rich. A story told is something to be treasured, but to hear it sung is like magic. With it words are not only heard but can be danced, their passions relived, all who take part become part of the story. With the music of Tiéga what once was can be brought back to life, and what has never been might also be made real.'

He turned to look at me and smiled. A smile uncustomary on that young, old man's face. Its tenderness reminded me of Ma-Jo, and with that thought tears came to my eyes. The realisation I had come so far and still could not out pace her death; that its scar would never be fully healed, would always be part of me, was both a heartache and a salve. For though I would never see her again, forgetting her would have been a greater tragedy. I could not avenge her death, if in fact there had ever been any other to blame, but it was a blessing that she had passed in the tranquillity of her market garden and not in the field or by bullet or during the throngs of labour. She might not have died an old woman, but she died free.

Vier Bolom took hold of my hand, squeezed it.

I cannot tell you when he left, only that I found myself clasping my own hand. Vier Bolom disappeared from my life with the suddenness that he entered it. Was he man or spirit or a figment of my imagination, or even a mixture of all three? I cannot say for sure, though my memory of him is very clear. The rascality of his smile, that glint in his eye that left me unsure whether to believe him or not; the wisdom that emerged from his cocoon of folly; let's not forget the stench that had at first made me wretch. So then, do I need further proof of his existence? It wasn't through accident or good fortune that I travelled the paths I did, that I navigated forest and mountain and brook. It wasn't empty air that furnished me with stories and dragged me on though my heart and body protested. Or made me realise that a man's destination is not always the same as the place as he is searching for. This might not be conclusive evidence but for me, it's good enough.

And of the other things, namely that love story you saw ready to emerge. Well as you might have gathered from my earlier remarks, me and the young lady with the beautiful taluses were not fated to be strangers. Never again did I have to seek out that anklet, though her beauty caused me to drop many a guava, and not only guavas but soursops and mangoes, too. And when I was not off a-wayfaring, wearing down both dirt and macadam, I could be found wherever she might be.

What now, you might ask? Where did life take us next? Well, my friends that is a tale for another fireside. And maybe, just maybe we will meet up there.

Epilogue

The Ol' Storyteller

Rainwater streams from the rooftop. Pools of water form on the baked earth. Its smell is everywhere calling people out from their houses to stand on verandas and under trees. Men squat beneath eaves looking up into the grey, haunches on heels palms held outward and cupping the rain. The ground is pummelled as the drops turn into the white spears of rain-beams, and the puddles are gone leaving a shifting, swirling stream. And the sounds are river sounds, splashes and running water striped with lines of its movement and the impact of the downpour. The red earth is blackened and the yellow dust is washed away. Everything is veiled in white. Nothing exposed is vivid. The rain is so hard that the only response is excitement. Grown-ups run for cover. Frenzied children run naked or in their underclothes, their cries lost among the zipping arrows of rain. Sound is absorbed and distorted, watered down, everything secondary to the rush of the inundation. As it pelts with the urgency of long held secrets freed from their binding vows.

Out of the grey appears a streak of blue and the beating rhythm of the rain begins to subside, becomes a patter and then ceases. The sights of the world are restored, the thatch and clapboard of a neighbour's house can be clearly seen and gable end shutters are opened. Children are still running and jumping. Feet skip through shallow streams and kick up fans of water. A small boy cries, tears invisible on his wet face as he is dragged home limping by an elder child.

Once released from behind the clouds the sun immediately reasserts itself, reminding its subjects of its sovereignty. Steam rises from the thatch of roofs as if from a cooking pot. Palm fronds which had sheltered heads during the rain resumed their lives as fans. People are walking now, have taken to the muddy streets, all except a man sitting under a tree.

He is old and barefoot and squats with the suppleness of a child. He wears a singlet of unbleached cotton which ties at the neck like a sack. His sleeves are rolled above his elbows, black and bony and resting on his knees, as his hands capture the sun's rays. Rain still falls on him, gently, dripping from the branches and leaves above. On his wet face there is a smile, the kind of smile that comes from inside, spurred by some memory or the happiness of just being alive. And in that smile there is youth, a hint of childish spirit so often lost when one has come of age. There is dancing in that old body, which is not so much ravaged as well worn. All of this evident, despite his easy repose, because of it.

People greet him.

'Ey, papa, ki mannier.'

He nods and might raise up a hand, but always smiles. The same smile with which he greets almost every eventuality. It seems like he never speaks, except to the children.

They shout to him.

'Ey, bolom, to pe fair caca?'

Hey old man, you taking a shit?

They're laughing, he's laughing and he shakes his head.

'Yes, yes, I'm giving birth to your brother.'

And his voice is full of the same mischievousness as theirs, absent of malice or reproach. Laughter floods up from their bellies and they push each other and stumble and grab onto shoulders, tripping over their own feet.

But at other times they come to him, whisper into his ear and nod and shake their heads in time to his muted responses. Their faces are grave and serious and occasionally break into a smile. This might lead them to sitting about his feet as he recounts some tale of the days of yore. A history that excites them about their own line, about the histories that preceded their histories, a time that might appear blank in their minds and even their fathers minds if not for him. For he sees. He sees what he has heard, the recounting of older voices, gruff and croaking and straddled by age. The skein appears to him, all of their histories intertwined threads, bound and twisted and confused. But beyond that the lines become clear, or as clear as the lines of history might ever be. He sees the gaps that those older griots thought fit not to tell him, and those scraps lost as fallen leaves in the detritus of the forest. Either degraded and mouldering away, or hidden beneath composting earth and soil.

'Ey, papa, c'est vrai?' *Hey father is it true?* You might hear the *pitis* say, as their eyes grow wide and whites expand leaving their irises like so many black and brown planets in ivory skies.

He rises, standing without the aid of stick or hand, and he is wet, a light drizzle still falling from the branches and leaves above him.

The streets are now full of movement, full of the commerce of village life; greetings, extended greetings, exclamations regarding the storms ferocity and memories of tempests of the past, when houses, livestock, crops and even people were blown away. Men lean against verandas and storefronts, in congregations whose very languor pays homage to the great smile of the re-awoken sun.

A cariole passes by, the donkey's head lightly bobs, its sodden coat steaming, and its eyes look to nowhere and seem oblivious to where somewhere might be. The driver, who looks no more than ten years younger than the old man, appears to be no more aware of his destination than the donkey. He has the look of one wearied by the journey, yet still has many miles to cover. Or maybe it is life's many miles, and yet another of his countless journeys which has fatigued him so.

But at the sight of the old man beneath the tree, a light touches the man's face. This brightening is not the work of the newly returning sun, no, for the brim of the driver's straw hat, drooping from the rain, shades his face to below his chin. And the lines of his face all rise in inverted arcs, making those thin lines seem deeper and more ruffled, and the slackness of his face is excited into the tight lines of a smile.

'Ey, Liberté, ki mannier?' *Hey, Liberté, how are you?*

'Cava, Alfred, Cava,' *fine, Alfred, fine*, the old man says, raising a hand to the cariole driver. 'E ou?' *and you*, 'if you don't watch out that old cart is going to outlive you.'

The man in the cart laughs, and pushes his hat towards the back of his head, revealing a reddish-brown face with big papaya cheeks and a nose so large it is only his heads exaggerated width that saves it from being ridiculous. But it is a good face, with shining dark eyes, its many lines those of laughter and good humour, and of course age.

'Hein, she's keeping up. Her old frame creaks and moans, but her spine is strong and her wheels run true.'

The man beneath the tree chuckles.

'Ah, you're a lucky man.'

'Vrai, vrai. She's a good woman, there's no better thing. Can I take you anywhere, papa?' The carter asks, with the deference of a child to an elder.

'No, no. I have nowhere to go that my feet can't take me.'

Above them the sky is now cloudless, flat and blue and seemingly never-ending. And the burning yellow pearl at its centre beams down relentlessly hardening the ground so lately softened.

Both of the men's hands are lifted again and the smiles remain, as their paths diverge.

The old man hums a tune, his right hand tapping out a rhythm on the top of his leg. Words are gradually revealed from among the mumbling sounds, but they are still quiet, his lips barely moving as if he is holding a conversation with himself he wishes no one else to hear.

He begins to walk, nodding his head gently. This could be as a result of his rolling gate, still fluid and graceful for an old man, but coupled with the tapping hand and his muted chant it is more likely caused by the song his head sings to him.

Glossary

Arpent. An old French unit of linear measurement equivalent to 190 feet or approximately 58m.

Brède. Leafy greens

Bouillon brède. A traditional broth or bouillon made with leafy greens, onions, garlic, ginger and herbs. A Creole favourite in Mauritius and The Seychelles.

Calebasse. Calabash, a bottle gourd. A vine fruit that can be harvested young as an edible squash or be allowed to mature and dried for use as a container.

Détachement des noirs. A detachment of arm slaves used to hunt down maroons.

Fleur de lys. A heraldic symbol depicting a stylised lilly. The symbol of the *fleur de lys* was often used to brand captured maroons.

Gris-gris. An amulet or charm said to bring luck or protection to the bearer.

Gens de couleur. Free blacks. Often used to refer to people of mixed African and European heritage.

Habitation (italicised). A French term for plantation.

Malabar. From the Malabar Coast. A person of Indian descent.

Malgache. Malagasy. A person from Madagascar. The Malagasy language.

Maréchaussée. A division of the French armed forces formally responsible for policing.

Manze-poule. The Mauritius Kestrel. From the French *mangeur de poules*, chicken eater.

Maroon. From the Spanish *cimarron*, wild. A runaway slave.

Marronage. Maroonage. The act of becoming a maroon.

Mulâtre. Mulatto. A person of mixed black and white ancestry.

Phrenitis. Inflammation of the brain, often accompanied by fever and delirium.

Ravanne / Tambour. A large, flat, tambourine-like drum made of goat skin. The most important instrument in Séga Tipik, traditional Mauritian Séga.

Séga. Also formally referred to as tiéga, tchéga tschiéga and céga. A traditional form of Mauritian music and dance, with roots in East Africa.

Tang. Common Tenrec. A hedgehog-like mammal introduced to Mauritius from Madagascar

Tilambik / Ti-lambik. A raw, unrefined, locally brewed rum with higher levels of alcohol than mass produced varieties.

Zambiques. From Mozambiques. A colloquial term for slaves purchased from Mozambique, Mozambique island and East Africa in general.

Afterward

The world I attempted to create in The Magic of Tiéga was one of transition, a time of possibility still weighed down by the sins of the past. The end of slavery did not usher in a new era of equality, nor did the perpetrators of slavery seek atonement for their iniquities. In fact the only reparations ever dispensed were those received by slaveholders.

What was sort by those in authority was a refiguration of business as usual, an attempt to attach some semblance of morality to a mode of production dependant on exploitation. The hope being that slaves would become paid labourers, peons whose wages would amount to little more than their upkeep as slaves.

When the majority of freed Africans, Creoles and Malagasy chose not to work for their former masters, when they refused to follow the patterns of work proscribed by Europeans and shackle themselves to the old life of toil, they were labelled lazy, ungrateful and indolent. The island's governor at the time was 'baffled not only by the fact that the aged and infirm ex-slaves were glad to exchange a life of "certainty" and "comfort" for the uncertainties of the world outside, but also by the disinclination of the able-bodied ones to work on the plantations for hire.' (Nwulia, 1981.) This incredulity was expressed by many who sympathised with the plight of the emancipated, as well as those who bemoaned the end of slavery.

The solution to this crisis of labour, in Mauritius as in many colonies formally dependant on slavery, was the procurement of indentured workers. The desperate and destitute of British India were enlisted to fill the vacuum left by the great exodus, people whose use value could be procured for next to nothing and whose very numbers yielded the possibility of huge profits. Then, as today, fortunes were made off the backs of black and brown bodies, and those of the poor and expendable.

Those souls who took to the road and forsook plantation life, sought out new beginnings. They took satisfaction in the act of living: fishing, cultivating market gardens, working trades and odd jobs, and when they could, doing no work at all. Many chose an itinerant existence, refusing the constraints of settled life, altogether. It is into this space of potentiality that I placed Liberté, Ma-Jo, Vier Bolom and even Mme Lousteau. The intention of my story was to re-imagine this time, one largely overlooked in the history of the island. Because, although there are folk tales and sirandines, and chronicles of historical events, there is very little in way of firsthand accounts. Through research I hoped to give my work some historical and cultural grounding, but in the end it is a work of fiction and should be treated as such. There are no doubt mistakes and liberties have been taken, but I hope I will be forgiven these indiscretions in light of the sincerity with which I undertook this project.

Finally, as is customary, I must assert that all characters and events depicted in this work are fictional, and any resemblance to persons living or dead is purely coincidental.

Acknowledgements

It is hard for me to separate the writing of this book from the rest of my life. Of course, it was its own process and demanded that specific time be set aside for the tasks necessary for its creation. But without everything that came before, there would have been no after. So, it would be easy, and not unwarranted, to thank everyone who has impacted my life. And I do thank every one of you.

However, there are those whose input or encouragement directly influenced this work, and it is to them I would like to give special thanks.

Firstly, and to echo the book's dedication, I would like to thank my wife, Sabrina. Not only has her belief in me been unerring, but she never once questioned the validity of my work, nor did she urge me to follow some more profitable pursuit. Even during the leanest of times, when money was at its tightest, she encouraged my writing. Neither was her role limited to moral and emotional support, as she assisted me with Creole diction and phraseology, as well as matters of culture, reaching out to others for me when she was unsure of answers, herself. To this end, I also thank Dominique Farla for his assistance. Along with Sabrina, I thank my children: Shola, Cybele and Kweli for giving me the will to live, a necessary condition for the completion of this book.

Thanks is also so due to my mother Rosalind Souris, and Sabrina's parents Josiane and Jean-Claude Farla. For, it was their generosity that enabled me to journey to Mauritius and begin the initial research for my book.

Likewise, I am grateful to those who gave me confidence in my work. To Stephen Carver and Ashley Stokes, of the Unthank School – Ashley, your advice and direction was invaluable – and of course to all the 2014-15 Monday night Unthank workshop crew. A thoroughly talented bunch, one and all. Not to forget Angela Birchnell, who after reading some of my earliest attempts at fiction, replied with resounding yes to my question as to whether or not I could make a go of this writing lark. I never doubted your sincerity. And last but not least, Lynsey Dorman, who from the beginning believed I could produce this whole thing, myself.

I must make honourable mention to Stephen Powers, Eshe Kiama Zuri and Kata Martell. Thank you all for taking the time to read this book, for making me feel it was worthwhile and inspiring me to finally do something with it. It was your appreciation that made this book real to me.

Gary Bishop, thank you for your advice and for giving up your time to help me with the pre-press work.

Then there are those whose cultural grounding laid the foundations for this book. Ti Frère and the unnamed ségatiers of earlier times, as well as the host that followed, I owe you all a debt of gratitude. My late father, Paul Souris, the first to pique my interest in the history of Mauritius, slavery and black history in general. I wish you were here to read it. Bingi Bingham, who along with his friendship brought rasta, reggae and dub poetry into my life. Paul Taipow, Benjamin Wachenje and The Uninvited, truly foundational. Paul, I love you, brother. Ras Bobbie, Sister Tegeste Selassie and Ronford Reid, family in my heart forever. And out of the great many literary influences I am indebted to, I cannot finish without paying homage to Toni Morrison and Patrick Chamoiseau. The beauty of your words, stories and imaginations made it impossible for me not to write.

It would be remiss of me not to mention the people of Mauritius, Mahébourg, my family by blood and by marriage, this book would have been impossible without the love, inspiration and wonderful memories you have given me.

Finally, I must acknowledge those whose work on Mauritius, the Mascarenes and the Indian Ocean world, helped me to add some social and historical sense of place to The Magic of Tiéga. Megan Vaughan whose work gave me the wonderful name Lousteau and the sketch of a slave hunting mistress. Not to underplay the profound and enlightening nature of her work on slavery in Mauritius. Rosabelle Boswell whose anthropological writings provided insight into Creole life, past and present, and inspiration for the village of Pas-Cousin. Also thank you to Edward A. Alpers, Richard B. Allen, Philip Baker & Guillaume Fon Sing, P. J. Barnwell & A. Toussaint, Patrick Beaton, Jacques-Henri Bernardin de Saint-Pierre, Anthony Cheke & Julian Hume, Ameenah Gurib Fakim, Lee Haring, Pier M. Larson, J.-M G. & Jemia Le Clézio, Jacques K. Lee, Amédéé Nagapen, George Norvill & R. Bell, Moses D. E. Nwulia, Deryck Scarr, and Sydney Selvon. All that is authentic in this book is down to your expertise, all incongruities are my own.